Mollie Hardwick was born in Manchester. She worked there as a BBC announcer and then moved to the Drama Department in London, leaving in 1963 to become a full-time freelance author, playwright and broadcaster. Alone or with her husband, Michael Hardwick, she has written and adapted several hundred plays for radio, television and the stage, and written some fifty books, ranging from best-selling novels to biographies and several studies of the works and lives of Charles Dickens and Sir Arthur Conan Doyle – she and her husband advised BBC Television on its series about the great detective and wrote some of the scripts; they also wrote the novel based on Billy Wilder's film *The Private Life of Sherlock Holmes*.

Mrs Hardwick contributes historical features to leading women's magazines and reviews books regularly for a group of newspapers. Her own books include *Emma, Lady Hamilton, Mrs Dizzy*, and *Sarah's Story*, the third book in the highly successful *Upstairs, Downstairs* series.

Also available from Sphere Books

UPSTAIRS, DOWNSTAIRS John Hawkesworth
ROSE'S STORY Terence Brady & Charlotte Bingham
SARAH'S STORY Mollie Hardwick
MR HUDSON'S DIARIES Michael Hardwick
IN MY LADY'S CHAMBER John Hawkesworth
MR BELLAMY'S STORY Michael Hardwick

The Years of Change

MOLLIE HARDWICK

SPHERE BOOKS LIMITED
30/32 Gray's Inn Road, London WC1X 8JL

First published in Great Britain by Sphere Books Ltd 1974

Reprinted August 1974

TRADE
MARK

Set in Intertype Baskerville

Printed in Great Britain by
Hazell Watson & Viney Ltd
Aylesbury, Bucks

ISBN 0 7221 4299 4

This book is based on the third television series of UPSTAIRS, DOWNSTAIRS, produced by John Hawkesworth for London Weekend Television Limited, and created by Sagitta Productions Limited in association with Jean Marsh and Eileen Atkins.

Rex Firkin was the Executive Producer, and Alfred Shaughnessy was Script Editor of the series.

The author wishes to acknowledge that in writing this book she has drawn largely on material from television scripts by the following writers:

John Hawkesworth
Deborah Mortimer
Jeremy Paul
Alfred Shaughnessy
Rosemary Anne Sisson
Anthony Skene
Fay Weldon

The author is grateful to them; and to London Weekend Television for the opportunity to attend rehearsals and recordings, to meet the actors, directors and technicians concerned, and to become a part of the world of UPSTAIRS, DOWNSTAIRS.

CHAPTER ONE

Mr Hudson laid down the daily paper with a sigh. It had been one of those days at 165 Eaton Place, Belgravia, when a series of minor but irritating incidents had disturbed the domestic routine he so much prized. The telephone had gone wrong again, as a consequence of which two persons in overalls, exuding an unpleasant aroma of strong pipe-tobacco, had spent the morning fiddling about with the instrument in the hall and getting in the servants' way, and going in and out of the front door 'like dogs at a fair', as Mrs Bridges the cook put it.

'As if the place wasn't cold enough with this dratted Coal Strike on,' she complained to Mr Hudson. 'April it may be, but February's the way it feels, and I'd like to know how I'm expected to cook the dinner with a miserable bit of gas and two penn'orth of coals?'

'We must put up with small inconveniences when the country demands it, Mrs Bridges,' Hudson replied. But his private feelings were in tune with hers. In all his years of serving the Bellamy family as butler he had never known a year like this, 1912, when the old order of things seemed to be so much threatened. People simply didn't know their place any more. In China the great Manchu dynasty had been overthrown by a middle class demanding rights they had never known before; while at home ordinary working men were presuming to disrupt society with behaviour which, in Mr Hudson's opinion, merited the strongest processes of the law. Last year a Railway Strike and a Taxi-cab Strike, and now this, a hit at the very heart of England. (Mr Hudson, though a Scot to the backbone, never veered for one moment from his loyalty to the country in which he had spent thirty of his fifty-six years.)

Why, even their present Majesties, King George V and Queen Mary, had broken away from protocol by visiting India, where such dreadful events had happened only fifty years ago. A nice thing it would be if they were both trampled on accidentally by those great brutes of elephants which the natives actually considered suitable means of transport.

And that reminded Mr Hudson that even less exotic transport was not what it had been. Look at all the trouble the coming of the motor-car had caused in the Bellamy household; all that upset with that slippery Welsh chauffeur, Thomas, and the final scandal which led to his marrying Sarah Moffat and removing her from the household; not but what that had been a relief to all. And Miss Elizabeth had never been the same, in Mr Hudson's opinion, since she started going out alone with Thomas in the motor. Who could tell how much of her distressingly fast behaviour was not directly the result of that breach of etiquette?

'Flying machines next, I suppose,' reflected Mr Hudson glumly. 'Young people thinking no more of crossing the Channel in those unnatural things than riding in the Park; and bringing nasty Continental ways back with them.'

But at least, he reminded himself, Miss Elizabeth was no longer a worry to her parents, Lady Marjorie and Mr Bellamy. After her first unfortunate marriage, and that shocking affaire with Julius Karekin, she had settled down at last, it seemed, and was living happily in New York with her American lawyer husband, Dana J. Wallace.

And even Mr James, her brother, appeared to have forsworn his wild ways. Since he had left the Army and come home from India he had taken a post as clerk at Jardine's trading office in the City. It seemed to have quietened him down a lot, the servants felt; and they were relieved that his engagement to Miss Phyllis Kingman had proved to be a mere shipboard romance.

'Pity,' Mrs Bridges had said. 'Healthy stock, that's what she'd have brought into the family. But I can't really see her as Mrs James.'

Rose sniffed. 'Only a vet's daughter, for all she kept on about her father's polo horses, every blessed mealtime. Downright common, I say.' Rose herself was a lodge-keeper's daughter, born on the Norfolk estate of old Lord Southwold, Lady Marjorie's father. Her resentment of Miss Kingman was based less on class prejudice than on simple feminine ire at being addressed by a woman younger than herself as if she were a mere servant – she, who had been Miss Lizzy's friend and confidante throughout her young mistress's girlhood and unhappy first marriage – and, subconsciously, on the fact that her own dark wistful prettiness had brought her not even the glimmer of an engagement ring, only a few advances from the faithless chauffeur Thomas. Not that she fancied Mr James herself; not a bit.

As for Mr Hudson, he had borne with dignity Miss Kingman's habit of addressing him as if he were some turbaned native who should jump to attention at the lightest clap of her rather large hands, and her sharp barks at Edward the footman. He had guessed that her reign would be short. Clean, white and little more than twenty-one she might be, but Mr James could do better. It was a pity that since parting with Miss Kingman and embarking on a mercantile career he had become noticeably more gloomy and almost rude to his long-suffering parents.

At this moment in Mr Hudson's reflections sounds of arrival were heard in the hall above, at the same time as the rattle of porcelain and silver betokened Rose's journey upstairs with Lady Marjorie's tea-tray. He glanced up at the clock – 4.30. He darted off in Rose's wake, and, seizing the silver kettle while simultaneously whisking a lace table-cloth over his arm, he arrived at the pass door to the hall in time to usher Rose through it.

James Bellamy was hanging up his bowler hat, the symbol of civic servitude, as he bitterly thought of it. The elegant hall mirror reflected a face handsome, only too attractive to women as time past had shown, with a touch of innate weakness in it. This afternoon a cloud of discontent and boredom had descended on James's brow. He nodded to Mr Hudson and Rose without a greeting, jamming his rolled umbrella with a jarring clatter into the green pottery umbrella stand, ornamented with thoughtful storks musing among reeds.

'Good afternoon, sir,' said Hudson. 'Will you be joining her ladyship for tea?'

James appeared to be about to refuse, then sniffed as an alluring fragrance crept from beneath the silver dish-cover.

'Is that crumpets, Rose?' he asked.

Rose revealed a corner of the contents. 'Hot buttered teacake, sir.'

'Then I will,' James decided. He preceded them into the morning-room, where his mother, perched straight-backed on the sofa, was engaged in embroidery. She raised her still-lovely face for his kiss.

'You're home early, darling.'

'Well, I told the head clerk that as I'd finished the cargo lists he gave me to check I saw no reason to stay on until five o'clock twiddling my thumbs, so I came home. And I'm going to have tea with you.'

Lady Marjorie's eyebrows arched slightly at her son's arbitrary dismissal of statutory working hours, but she only said: 'Well, that's nice,' and asked Hudson for another cup. 'Oh,' she added, 'and tell Mr Bellamy tea's ready, would you?'

Hudson paused at the door.

'I understand the master will not be requiring tea, m'lady. He's working on in the study and not to be disturbed.'

'Why, hasn't Miss Forrest left yet?'

'Not yet, m'lady.'

'I see. Then we shan't need another cup, thank you, Hudson.'

When the servants had left James drank the tea his mother poured for him with enjoyment, his bad temper beginning to ebb. He visualised his father toiling away in his study at the monumental life of his father-in-law, the eminent statesman Lord Southwold, which he had been commissioned to write. It was no secret to Richard Bellamy's family that authorship came hard to him, after a lifetime of politics, and that sheer conscientious determination rather than literary zeal kept him at it. So arduous was the work that he had engaged a young woman to assist him by typing the manuscript, keeping his notes in order, and generally allowing him to concentrate on making a coherent whole from the immense amount of material yielded by the late Lord Southwold's long life. It was becoming quite acceptable for a professional man to engage the services of a private secretary, as such ladies were now called; not very long before, all females who earned their living by typing, shorthand and bookkeeping had been confusingly known as Lady Typewriters.

James smiled over his teacup.

'I'll bet Father wishes he'd never started on Grandpa's biography,' he said.

'Oh, I think he's enjoying it. It's just that the publishers want the manuscript by the end of the month and he still has a few chapters left to write.'

'Damned hard work.'

Lady Marjorie's eyes met her son's in a level look.

'Yes, darling,' was all she said. The teacake James was eating ceased to soothe his temper.

'All right, Mother,' he snapped. 'I've stopped work early and come home for tea. Father's still working and hasn't time for tea.' He jumped up and began to pace about the room, to the peril of several small elegant tables and their knick-knacks and silver-framed photographs, watched anxiously by his mother.

'Well, do you blame me, with a dreadful boring job like mine? It's not living, it's existing. Thank God for the weekend.'

'I'm afraid you'll have to amuse yourself this weekend, darling,' said Lady Marjorie. 'You know your father and I are motoring down to Syon tomorrow.'

'Yes,' said James, who had forgotten. He stared gloomily out of the window at the familiar, uninspiring view. A lot of stuffy houses full of stuffy people. His mouth, below the neat Guards moustache, was set in a droop which his mother knew all too well. She searched her mind for something to change his mood, and found a hopeful topic.

'Oh, by the way, *such* a happy letter and a parcel, from Elizabeth. She's sent a pair of gloves for me from Macy's in New York, and a book for your father, and a phonograph record for you.' She produced from the opened box at her side a small disc wrapped in tissue paper and tied with a smart bow of silk ribbon. James unwrapped it, read the label and gave a sharp bark of laughter.

'Everybody's Doing It!' He dropped the record on the sofa. 'Everybody except me.'

Lady Marjorie's natural sweetness of disposition kept exasperation out of her tone.

'What *do* you mean, James?'

He was staring out of the window again, hands in pockets. 'Nothing.'

'Elizabeth says it's the latest craze in America, this "ragtime",' ventured his mother brightly. She put on her spectacles and referred to a letter on the table. 'She and Dana and little Lucy are to meet us off the boat on the 16th, when we land in New York. Won't that be lovely, to see them!'

'Lovely,' replied James sarcastically. 'For you and Uncle

Hugo and Aunt Marion.' Relations had never been cordial between him and his uncle, whose privileged life as a Southwold appeared to James to have been one long round of giddy pleasure.

Lady Marjorie determinedly ignored his tone, and went on: 'Then we go up to Montreal, where the President of the Canadian Pacific is giving us the use of his private railway coach right across to Alberta, and we shall stay there at Uncle Hugo's new ranch in Calgary, then . . . James, what *is* the matter?'

'Nothing.'

'Oh, I know you'd like to come with us. So would your father. But he's got work to do and you have, too.'

'Father's work is at least interesting.'

Lady Marjorie allowed herself to lose her temper. 'Any work is interesting, if you let it be. I'm sorry if you're bored, darling, but you've got to realize that thousands of young men slave away in offices every day to earn their bread-and-butter. Why should you complain? Especially after the trouble your father took to get you into the firm.'

James turned round, almost shouting. 'I will *not* spend the rest of my life worrying about how much tea we can ship from Hong-Kong to London just to be gulped down by silly women in drawing-rooms!'

'You're drinking tea yourself, aren't you?'

'Only because it's too early for whisky.' He slammed the delicate Coalport cup on to its saucer, like a boy smashing a butterfly.

'It was your decision to leave the Army,' his mother reminded him. She forebore to remind him of all the other worries he had thrust on them: the liaison with the attractive under-housemaid Sarah; the resultant baby which had died at birth; the shock of his sudden engagement to Phyllis Kingman and of the girl's utter unsuitability to be their daughter-in-law. She only added: 'You wanted to leave to make some money, you said.'

'Yes,' her son retorted bitterly, 'by the time I'm forty and half dead out in Calcutta with malaria and a rotten liver.'

Lady Marjorie's head was bent over the embroidery she had taken up again. When she spoke her voice was very quiet.

'It's not very considerate of you to talk like this, darling, just when I'm about to go abroad for a month or more. You know I worry about you.'

James flushed. 'I'm sorry, Mother.'

She laid her hand on his briefly.

'When I'm away, you'll help your father and the servants, won't you – let them know about being in or out to meals and that sort of thing.'

'Yes, of course.' She knew he was not listening.

'Darling, something else is troubling you. Is it Phyllis?'

James looked surprised. 'I don't think so.'

'Only I noticed you'd written to her. Didn't I see a letter on the hall table?'

James's reply could not have been less like that of a broken-hearted lover. 'Yes, I thought I should congratulate her. She's got herself engaged to a chap in the 4th Hussars – chap called Jack Pettifer, on the Governor's staff out there. An awfully worthy fellow – with a ginger moustache.'

'Oh, I'm so glad,' said her mother politely.

'So am I,' said James, meaning it.

'You were right to be honest with her before it was too late.'

'I hope so.' He was twirling the phonograph record between his hands, frowning. His mother made one more effort to cheer him.

'There are plenty of other girls, you know.' For James, there would always be plenty of other girls, she reflected ruefully.

He got up abruptly and made for the door, the record in his hand.

'I'm going to take this up to my room and play it.' At the door he paused. 'Thank you for my tea.'

It was what he had been taught to say as a little boy, by Nanny Webster. The polite little sentence brought a sting of tears to Lady Marjorie's eyes as the door closed behind the son she loved much more, if the truth were told, than her daughter. She forced the tears back before they could fall and spoil her delicately-powdered cheeks. She took a small mirror from her vanity bag and touched her face with a leaf of the papier poudré which was all a lady might officially allow herself in the way of a 'complexion aid'. Her beautiful eyes were as lustrous as ever, though there were a few lines around them now, and her famous smile had a certain strain.

But the magnificent auburn hair, high-piled in clustering curls and graceful waves, showed not one grey thread. If any lurked beneath its autumn russet, only Lady Marjorie's hairdresser and Miss Roberts, her maid, knew of it.

She rang the bell for Rose to remove the tea-things.

'Everybody's doing it, doing it, doing it,
Everybody's doing it, doing it, doing it . . .'

The manic rhythm of ragtime thumped its way through the panelled walls and parqueted floors of the old house which had known no music more violent than the long-ago tinkle of harpsichord and spinet, and the well-tuned voice of Lady Marjorie's Bechstein grand. Scratchy and aggressive, it assailed Rose's ears as she descended the stairs, and followed her into the servants' hall, faint but pursuing.

'Whatever's that?' queried Mrs Bridges. Rose pointed heavenwards.

'Him. In his bedroom.'

'If you mean Captain James, Rose, kindly use his name,' put in Mr Hudson. Rose sighed. 'You'll be telling me next that *he*'s the cat's father, Mr Hudson.' Ruby, the kitchen-maid, giggled, and Mr Hudson quelled both girls with a look. But his gaze, too, strayed towards the ceiling.

'Yankee tomfoolery,' he muttered. At any moment he expected to be summoned by Mr Bellamy to find out the reason for the unseemly racket.

But Richard Bellamy, working in his study, was too absorbed to hear even the clicking of his secretary's typewriter. His handsome silvered head bent over his paper-littered desk, his pen scratching away, he had no eyes for the young woman who sat at a small typing table on the other side of the room, her fingers moving briskly over the keys of her Royal Portable. Yet Hazel Forrest was well worth a man's regard. Her plain high-necked blouse and long tweed skirt subtly flattered her slender figure, and the simple dressing of her cloudy red-gold hair set off a face that might have belonged to one of Rossetti's pale dreamy beauties, though its expression was usually one of business-like calm rather than of romantic meditation. She had, in fact, a curious air of either being unconscious of her looks or ignoring them that was strange in a pretty young woman.

The vinegary Miss Roberts had been heard to observe tartly: 'Whatever they may think nowadays, it doesn't seem at all proper to me, Mr Bellamy in there alone with that girl all day. Lord Southwold would never have done such a thing. What *would* he say to it?'

'Wish he'd been as lucky himself, if you ask me,' rejoined Mrs Bridges. 'When I was at Southwold as a girl there used to be a young fellow called Cyril Clumber scribbling away in the study with his lordship. Terrible spots he had, and bad breath.'

'Anyway,' said Rose, 'you can see Mr Bellamy's as much in love with Lady Marjorie as the day he married her.' She breathed a romantic sigh over the lacy petticoat she was mending for her ladyship's voyage.

In the study, Miss Forrest wound a sheet of paper from her typewriter. 'That's Chapter Fifteen typed, Mr Bellamy,' she said, laying it on his desk.

'Thank you.' He glanced at it. 'Capital.'

'Oh, and I've managed to find the two passages you wished to quote from the Lansdowne correspondence. They're both marked there.'

'Ah, thank you. Well, I think you've done enough for one day. You'll be wanting to get home.'

Miss Forrest seemed reluctant to leave. 'I'd like – I'd like to come again tomorrow, if it's convenient,' she hesitated, 'so that I can finish off the last two chapters, ready for you to collect on Monday.'

Richard looked mildly surprised, but said 'Well, if you're sure you don't mind giving up part of your weekend.'

'Oh, that's all right. I've nothing particular to do.' (And Heaven knows, she thought, that's too true.)

'I see. Well, by all means. Just ring the bell and Hudson will show you in here.' He glanced at the typewriter, deceptively small. 'Perhaps you'd care to leave your machine overnight – I know it's heavier than it looks.'

'If I may, please. It *is* a weight to carry, and if my train's crowded . . .'

She was putting on the round felt hat, so unlike the ornate cartwheels worn by Lady Marjorie, and the neat cloth coat. Richard had begun to write again, but a sound which had been going on for some time finally penetrated his consciousness. He looked up irritably.

'What on earth is that noise?'

'A gramophone, I think, Mr Bellamy – it's coming from upstairs.'

'Must be my son,' grunted Richard. 'He's keen on all this ragtime music. Dreadful syncopated "jazz", like everything else from America – too fast and too noisy.'

Hazel Forrest's look was just a shade wistful. The cheerful, foot-tapping rhythms of ragtime were rather jolly, if you were young. She couldn't really agree, and it was a nasty thought that when she was Mr Bellamy's age she would certainly be saying the same sort of things about the popular music of the time. She drew on the gloves without which no lady could be seen in the street, and wished her employer goodnight. He held the door open for her exit.

Mischievous Fate so arranged it that as she was passing through the hall on her way to the front door, James was coming downstairs, the offending record in his hand. At the foot of the staircase he nearly collided with her. Both smiled.

'Good evening. Just off?' he enquired unnecessarily.

'Yes. Good night.'

James was bored and inclined for conversation, even with underlings. 'I hope my father isn't working you too hard.'

'Oh no, not at all.' If she was kept talking she would miss her train. She edged towards the door, and James followed her.

'Got far to go? It seems to be raining.'

'I've my umbrella, thank you, and I'm only going as far as Sloane Square.'

'You live in Sloane Square?'

Hazel laughed spontaneously. 'Oh, dear me no. I catch the Metropolitan there, to Wimbledon.'

'Ah yes. Er – well, I wish you a – restful weekend.'

'It won't be altogether that. I'm coming back tomorrow to finish Mr Bellamy's typing.'

'Oh. Then you must – er – rest on Sunday.'

'I expect I will. And now I really must go, if you'll excuse me. Goodbye.'

James watched her neat figure proceeding down Eaton Place, till she turned the corner and vanished. Nice girl, if rather dull. Pity she had to go, just when he felt like chatting to someone. He sauntered into the morning-room, found his mother too absorbed in letter-writing to take much notice of him, and drifted out again. Life was really horribly boring.

The Saturday mid-morning cup of tea in the servants' hall was a pleasantly relaxed occasion. The family car had left on its journey to Syon House and the weekend with the Northumberlands, and everybody, including Miss Roberts, was figuratively unbuttoned.

'Thank goodness!' that lady exclaimed. 'I'm badly behind with her ladyship's packing.'

'Well, I *have* offered to help you, Miss Roberts,' said Rose.

Miss Roberts sniffed. '*You* wouldn't know what to put in. She doesn't know herself what to take.'

Mrs Bridges, who had never travelled farther west than Hampshire, meditated. 'I expect it'd be warm in Canada, this time of year.'

'Not in the Rockies. They have snow in the Rockies, all the year round. And grizzly bears.' Edward growled realistically.

'How do *you* know?' enquired Rose.

'Oh, I've seen pictures, in a mag. It says in spring it's always hot in America and cold in Canada. So you'll have to pack everything she's got, eh, Miss Roberts.'

'Hardly. We're only taking four cabin trunks.'

Edward hooted. 'Four? What, three for her clothes and one with you in it – save paying your fare?'

Miss Roberts glared at him over the teacup she was holding genteelly, little finger slightly crooked. 'Don't be ridiculous, Edward,' she snapped. She was sensitive about many things connected with herself, including her small size, which Edward was now weighing up, insolent fellow.

'Oh, I don't know – if they packed you in a trunk across the Rockies the grizzlies wouldn't get you, nor the Red Indians, when they hold the train up.' Rose and Mrs Bridges laughed.

'Oh, really, Edward!'

'Honest.' Edward was enjoying the centre of the stage, which he seldom held. 'They swoop down from the rockies on to the railway line and scalp all the passengers – so if you're not hidden in a trunk, Miss Roberts, you mind you keep your hair on.'

Miss Roberts gave one of her derogatory snorts, but her hand automatically flew up to her stiffly-dressed iron-grey hair. The laughter was abruptly stopped by the entrance of Mr Hudson. Ordered by Mrs Bridges to pour a cup of tea for him, Ruby remained lost in horrific visions of gigantic bears and feathered savages, until the sharp tones of Mrs Bridges broke in on them.

'A cup of tea for Mr Hudson or I'll have *your* scalp! Step lively, now!'

Ruby stepped lively.

It was half-past eleven, but James had had no breakfast. In his bedroom, full of schoolboy and Army trophies and photographs, he sat on the side of his bed, unheeding the strains of 'Everybody's Doing It' from the record on his gramophone. Only when the tune ended and the needle began to scrape round and round the final groove did he reach out and lodge it at the beginning of the record. His gaze came to rest on the H.M.V. trademark picture of the faithful terrier with one ear cocked for His Master's Voice.

'Silly-looking beast,' said James. He snatched the needle off again, fastened his tie and went downstairs. In the hall he met Edward, carrying an empty tray.

'If you were requiring breakfast, sir, I've just cleared the dining-room,' he was told; and, reluctantly, 'but I can get you something if—'

'No, no, that's all right, Edward. I'll wait for lunch now. Overslept.'

'Yes, sir.' Edward departed downstairs, and James pottered about in a desultory way until he was struck by a sound which had been heard continuously that morning from his father's study – the regular tap-tapping of a typewriter. With sudden resolution, he moved briskly to the study door.

'Oh!' Hazel Forrest looked up from her work with a start.

'Hope I'm not disturbing you,' James said. 'I was just looking for this week's *Punch* . . . ah, here it is.' Hazel suspended her typing politely in case he had any more to say. He had.

'Been hard at it all morning, have you?'

'Oh, I've disturbed you. I'm so sorry. This machine is noisy.'

'Good Lord, no. I – well, I just thought I'd look in and see if you were all right.' And all right she certainly was, he thought. In the morning light her hair and skin glowed with youth and health, and there were no shadows of tiredness round her clear blue eyes. Pretty figure, too. He began to ask her about her work, and she responded enthusiastically.

'It's very interesting. I'd no idea Lord Southwold was such a progressive . . .'

James, who could not possibly have had less interest in his grandfather's political career, hardly listened to her as she talked on, but, lounging in an armchair, surveyed her thoughtfully. The black basalt clock on the mantelpiece struck twelve.

'I say, it's getting on,' he observed. 'What about your lunch?'

'That's all right – the butler's arranged something cold for me on a tray.'

'Oh, good. Er – have you been doing this kind of work for long?'

'About ten years. Of course, I've only been trained to typewrite for three years. Before that I worked at a draper's in Surbiton, looking after their accounts.'

'I see. *I*'ve only just started work.'

'You were an officer in the Life Guards, weren't you?'

'Yes. Now I'm a clerk with Jardine Mathesons in Lombard Street. In the tea department.'

Hazel responded politely. 'That sounds very interesting.'

James left his chair and perched on a corner of his father's desk. 'So, having that much in common with you, would it be too forward of me to ask you your Christian name?'

A slight blush touched her face and neck. 'Well, I . . . I was christened Hazel Patricia.'

'Hazel . . .' He bent forward and scanned her face; her blush deepened. 'But your eyes are blue.'

'Yes. I – I think it was my father's love of shrubs that . . .' Her voice trailed away and she bent her head to avoid his admiring stare.

'Please don't think me discourteous, Mr Bellamy. But I must get on with my work. Your father's most anxious to revise these chapters on Monday morning.'

'I'm sorry. It was wrong of me to ask you personal questions. But I want to know more about you – about your home, your family, your life, what you think and feel.'

Her tone was edged when she answered. 'I find it difficult to believe that someone in your position in society should be in any way interested in someone like me. Unless you're making a study of ordinary middle-class life in the outer suburbs of London.'

'No, I'm not. I just feel a desire – to know you a little better. Might I call you Hazel – at least during the weekend?'

Their glances met, hers puzzled and a little alarmed, his openly amorous. The awkward moment was interrupted by the entrance of Hudson, bearing a tray, and obviously not prepared to find James present.

'Excuse me, sir,' he said stiffly. 'Miss Forrest's luncheon.'

James lifted the dish-covers, revealing a plate of cold tongue and an uninspired side-salad. He dropped the covers.

'You can take that stuff downstairs, Hudson, and lay up for two in the dining-room.'

Hudson's face could not have registered more shock if James had requested him to call in a street-hawker for luncheon. He could only stammer: 'In – in the dining-room, sir?'

'Yes. I shall be lunching at home today after all, Hudson, and Miss Forrest will be joining me.' He turned to her confidently. 'Won't you?'

It was a coldly angry Mr Hudson who announced to his staff:

'Captain James has ordered luncheon in the dining-room for himself and the typist.'

Before Mrs Bridges could give utterance to her astonishment, he had sharply ordered Edward to lay two places in the dining-room. 'With tumblers. And a jug of barley-water.'

Flustered, Mrs Bridges ordered Ruby to fetch two more pork chops from the larder, to be served with spinach and apple sauce, and to peel more potatoes. Mr Hudson's rage was exacerbated when James rang from the morning-room for a decanter of sherry. In an expressive silence, he bore it upstairs, to find James and Miss Forrest side by side on the sofa, she looking embarrassed but not displeased. Hudson heard her say 'James' as he entered the door. 'On Christian name terms with the typist! Whatever next?' he mentally exclaimed. To James's thanks for the decanter he made no reply. But as he was leaving James called him back.

'Oh, by the way, we'll have a bottle of the Cantenac '93 with lunch.' Ignoring the butler's horrified look, he turned to Hazel. 'My father has this marvellous claret – wait till you taste it! It's really –' Hudson interrupted, his normally light Scots accent thicker with emotion.

'Begging your pardon, sir, but I'm afraid I cannot serve the Chateau Brane Cantenac '93, sir.'

'Oh? Why not?'

Hudson hesitated. 'There are – certain difficulties . . . If I might see you in private, sir.' He glanced towards the door. James shrugged.

'Excuse me, Hazel.' He followed Hudson into the hall and saw that the butler was shaking with fury, his face pale and set.

'What *is* all this, Hudson?' he asked impatiently.

'I preferred not to speak of it in front of the – secretary, sir. But I must point out that I cannot serve the master's best claret. There are only two bottles left.'

'I ordered one bottle, Hudson. And I expect you to serve it.'

'Are you asking me to go against the Master's wishes, sir?'

'Did my father forbid you to serve that claret?'

'He would not wish it to be served at luncheon – especially in his absence and in the circumstances.'

Their voices were raised now. The embarrassed Hazel could hear the angry voices through the closed door. James was almost shouting.

'Let me remind you, Hudson, that whatever your private views may be, and in the absence of my parents, I'm in charge of this house. Miss Forrest is my guest for lunch. In such a situation I expect my orders to be obeyed!'

'Yes, sir.' If an iceberg had uttered the words they could not have been chillier.

Luncheon in the servants' hall was a silent, cheerless meal, dominated by the thunderous brow of Mr Hudson. An attempted defence of James's behaviour by Rose was counteracted by Miss Roberts.

'I'm sure Mr Bellamy's typist is a perfectly respectable young woman, Rose, but she is Not a Lady. Now would someone kindly pass me the apple sauce.'

In the dining-room the luncheon conversation was less than sparkling, in spite of the Chateau Brane Cantenac '93, to the glory of which Hazel's palate was not trained. James chatted of his experiences in the Far East, of the Himalayas at sunrise, and other exotic scenes; to which Hazel could only reply that she had once been on an Easter Monday excursion to Margate. On James's expression of disbelief, she further admitted to having visited Newcastle-on-Tyne. Snatching at any chance of learning more about her, James enquired what she had been doing in that unlikely spot. She flushed.

'Oh – it was just . . . something. I'd rather not talk about it.'

When they reached the coffee stage, during which Hazel felt Mr Hudson's eyes boring through her back like knives, she excused herself and went back to her work. Once again thrown on his own resources, James telephoned his friend 'Bunny' Newbury and arranged an afternoon of tennis and an evening party at the Trocadero, if any suitable companions could be raked up from the ranks of ballet-girls and pretty young actresses of their acquaintance. Then, whistling, he went off to assemble his tennis gear, sublimely unaware of having dropped a bomb into the calm territory of his butler's life.

For Mr Hudson, so long cushioned in the ordered existence of 165 Eaton Place, was for the first time assailed by a horrid fear: the dread that the old order of things might be changing, giving place to new, and highly distasteful new at that. All his life he had accepted thoughtlessly the optimistic views on social reform held by his national poet.

'For a' that, and a' that,
It's coming yet, for a' that,
That man to man, the warld o'er,
Shall brothers be for a' that.'

Could the man have been a dangerous revolutionary, after all? Was the day not far off when underlings like Edward would be slapping the Master on the back and calling him Old Cock, while Ruby took afternoon tea upstairs, rambling on to Lady Marjorie about the shocking time her sister in Bradford had had with her last baby? Mr Hudson shuddered.

The chill of angry fear was strong on him as, later that afternoon, he encountered Hazel Forrest in the hall, in her outdoor clothes. Their eyes met, his steely. Without speaking, he opened the front door for her. At the threshold she hesitated, turned to him, and said falteringly:

'I would like to thank you for . . .'

A motor-car rattled past, drowning her soft voice.

'I beg your pardon, Miss?'

The tone of his reply destroyed her courage. She had meant to thank him for serving lunch, in spite of his obvious great disapproval of her presence in the dining-room and of the squandering upon her of Mr Bellamy's precious claret. She had wanted to say that she understood and bore him no resentment, that she wanted to be friends with him and his staff, and had no intention of putting on airs just because Captain James had taken a fancy to her. What she actually said was so abrupt that it sounded to Hudson's ears like stand-offishness.

'I've left my typing machine in the study. Mr Bellamy said I might.'

'Yes, Miss.'

'Good-day.'

He shut the door behind her.

As James was preparing for his departure to Hurlingham the butler requested a word with him.

'I fear, sir,' he said, standing straight and inflexible, his eyes fixed as a butler's should be on a point somewhere about the middle of James's forehead, 'today has proved that I no longer enjoy the authority of a butler here, which makes it impossible for me to continue in your parents' service. I shall see the Master and her ladyship on their return tomorrow and ask them to accept a week's notice. That is all I have to say, sir, if you will excuse me.'

Before the shocked James could speak, Mr Hudson was gone.

CHAPTER TWO

The following evening, Sunday, James spent at his club, remaining there until well after dinner in the faint fond hope that his parents might have returned before him and gone to bed. His heart sank as he saw Hudson emerging from the morning-room, wearing a stern, set expression. He called a cheerful greeting, and was answered briefly and coldly. Like an aristo jauntily mounting the tumbril, James entered to face his parents.

Richard came straight to the point.

'What the devil do you think you've been doing, James?'

James went pink, but asked innocently 'What?'

'You know damned well what I mean.'

'How can I, until you tell me?'

'And don't you be flippant.'

James's glance strayed towards his mother, always his defender in time of trouble. Her look promised little support.

'Hudson has just been in to see us, James.'

'Well?'

'He's given us a week's notice.'

'And you know why,' added Richard.

James shuffled his feet. 'Well, he did mutter something yesterday about leaving, for the simple reason that I ordered lunch in the dining-room, which evidently didn't suit his plans; and I think because I ordered him to serve a bottle of wine from the cellar. Frankly, I didn't believe he'd carry out his threat.'

'Well,' said Lady Marjorie, 'he has. And *I'm* leaving for Canada on Wednesday. That means your father will be left here with no butler.'

James still tried to brazen it out. 'Well, all I can say is, he'd be better off *without* Hudson, if the man continues in his present mood.'

His father's fury increased. 'Hudson happens to be a dam' good butler, James, as good as you'd find anywhere. He's served your mother and me well since before you were born. He's a man of high principles and, as you well know, he cares deeply for the welfare and honour of our family, and he expects things to be done correctly.'

'Then he ought to obey my orders,' James retorted.

'*Your* orders!'

'Yes, my orders. I live here.'

Lady Marjorie hated scenes at any time, and could see that her son was going to be the vanquished in this one. She interposed.

'You did put Hudson in a very difficult position, darling, by inviting your father's typist to lunch in our dining-room. *And* by ordering that bottle of wine.'

'What was the wretched man to do?' Richard raged. 'He knows I don't allow my best claret to be drunk at luncheon. You were showing off to Miss Forrest, weren't you?'

'I was *not* showing off. I was showing *her* the common courtesy of lunching with her as a token of what I hope is *your* gratitude, Father, for the extra work she did for *you* over the weekend.'

'It is not for you to extend courtesies to my secretary!'

'Well, I thought it was time somebody did. Her lunch – if you can call it lunch – was brought up on a tray.'

'Those were my orders, James!' said his mother. 'How could you of all people possibly think it suitable for Miss Forrest to lunch in the dining-room?'

'She happens to be an extremely nice person and very respectable,' James snapped back.

'I've no doubt she's respectable, but she can't have much sense or judgment to have accepted your invitation, in her position. If you'd decided to invite her out to supper at a restaurant, well . . . But to take her into our dining-room and to humiliate Hudson in front of a woman of her class—'

'I didn't humiliate him. And if he chooses to leave on account of so trifling a matter, let him go.'

'I have no intention of letting him go, James. You're going to see him and apologize to him.'

Lady Marjorie intervened. 'Richard, no. I will not have my son apologize to a servant in any circumstances.'

'Hudson is not an ordinary servant!' Richard blazed. His wife ignored the interruption. 'It seems to me if anyone should apologize it's your typist, for daring to think it would be right for her to lunch in the dining-room. She could have refused. I blame *her*.'

'Marjorie—'

'In fact I think in view of what's happened, you ought to terminate her engagement here at once.'

'I will do nothing of the kind. And I shall not allow Miss Forrest to be made a scapegoat for James's grossly stupid and unthinking behaviour.'

James cleared his throat. 'Look, Mother, I'm perfectly prepared to go and see Hudson, admit I made a mistake, and ask him—'

'No, James. I don't want anything more said about it tonight. I shall probably speak to him in the morning. You must leave these things to me, Richard.'

In the glum silence that fell, James excused himself and went to his room. Soon afterwards, Hudson appeared, uncompromising of aspect.

'Supper is served, m'lady.'

Lady Marjorie bestowed on him a smile of unclouded charm, as though the atmosphere of the room was not heavy with the smoke of battle.

'Thank you, Hudson,' she said.

With a sigh, Mr Hudson sat down at the table in the servants' hall, which was half-covered with the newspaper Mrs Bridges was scanning with a magnifying glass. She glanced up.

'They've not spoken a word to each other, since they went into the dining-room,' he told her.

'Seems to me everyone's upset in this house tonight, Mr Hudson.'

'And whose fault is that?'

Mrs Bridges shook her head. 'I still can't see why you had to go and give notice. You're not telling me you're going to walk out of here with her ladyship off to Canada Wednesday. Nice thing for her to go off for two months, leaving a nasty atmosphere like this in the house.'

Mr Hudson drummed his fingers on the table. 'I daresay I shall consider my position carefully, between now and Wednesday.'

'I should hope you will!' She couldn't bring herself to make a personal appeal to him, but behind her sharp tone was a world of fear. So many years in service together, at Southwold as footman and young kitchen-maid, here in London as butler and cook, twin pillars of strength to the

Bellamys. In that shameful time when middle-aged resentment at her spinsterhood, disguised by the cook's courtesy title of Mrs, had driven her to borrow a baby, Mr Hudson had been her advocate and had even publicly declared his wish to marry her – one day. Perhaps that day would never come; but meantime he was her ally and her best friend. If he left, Kate Bridges's life would be a desert.

Her eyes were misted as she focussed them again on her newspaper.

Miss Roberts, clad for travel, was ticking off items on her fingers.

'Let me see, what else? Oh – I've put the key of your jewellery-case in your brown handbag, m'lady.'

Lady Marjorie, serenely beautiful in an elegant coat and one of the hats for which she was famous, might have been about to embark on a journey to Southwold instead of to the wilds of Canada, so calm was her appearance in contrast to the worried lady's maid, who was surveying her with anxiety.

'I just hope you'll have enough warm clothing for the boat in the one cabin trunk, m'lady. The others go down into the hold I understand, and we shan't see them again until we get to New York.'

'I'm sure I shall be warm enough, Roberts. After all, it's spring already – April 10th, isn't it? – and they say the liner is like a floating palace. Is all the luggage down?'

'Yes, m'lady.'

'And you know that the brake is coming here at ten to take you and Lady Southwold's maid and Lord Southwold's valet to the station, and Edward will go as well to help them with the luggage.'

Miss Roberts was hardly listening as she fidgeted about the room, taking her gloves off and putting them on again and consulting her fobwatch.

'Try not to worry, Roberts,' said her mistress kindly. 'We shan't miss the boat-train, I promise you.'

'Yes, m'lady. It's just that I get train fever, m'lady.'

'Then I should go and sit in the servants' hall until the brake comes.'

Miss Roberts, her gloves off once more, took herself and her apprehensions downstairs. Mr Hudson passed her in the hall and joined Lady Marjorie, closing the door behind him.

'I was hoping to see the Master and yourself today, m'lady, before your departure—'

'Mr Bellamy has gone round to the chemist in Pont Street to get me something for sea-sickness. Would you like to speak to me alone?'

'In the circumstances, m'lady, I would. I just wanted to say that I acted in haste, giving notice on Sunday night, and I would now ask you to consider the whole incident closed.'

Their eyes met, hers smiling.

'Nothing would please me more, Hudson. What made you change your mind?'

'Only one consideration, m'lady.' He drew a deep breath for what was probably the longest speech he had ever addressed to her. 'Whatever may have been done and said in this house, since the weekend, and some bitter things *have* been said, m'lady, both above and below stairs, I could not on the eve of your departure for Canada abandon my post here. I am aware that my resignation, prompted by momentary anger and pique, has not only caused trouble for Captain James but a certain difference of opinion between the Master and yourself. And I would not care to see you leave behind any sense of disharmony in your house, m'lady.' He stood as if to attention, his justification expressed and his pride saved.

'That's very thoughtful of you, Hudson, and I'm most relieved.'

Indeed she was; but she had known all along that he wouldn't let the Family down.

A few minutes later the tension which had hung over the house was transformed into action. Miss Roberts, her veil firmly down and her gloves firmly on at last, was being seen off to the waiting brake by her fellow-servants with cries of 'Good luck!' 'Send us a nice postcard!' and 'Don't half envy you!' while in the hall Lady Marjorie, who had already said goodbye to the staff, was having a final word with Mr Hudson, her husband and son at her side, ready to accompany her to Southampton and see her aboard the liner.

'Goodbye, Hudson. Look after everything, won't you?' (But I know you will, her eyes said.)

'Indeed, m'lady. A pleasant voyage, m'lady.'

On Richard's arm, she moved out to the motor car, turning, as she reached it, to look back at her house. Richard beckoned impatiently to James, who had turned back to say something that he knew must and should be said.

'My apologies, Hudson. It won't occur again.'

'Sir.'

They understood each other; the war was over. Behind him, Hudson went out to see his Family safely into the car.

The house was strangely quiet after Lady Marjorie's departure. Richard and James, returning from Southampton that evening, found themselves eating their dinner in an embarrassed silence varied with stilted remarks.

'Magnificent ship.'

'Yes.'

'Very luxurious cabin, wasn't it.'

'Very. I could see even Roberts was impressed,' said James. 'Seems odd without Mother.' He looked round the room, which seemed to have grown larger and less welcoming – even colder, though the chill might well proceed from his unsmiling father. Richard had not heard James's muttered apology to Hudson, and was thinking with grim satisfaction that a month without his mother to help him out of scrapes might be very good indeed for James.

James, as he toyed with a lemon soufflé, of which he was not fond at the best of times, sought desperately round in his mind for further topics of conversation. Enquiries about his father's book would inevitably mean a mention of Miss Forrest, which would certainly be unfortunate. He left half the soufflé on his plate, to the indignation of Mrs Bridges when it went downstairs ('All that good cooking wasted!'), gulped down his coffee, and escaped to his room.

In the servants' hall silence also reigned. Mrs Bridges was meditating that there'd be less work to do for all of them with her ladyship away, no entertaining and the Master and Captain James out at their clubs as often as not; plenty of time for practising some new recipes and trying to get some sense into Ruby's head. It would be nice, but still . . . she sighed.

Rose, at the ironing-table, was dreaming as she expertly goffered a frill. Dreaming of Miss Lizzie so far away, and the talks they used to have that she missed so much. Seemed to bring it all back, her ladyship going away too; how she'd cried all night after Miss Lizzie went, and again when the letter came saying that she was getting married again to an

American, and how sweet he was with little Lucy. 'You needn't have any more worries about me, dear Rose.' Perhaps Lady Marjorie would bring some photographs back. Perhaps Miss Lizzie and her husband and Lucy would come over themselves next year . . . a sharp smell of burning recalled her to the present. 'Drat!' she said.

Mr Hudson looked up from his newspaper, but made no comment. He too, was finding it quiet.

The next day, Thursday, of Miss Forrest's last week with Richard, James strong-mindedly gave himself few opportunities for meeting her, much as he wanted to see her again. He went out with unusual celerity in the morning and lingered on the way home from his office in case she happened to be working late. His father's temper was improving, and James was not anxious to provoke him again.

But his mind constantly returned to her, the girl with the face and hair that reminded him of a picture he'd seen somewhere of a young woman floating in a pool under a willow-tree, singing and holding some flowers in her hand. Yes, by Jove, he remembered where it had hung; in his tutor's room, where he had sometimes been privileged to take tea with other Seniors. He'd always thought she was a pretty girl, though it seemed a rum thing to be doing. And tunes kept coming into his head when he thought of Hazel. Tunes like that thing from *The Merry Widow*.

> 'Hear sweet music softly saying
> "I love you",
> While from your heart come these words
> "I love you too . . ."

And one that Sarah used to sing when she was feeling melancholy, something her father had taught her.

> '. . . Then pretty Jane, my dearest Jane,
> Ah, never look so shy;
> But meet me, meet me in the evening,
> When the bloom is on the rye.'

Hazel was shy too, and she had the most ripping blush . . .

The next day, Friday April 12th, his resolution broke

down after a restless night. 'Dammit, I *will* see her,' he told himself, and marched resolutely towards the study.

Hazel was sorting through papers, Richard opening his correspondence, when James knocked and entered.

'Sorry to disturb you, Father.'

'Yes,' replied Richard abstractedly, his mind on the letter he was reading.

'Just thought I'd return your *Punch*. I borrowed it,' he added unnecessarily.

'Thank you. Off to work?' His eyes still on the letter, he didn't see those of his son dwelling on Miss Forrest's face, and her ripping blush once again manifesting itself.

'Yes,' said James. 'It's such a fine morning, I thought I'd walk part of the way, I need the exercise.'

'Better be off, then.' Richard was reading the letter through again. James bade him a goodbye which he didn't hear, and to Hazel he made a gallant bow which brought him the reward of a smile. Her gaze followed him to the door, and rested on it until the front door banged. Richard raised a face glowing with pleasure from the letter.

'This is wonderful news, Miss Forrest! It's from Mr Sayers at Macmillan's.'

'They've received the manuscript, then?'

'Not only received it but read it.' He handed the letter over to her. She scanned it quickly.

'Oh, what good news, Mr Bellamy! "... Unanimous in our praise of the work – informative, entertaining, well-documented – in every way a most excellent and acceptable political biography." How splendid!'

'I must say I'm delighted – and relieved. If only this news had come three days ago, before my wife left for Canada. How thrilled she'd have been.'

'Oh, do write and tell her at once.'

'I'm afraid there's no point.' He was looking at the calendar. 'By the time a letter could reach New York, my wife will be half way across Canada.'

'Oh, what a shame. But – couldn't you send a wireless message to the ship?'

'A marconigram! Yet – that's what I shall do. She'll get it at sea. Bravo, Miss Forrest! Edward can run round with it to the Marconi office.'

Hazel reached for her notebook and sat with pencil poised,

while Richard, pacing about excitedly, began to dictate.

'To Lady Marjorie Bellamy, State Room No. 6, on board White Star Liner R.M.S. TITANIC, en route from Southampton to New York. Date, April 12th, 1912 . . .'

CHAPTER THREE

Nobody at 165 would ever forget the impact of the terrible news which shocked the world only three days after Richard's marconigram had been dispatched. The TITANIC, the largest liner afloat, on her maiden voyage, had struck an iceberg at full speed, in the early hours of the morning of April 15th. When day came, the great ship, pride of her builders, lay at the bottom of the Atlantic, with horrifying loss of life. No figures were available at first, as survivors were rescued by other craft, but it was believed that over 1500 people had drowned – about half the number of people on board, passengers and crew.

Not even the calm order of the Bellamy household could survive such a blow. Richard, when the newspaper with its banner headlines had been brought to him by a white-faced Mr Hudson, had looked at it like a man reading the order for his execution; and then, without word, had left the breakfast-table and gone up to his bedroom. After an hour, the butler had knocked gently at the bedroom door and called to his master that he had brought up the brandy decanter, in case Mr Bellamy felt in need of it. A muffled voice from within had replied: 'Thank you, Hudson. Leave it outside.'

James, who had left early for the City, rushed home at once. Shaking and incoherent, he had waved the paper at Hudson.

'It's not true, is it? It can't be. Not Mother. Oh, not Mother!'

Mr Hudson, not given to tender gestures as a rule, put a hand on the boy's shoulder and gently pushed him into a chair.

'We don't know yet, sir. We can only wait, and pray.'

He said the same to the weeping women downstairs.

'It's early days yet. If many poor souls have gone down, many have been saved. By the Lord's goodness Lady Marjorie may be among them.'

Then, when their first burst of grief was over, he quietly organised them into a semblance of their usual tasks, knowing that work was the only remedy; for himself as well as for them. Even the blubbering Ruby managed to wash up and peel potatoes, while Mrs Bridges and Rose sensed Mr Hudson's wisdom, and obeyed him. The lunch must be prepared, whether anyone ate it or not, the house swept and tidied, the general work done as usual by Edward, whose normal cockiness had left him. He kept murmuring dazedly: 'I saw her on to the train. She looked all right then,' as though a journey begun so well could not have ended in tragedy.

Hazel Forrest, shocked as she was, had the tact to carry on with her work as though everything were as usual, refraining from intrusion on the household's sorrow. Richard Bellamy appeared late in the afternoon, looking ten years more than his age. Her quiet words of sympathy he accepted with a pretence at a smile, sat down at his desk and began to sort out a pile of documents to be returned to those who had lent them. At her usual departure time, Hazel went home, leaving him still at the desk, sometimes reading or making a note, sometimes staring blankly into space.

James came down from his room red-eyed in the evening, and without a word to anyone left the house. At one-o'clock the next morning he was brought home in a cab, dead drunk, unconscious and snoring. Mr Hudson, who had been waiting up, paid and tipped the driver after they had carried James's inert form in between them, and single-handed got James to bed. Then he retired himself. He was exhausted, and glad to be.

In the days that followed they all reminded themselves that news was slow to come, that they mustn't despair yet. Richard was snappy with strain, barking at Hazel over trifles, and careless as he never had been about his staff. Hazel, without asking, had stayed on.

They had. Mrs Bridges, informed during her dinner preparations that the Master would be dining out, broke into righteous indignation.

'But I've made Filets de Veau Talleyrand! It's the Master's favourite, and I made it specially to tempt his appetite. I think he might have let us know!'

'It seems the Master did inform Miss Forrest,' said Hudson, 'but she didn't think to mention it.'

Mrs Bridges's arms were akimbo. '*Well*!' she exploded. And Hazel was blamed, as she so often was.

The suspense of the household was ended one afternoon when a telegraph-boy delivered a marconigram. Edward answered the door, but Hudson intercepted him on his way to the study.

'I'll take that in, Edward.'

Rose, on her way up the staircase, saw the encounter. Holding tight to the handrail, she shut her eyes and prayed.

Richard looked at the envelope for a moment as it lay on Hudson's salver, a messenger of joy or despair. Then he ripped it open, as Hazel and Hudson watched. His face told them its contents.

'From the White Star Company,' he said, his voice flat. 'Regret to inform you – Lady Marjorie Bellamy – Maud Roberts – unaccounted for, presumed drowned.'

It was a kind of relief for the staff to know the worst. They had never dared to have much hope, and the worst violence of their grief had spent itself when the news of the disaster broke. They would miss her more and more as time went on, but now at least they could talk.

'What I can't understand,' said Rose, 'is how a great ship like that could go down, just hitting a little iceberg.' Mr Hudson quelled her.

'It was not a little iceberg, Rose. From all accounts, it was nearly as tall as the ship.'

'Yes, but it seems so – I mean – we make the biggest ship in the world, and we say it's so big, there isn't anything could make it go down. And then along comes this ice-berg ...'

He shook his head. 'I believe it was the Captain who said "Even God Himself could not sink this ship." '

'Tempting Providence,' pronounced Mrs Bridges.

They sipped their tea, meditating.

Suddenly Rose spoke. 'I remember the first time that ever she spoke to me. It was at Southwold, and she was out riding, and my father was opening the gate to her, and I went out to help him. I can't have been more than five. And I remember her leaning down from her horse and saying "You must be little Rose." I remember that as clear as anything.'

Mr Hudson's eyes were dreaming, for once. 'I mind well my first meeting with her ladyship when I was a raw young lad from Scotland. She was no older than I was, and I was able to do her some slight service – she had got her dress muddy when Lady Southwold had guests, and I helped her to get up the back stairs before anyone saw her. And she said to me "You must be the new footman." And I forgot myself and said "Aye, I am that," whereas what I should have said was "Yes, my lady." And she smiled and said "I hope you're not too homesick for Scotland." There's not many young ladies of her age who would have considered the feelings of a servant.'

Ruby and Edward exchanged awed looks at these revelations. It was as though God had descended and casually revealed details of His private life. They would have been even more astonished if Mr Hudson had gone on to tell them of another memory, the heartless and scandalous behaviour of Miss Adela Rennishawe, in a previous household, and how relieved he had been to find Lady Marjorie so different.

Mrs Bridges was gazing into the fire. '*I* always think of her as she was when she came here as a young bride. She had a pink hat with feathers on it, and she and the Master came back from their honeymoon, and we were all lined up in the hall – remember, Mr Hudson?'

He nodded. He had been such a young butler, and so nervous.

'And you said "May I make so bold as to wish your ladyship and the Master every happiness in your new home?" and her ladyship said "I hope you will all think of this as your home, too. I'm sure we are all going to be very happy here." '

Ruby, overcome with emotion, broke into loud sobs.

Later that week Richard was having a disturbing interview with his solicitor, Sir Geoffrey Dillon. That grave and formal gentleman had called to remind Richard that his financial prospects were now far from rosy.

'You remember that the terms of Lady Marjorie's Will were, to a great extent, conditioned by the terms of the Marriage Settlement. Now: the main source of income for yourself and your late wife has been the interest on the £100,000 of the Settlement.'

'Yes.'

'That was, of course, tied to the children, and is now inherited by James and Elizabeth, in equal parts of £50,000.'

On Richard's face realisation dawned. He had known, of

course; but money had been the last thing in his mind recently.

'Your own income is not large,' continued Dillon.

'No . . . hardly sufficient to maintain this household as it should be. Stupid of me. I've never thought of it as her money or my money. We planned our expenditure together.'

'Naturally.' Sir Geoffrey sailed complacently towards disaster. 'Of course, in an ordinary marriage, a husband and wife sink or swim together, but—' Richard's face brought him up short.

'I wish to God we had!'

'Forgive me.' There was a pause. 'Will you continue in politics?'

'I don't know if I can afford to. At least, if I do, I shall be free to follow my own conscience, without being hampered by considerations of the Southwold patronage.'

'Yes.' Sir Geoffrey's expression was thoughtful. He got up. 'Well – I must be on my way. Oh – the lease of this house will be yours, of course. It was made over to you and Lady Marjorie by a deed of gift, and therefore it will now belong to you.' He was in the hall, Hudson helping him on with his coat, and Rose coming downstairs with a tray. Smiling, he called back: 'If things *do* get sticky, you can always sell the house, get rid of your servants, and rent a flat somewhere. Don't be too down-hearted, old chap.'

Sir Geoffrey's excellent brains were not accompanied by any high degree of tact.

Some days later he called again, with a proposition.

'Lady Southwold has a number of shares in a large tobacco company, of which Hugo Southwold was on the board. His Directorship is now, of course, vacant, after his lamented decease, and Lady Southwold wondered if you would care to have it?'

'Well . . .'

'She would make over to you a substantial proportion of her shares, and in addition you would receive quite a handsome Director's Fee.'

Richard had never been a favourite with his domineering mother-in-law, nor she with him, but he was compelled to admit that it was most generous of her. Sir Geoffrey extracted some documents from his brief-case.

'I have some papers here which you might care to glance

at, at your leisure. If I have your agreement in principle, then I will draw up the necessary document. The income should be more than enough to take care of the upkeep of this house.'

Richard heaved a sigh of relief. 'That's a great weight off my mind, Geoffrey.' The solicitor gave one of those expressive coughs which politely indicate a reproof.

'Hrhm. Lady Southwold was rather distressed to hear that you voted with the Government last week. She felt that it reflected upon the honour of a great Tory family for one of its members to—'

Richard put the documents down. 'I am not exactly a member of the family.'

'Oh, come, Richard!'

Richard was remembering, all too clearly, a painful scene with James before the third reading of the Home Rule Bill. He had mildly observed that on several recent questions he had found himself on the side of the Liberal Government, and James had burst out in protest. How could his father even contemplate crossing the floor of the House – joining the company of the Hooligans, people like Winston Churchill, who was simply out for his own ends? How could he disregard his debt to his electors, and to the Southwolds?

'You *won't* vote with the Government, will you?'

'Yes,' Richard had answered, keeping his temper. 'I probably shall.'

James's voice was choked with fury and reproach. 'I hardly think Mother would have liked *that*!' he flung at his father, and rushed out of the room in tears.

The boy had been under the same emotional strain as Richard himself, and Richard was sorry to have hurt him. But independence mattered greatly to him; political independence more than the financial kind. Politely, regretfully, he told the pained Sir Geoffrey that he could not accept Lady Southwold's kind offer.

Downstairs there was an uneasy atmosphere. Sir Geoffrey's flippant parting words, overheard by Rose and Mr Hudson, had caused Mrs Bridges to exercise a new concern about the economics of the household. She began to make leftovers of meat and chicken into savouries instead of putting them outside for the benefit of Old Matty. Sheets must be turned sides to middle instead of going into the ragbag; every little helped. When the butcher tempted her with some particularly fine chops instead of a piece of brisket, she succumbed, but guiltily; especially when she looked at the tradesman's book, which, together with the other accounts, had to be submitted to the Master.

They happened to arrive on Richard's desk as he was about to leave for an important meeting at the House. Hazel, clearing up the day's work, had just made up her mind to offer her resignation. There was virtually no more need for her presence in 165, now that all the research material had been filed or returned; correspondence was out of her hands, for Richard had insisted on answering personally the floods of letters of condolence, and the Memorial Service for Lady Marjorie had been arranged.

She began: 'Mr Bellamy, I wanted to ask you . . .' at the same moment that Richard was saying 'Oh, Miss Forrest, I wonder if you'd do me a favour.'

She subsided. 'Yes, of course.'

'The tradesmen's books – I wonder if you'd see Mrs Bridges and give her the money to settle them.'

It was the very last favour Hazel wanted to bestow. She knew only too well, from her occasional encounters with Mrs Bridges, how that lady would regard interference in her department by a mere typewriter. It was with a feeling of one trampling on holy ground that she timidly began to ask Mr Hudson to summon Mrs Bridges; and, as usual, when she was nervous her voice took on a sharp note.

The mere request was enough, she could see, to put his back up. But his resentment was nothing to that of Mrs Bridges, as she stood by Richard's desk, on which the books were laid out, and That Hussy sitting in the Master's chair, actually presuming to tell her that there was a mistake in the addition in the butcher's book.

'Oh?' Mrs Bridges' tone was dangerous.

'The meat bill is higher this week and last than it was,' Hazel went on. 'Of course, these chump chops were expensive—'

'Lady Marjorie never grudged good quality meat for the kitchen!'

'No, of course not.' Her appeasing smile was not returned.

She added up the figures, unlocked the cash-box, and handed over five pounds.

'That will more than cover it. You could let me have the change in a day or two.'

Mrs Bridges stuffed the notes in the pocket of her apron and turned to go. At the door she paused. 'If I might have the storecupboard key, *Miss*.'

'Storecupboard?'

'I'm nearly out of tea and sugar. And tinned salmon.' She saw with satisfaction that Hazel had no idea where the key was, and pointed out the drawer in which it was kept. Hazel hesitated.

'Shall I come and unlock—?'

Mrs Bridges held out a relentless hand. 'There's no need for that, *Miss*. I'm sure you have your *work* to do. I'll get the stores out, and give the key back – to the Master.'

Something made Hazel cling on to the authority Richard had deputed to her, in spite of the intimidating figure glowering at her side. She handed over the key, saying: 'Perhaps it would be better if you returned it to me. Mr Bellamy won't be back till late tonight.'

In the kitchen Mrs Bridges exploded with the fury she had barely bothered to conceal upstairs. She glared at the unoffending Edward, who was cleaning knives in the knife-machine, as though she were about to seize a carver from him and plunge it into anybody who came near her.

'Cheek!' she raged. ' "I'll come and get the stores out, Mrs Bridges. I don't trust *you*!" '

Rose paused in her task of checking the stores. 'She never said that, did she?'

'She implied it.' Mrs Bridges banged down a tin on the table.

'Going through my books – this is expensive, that's expensive – as though I hadn't tried my best to economise, as well you know, Rose. Perhaps she'd like to pay our wages next, and knock a few shillings off!'

Rose agreed. 'I don't think the Master should have asked her. It's not right – putting her in Lady Marjorie's place.'

Mr Hudson agreed too, but loyalty prevailed. 'Now, Rose, it's not for us to criticise. I am sure we all want to make things as easy for the Master as we can, in this sad time.'

'Well, I think Miss Forrest's trying to take over,' said Rose defiantly. 'And I don't think it's right.'

Supper was a less enjoyable meal than usual. Mrs Bridges had economised on portions. When the after-supper pot of tea appeared, and Ruby asked for a third cup, Mrs Bridges snapped: 'You've had two already.'

'But Rose has had—'

'Two cups is quite enough for you. You keep your place, my girl.'

Outside rain poured down steadily, and there was a feeling of thunder in the air. Rose, who feared storms, looked apprehensively out into the area, dreading every minute to hear the approaching growl that would herald terrifying cracks overhead and flashes of forked lightning. She remembered how, when she was a child at Southwold, their dog Tatty would go under the table and howl during a storm; once her horrid old grandmother had kicked him for it, and her little brother Tim had cried inconsolably.

When the back door bell gave a loud peal she nearly jumped out of her skin.

'Whoever's that?' said Mrs Bridges. 'Can't be a tradesman at this hour.'

'Go and see, Ruby,' ordered Mr Hudson. 'And you go with her, Edward.'

They heard the area door unbolted and opened. And then, from Ruby, a loud scream.

'What on earth—' began Mr Hudson. Edward backed into the room, pale-faced, followed by a tiny bedraggled figure, clutching something Rose and Mr Hudson recognised: a large jewel-case. It was Rose's turn to shriek.

'Miss Roberts! No!'

Very much later tea was again being served. Miss Roberts was seated in the comfortable basket chair by the fire, taking sips from the cup in which she had refused the dash of brandy from the bottle Mr Hudson kept strictly for medicinal purposes. Bit by bit, they had learnt from her how she had come to appear at the door like a ghost, which at first they had thought her to be.

She had been one of the TITANIC passengers to be picked up by the CARPATHIA. Shock had deprived her of memory and speech, which came back to her in a New York hospital. As she couldn't tell anyone her name, news of her survival had not reached England. As soon as she recovered her memory she begged to come home; and here she was, straight off the ship. She told the story of the wreck to her hushed, breathless audience.

'There was this great noise, like a thousand trains letting off steam. And I said "M'lady, they say we ought to go on deck." And her ladyship said "It's much too cold on deck. I shall go and sit in the gymnasium." And the stewardess said "Oh, you must wear your lifebelts", and I said, "Oh, I don't want to wear that nasty bulky thing," and her ladyship said "Yes, Roberts, of course you must wear it. You can help me into mine, and then you must put yours on." And her ladyship sat with Lord Southwold and young Lady Southwold on the wicker chairs in the gymnasium. It got very quiet, and her ladyship said "Oh, Hugo, go and find out if anything's happening, or if we can go back to bed." And his lordship came back and said "You must get into the boats." Then we went out on deck, and everybody was running about, and there was a little girl there, crying, and her ladyship said "What's the matter, little girl?" and she said "I can't find my mother." So her ladyship gave me her jewel-case and said "Keep that for me, Roberts." Then she said to the little girl "I'll help you find your mother", and she took her hand and went away with her, and I never saw her again.'

Suddenly she looked wildly about her. 'Where is it? Where is it?'

Rose knelt at her side and lifted the jewel-case from the floor.

'It's here, Miss Roberts. We put it beside you while you had your tea.'

'No, no, I want to hold it!'

Rose laid it gently in her lap, and she grasped the handle tightly.

'How did you come to get into a boat, Miss Roberts?'

'There was an officer and two sailors, and they told me to get in the boat, and I said "Oh no, I must wait for My Lady," but they picked me up and threw me in and they lowered it into the water and rowed away. I said "Oh no, we must go back for My Lady," but they said "No, if we're near the ship when she goes down, we'll go down with her," and they kept rowing away.'

'Did you see the TITANIC go down?' asked Edward.

'There was a great roar . . . and then a crash and a lot of sparks. And there was – like it was a great black finger pointing down into the sea. And then it went down, and it took My Lady with it.'

Though Miss Roberts's body had survived the wreck, her mind had not. Obsessively she clung to the salt-stained jewel-case, refusing to be parted with it for a moment. When Rose found her in Lady Marjorie's bedroom, crooning over the dresses in the wardrobe and talking to their dead owner, she flew at Rose shrieking and clawing.

'Go away! Go away! Nobody touches My Lady's things but me!' And she pushed Rose and her dustpan and brush out of the room.

Her obsession raised a problem. Sir Geoffrey Dillon pointed out that the contents of the jewel-case must be checked and listed, then put into the bank as soon as possible, and Mr Hudson was sent upstairs to get it, very dubious of his chances of success. A few moments later the two men heard the air rent by Miss Roberts's manic screams and Hudson's pleading voice.

'Miss Roberts! You really must—'

'Leave me alone! No!'

Then Rose's 'Now, Miss Roberts, please—' produced a deafening volley of screams and sobs.

'What on earth—?' Sir Geoffrey shrugged, and Richard darted off upstairs, to be met outside his wife's room by Hudson, who informed him that Miss Roberts was not quite herself. Hazel, arriving on the scene behind him, found Miss Roberts at bay behind a chair, the jewel-box clutched in her arms and her eyes wild. Rose was pleading with her.

'Now, come on, Miss Roberts. Look, here's the Master.'

'You shan't have them! You shan't!'

Richard made an attempt. 'Now, Roberts, I don't know what all this is about, but—'

'My Lady told me to take care of them! You shan't have them!'

Helpless, they all stared at her. Obviously nothing short of violence would separate her from her sacred charge. Then, from behind them, came the clear, firm voice of Hazel.

'Oh, Roberts, I'm so glad you're here; we need your help,'

she said, as if the situation were the most normal in the world. The frenzied woman turned a puzzled gaze on her.

'Lady Marjorie left a spare key with the Master, and she wanted you to open her jewel-case.' She held out a hand to Richard, who detached a small key from his watch-chain and gave it to her.

Miss Roberts was quieter. 'Well,' she said slowly, 'if that's what her ladyship wanted . . .'

'Yes, it is. Perhaps if you put the case down on the dressing-table it might be easier.'

As if hypnotised, Miss Roberts did so. She unlocked the case, opened it, and looked down upon the familiar gems which had enhanced the beauty she would never see again, the bracelets and earrings, the carcanet of diamonds which had sparkled in the tawny hair. Hysterical no longer, she broke into tears. 'Oh, my lady, my lady!'

Hazel came forward and put her arms round the thin shoulders. Talking soothingly as if to a wounded animal, she led Miss Roberts from the room.

That afternoon Mr Hudson, of his own accord, brought Hazel coffee to the study.

CHAPTER FOUR

James glanced admiringly through the pages of the book he had taken from his father's desk. Handsomely bound, new and glossy, *Lord Southwold – a Life of Service* had just arrived from the publisher. Proud and slightly shy, Richard watched his son, curiously afraid of a critical reaction. James could be dauntingly chilly at times.

But this was not one of them. 'Well done, Father!' he said. 'I think it looks simply topping. Can I borrow this one?'

'You may keep it. I've inscribed the first copy for you.'

James turned to the fly-leaf and read the inscription in his father's neat handwriting. For a rare moment, there was affectionate understanding between the two men. 'Thank you, Father,' he said. 'I'll take it to the City with me. It must be more interesting than the price of tea!'

'Don't forget your letter.' Richard handed him the sheet of paper he had left on the desk.

'Thanks,' said James. 'It's only Bunny Preston, asking me to shoot next weekend. I don't think I'll go.'

'Why not? You don't go out enough these days. A change of scene will do you good. Who else is going to be there?'

'He doesn't say. Just "come down for the weekend. Bring your gun." He says he can supply me with a loader, but I don't know . . . I suppose I could take Edward, not that he knows anything about guns—'

'Why not take Hudson?' suggested Richard. 'He's an experienced loader, and I've always found him an excellent valet.'

'Hudson? He wouldn't want to go.'

'Why not? He's country born and bred. Whenever your mother and I took him to Chatsworth, he was delighted.'

'Possibly,' said James. 'But he'd think it far beneath his dignity to accompany *me*. He and I haven't always seen eye to eye, you know.' Memories of the recent clash inclined him to hope that Hudson would refuse any such offer. 'He thinks this house would fall to pieces if he wasn't here to look after it,' he added.

'In that case,' said Richard, 'it will do him good to know he's not indispensable.'

Mr Hudson graciously consented to accompany James. Though he replied to Mrs Bridges's observation that it would make a change for him 'Change is not everything, Mrs Bridges. I would much prefer to stay here at my post', he was looking forward to a temporary release from the sadness of Eaton Place. It would be pleasant to be in a great country house again. The young Marquis of Newbury, known to his friends as 'Bunny', was a rather rackety young man, certainly; but his mother, the Dowager Marchioness, still ruled his bachelor household, and it should therefore be a well-ordered one. Mr Hudson's Gladstone bag was packed, his key to the wine-cellar entrusted to Mrs Bridges; he was ready to leave.

James was rather less ready. The shock of his mother's death was still a cloud on his spirits, and the prospect of a weekend with Bunny and his frivolous, brainless friends was not exhilarating. If Hazel had been going with him it would have been different. He was surprised how much he disliked parting from her. Leaning over her desk, he said 'Shall I stay at home? Would you like me to?'

Hazel looked up in assumed surprise. 'Me? What have *I* got to do with it?' She began to wind paper into her typewriter. James tried again.

'Don't you think you'll miss me?'

She gave him a bright, formal smile. 'I doubt it. With the amount of work your father's given me to do, I shall be much too busy. Goodbye.' She began to type briskly and loudly. James turned to the door, a disappointed small boy.

'Goodbye,' he said. When he had gone she stopped typing, and sighed.

Somerby Park was a sturdy, stately Georgian house set in rolling acres of richly-wooded land. Approaching it through an avenue of beeches turned brilliant gold and glowing crimson by the touch of autumn, James sniffed appreciatively at the waft of wood-smoke borne to him on the crisp air, and his spirits began to lift. Mr Hudson, at his side, was less happy. James's driving was adventurous. When he took a corner too sweepingly Mr Hudson clutched his bowler hat and set his teeth. Not until the little tourer drew up before the imposing front door of Somerby did he relax. James tooted the horn sharply and continued to toot it while Mr Hudson began to unload their luggage and guns from the dickey-seat. At last the door opened. With cries of 'All right, sir, all right!' a stout figure wavered unsteadily down the steps. Mr Hudson disapprovingly surveyed the purple face and swimmy eyes of the old butler as he approached them, and James groaned.

'Makepiece has been at the port again,' he said.

The lounge-hall at Somerby contained an enormous fire-place, but the log-fire was powerless to warm the huge draught-riddled apartment. A number of small screens placed round the furniture helped to protect the guests from the worst of the cold; and there was always the exhilarating exercise of verbally dissecting other guests.

Kitty Cochrane-Danby's eyes were already alight with the joy of it. Brittle, elegant and worldly, Kitty delighted in gossip and conspiracy as much as in the stratagems by which she and her husband (known to all as Cocky) got the last ounce of value out of their hosts. Cocky's pension was chicken-feed compared with the riches of Somerby; it was only reasonable for Cocky and Kitty to scrounge, and scrounge they did. At this moment Cocky was exploring, with an absent-minded air, the decorative cigarette-boxes disposed about the room on tables and what-nots. He caught the amused glance of Lord Charles Gilmour following him from box to box.

'Er, just seeing if Bunny's got any cigarettes,' he murmured.

'Your case is empty, is it?' Lord Charles's tone was the ultimate in casualness. He was thirty-eight, a bachelor of some means, handsome and sophisticated. He would never lack for invitations to every kind of party. Like Kitty, he drew nourishment from the foibles of others; in this case from the baiting of Cocky, who was now nervously extracting his own cigarette-case.

'Oh,' he said, 'I do seem to have some, after all. That's lucky.'

Kitty, who had missed none of this, was smiling winningly at Charles.

'We're so glad to see you, Charles. We thought everyone was arriving this morning.'

'Well,' said Charles, 'I suppose "Come to lunch" and "Come to tea" *do* look rather alike in Bunny's handwriting.'

Kitty, with forbearance, confined herself to saying 'Yes, they do.' However illegible the schoolboy scrawl, Bunny's invitations were more than welcome when they plumped into the Cochrane-Danby letter-box, almost swamped by bills, reminders and Final Demands.

'And talking of tea—' said Cocky.

Kitty looked at her watch. 'I really do think poor old Makepiece is getting quite senile. I told him he could bring in tea a quarter of an hour ago.'

'Perhaps,' said Charles, 'he thought he should wait for the rest of the guests – or even for our hostess.'

Kitty laughed. 'Oh, Dolly will be having tea in her boudoir with Mr Weinberg. So much smarter to have a tame Jew than a poodle, and *much* more useful. Too funny to think of him sitting up there drinking tea and advising Dolly about her investments.'

Cocky's brow furrowed; his moustaches seemed to droop. 'I wish he'd advise us about ours.'

'Perhaps if Kitty is nice to him, he will.'

Kitty gazed at Charles, a gaze which conveyed that she was a beautiful woman – which she was not; and that Charles fully appreciated her charms – which he did.

'I admired his tweed suit,' she drawled, 'and I never once said that it made him look like a bookie's runner. I don't know what more I can do.'

They all thought of Weinberg, one-time adviser to King Edward, an astute and ambitious Jew whose chief preoccupation, apart from finance, was to be accepted as an English country squire, never so much at home as when hunting, shooting, and fishing. They despised him and were entertained by him.

'I suppose,' said Charles, 'darling Diana will be with us. Diana the huntress pursued by a Bunny! Quite a reversal.'

They all mused on Lady Diana Russell, beautiful, bright, something of a tomboy; and still single.

'Such a lovely girl,' purred Kitty, 'but not quite as young as she was. I suppose Bunny *does* mean to pop the question this weekend?'

'Well,' said Charles, 'there was another girl on the train. Very pretty little thing, golden hair and big blue eyes. Probably one of the Belvoir party.'

Cocky looked interested, a bloodhound scenting prey. 'I say! Golden hair . . .'

Kitty gave him a sharp look. 'Could be the youngest Grey girl – so pretty, but *almost* an idiot.'

'Possibly.' Charles concealed a yawn. 'Is anyone else coming?'

'Only James Bellamy. So embarrassing, his mother having gone down on the *TITANIC*. One feels quite inhibited about mentioning water. Cocky, you'd better drink soda with your whisky while you're here.'

'Wasn't James Bellamy rather keen on Diana at one time?' Cocky asked her.

Charles thought. 'In that case, I wonder why Bunny's asked him?'

'Perhaps it was Diana's idea,' put in Kitty.

They were all amused.

Later that afternoon a slightly more sober Makepiece was directing two footmen in the serving of tea to the now complete party of guests. The hall fire had been mended, a cheerful blaze roared wastefully up the chimney, and everybody was animated by the coming of tea and toasted scones. Their young host was talking to Diana Russell, enslavement written on his slightly vacuous face. She was, as even Kitty had admitted, a lovely girl, whose russet hair, big bright eyes and pointed chin gave her something of the look of a pretty fox-cub. At present the bright eyes were inclined to wander across the room, to where James Bellamy was seated on a sofa beside a young girl like a flaxen-haired wax doll, who was nervously stirring her tea.

'I say, Diana, I'm awfully glad you could come,' Bunny was saying.

'It was rather good of me, when you invite people like Kitty Danby. She's such a cat.'

Bunny looked surprised. 'I suppose she *is* rather awful.'

'So why do you ask her?'

'Oh, I don't know, really.'

Diana sighed impatiently. 'You never *do* know why you do things, Bunny. It gets rather boring.'

James extricated himself from Celia Grey and made his way to Diana.

'How perfectly splendid to see you!' he said. 'I thought you hated shooting-parties.'

The fox-brown eyes smiled into his. 'Do I? I must have forgotten. Come and have a scone – they're delicious.'

She put out a hand to him, and led him across to a laden trolley, watched with dismay by Bunny. Frustrated, he sat down by Celia Grey.

James and Diana were reminiscing, between bites of toasted scone, on their childhood days when she had been a visitor to Southwold.

'Do you remember the cinnamon toast?' he asked her.

'Yes! I remember my first weekend there, when I was so terrified, biting into a piece and spilling butter all down my dress, and your grandmother was beastly about it.'

'And said you were a hoyden.'

'I'm not really sure what hoyden means.'

James moved nearer to her, saying softly 'It means you're not in the least like Miss Grey.'

Her eyes teased him back. 'Do you think I could be, if I tried?'

'Never!' Both laughed. It was too much for the jealous Bunny, who came over and detached James with the excuse that Miss Grey would like a scone. But it was Cocky who sprang to attention and took the plate, while James and Diana, absorbed in each other, moved away together.

In the stone-flagged kitchen passage Mr Hudson was being welcomed by Breeze, the young Marquis's valet, and watching with some alarm the incompetent handling of his master's luggage by Henry, the young footman. As Henry prepared to go upstairs with the cases, Mr Hudson pointed sternly to one that remained.

'That bag is mine,' he pronounced. 'You may carry that, too, if you will.' And Henry, as a poor mortal obeying a god, scooped it up and departed.

'Well,' said Breeze, 'very nice to have you with us, Mr Hudson. Tea will be served shortly in the Servants' Hall, and we shall be very happy, I'm sure, to welcome you to the upper servants' sitting-room after dinner.'

Mr Hudson's sandy eyebrows shot up towards his receding

hair-line. 'Thank you, Mr Breeze,' he replied cordially. 'Er – Mr Breeze.'

Breeze turned. 'Yes, Mr Hudson?'

'Does Mr Makepiece take his tea in the Servants' Hall?'

Breeze was shocked. 'Mr *Makepiece*? Oh dear me, no. He has his tea in the Housekeeper's Room.'

'That would be Mrs Kenton,' Mr Hudson reflected. 'Mr Breeze, I wonder if you would be good enough to have a message conveyed to Mrs Kenton to the effect that Mr Hudson would like a word with her.'

With slow and serene gait he proceeded towards the staircase. Mr Breeze, puzzled, looked after him.

Mrs Kenton, trim, straight-backed and ladylike, was composing menus at her desk. Her black gown was free from ornament, her greying hair dressed in plain waves, but the aura of authority was about her, displayed in her assured gestures and her crisp voice. Next to the Dowager Marchioness, she ruled Somerby Park.

To a knock at the door she called, without turning her head, 'Come in.' Mr Hudson obeyed, and stood for a moment surveying with approval the cosy, warm sitting-room. His calm gaze slightly nettled Mrs Kenton.

'Ah, Mr – Hudson?' she said, in the tone of one identifying a rare insect. 'You are Captain Bellamy's valet, I believe. You wanted to speak to me?'

Mr Hudson carefully shut the door, and advanced.

'Mrs Kenton.' He greeted her with a courteous little bow, to which she returned a stiff inclination of her head. 'I think,' he said with a pleasant smile, 'there has been some – very natural – misunderstanding. I am not, strictly speaking, Captain Bellamy's valet. I hold the position of butler to Mr Richard Bellamy. Captain Bellamy's valet, Edward, would normally have accompanied him, but since there was shooting involved, and Edward is not experienced with guns, I offered to take his place for this occasion, and act as valet-loader.'

Mrs Kenton's gaze was as steely as her voice. 'I am sure Captain Bellamy appreciates it. Nevertheless, you are here in this household in the capacity of valet, and if you have come here to complain to me about your place in the Servants' Hall—'

'Complain about my *place*?' Mr Hudson appeared as shocked as though Mrs Kenton had uttered some unthinkable indecency. 'Certainly *not*. As far as my *place* is concerned, I think I should be content to quote the old Scottish saying, and remark that "Where the MacGregor sits is the head of the table.' He smiled charmingly.

Mrs Kenton's eyes opened wide and her thin brows arched. She seemed about to say something, but thought better of it as he continued.

'No, no, Mrs Kenton. In my own house in Eaton Place I am, as it were, master belowstairs. I don't expect my authority to be questioned there, and I would not dream of questioning your authority here.'

Like a bird fascinated by a snake, Mrs Kenton continued to stare at him.

'It was merely,' he went on airily, 'that I felt some slight embarrassment might arise later if it was realised that the situation had been misunderstood.' A whimsical little smile lurked about his mouth. 'I am sure I shall find it an interesting experience to take tea in the Servants' Hall. It will remind me of my old days as a footman at Southwold.'

Mrs Kenton scarcely noticed the entry of a maid with tea-tray and cloth, so riveted was she, but managed to say 'All right, Betsy. You can lay the table.' With a bow, Mr Hudson backed towards the door. The housekeeper pulled herself together.

'Mr Hudson. Perhaps you would care to stay and take tea with Mr Makepiece and myself – just for this afternoon.'

He shook his head regretfully. 'Thank you, Mrs Kenton, but I must unpack for the Captain. We travelled by motor, and it was rather dusty.'

'Well . . . perhaps you would care to return in half an hour.'

With no sign of unbecoming triumph, Mr Hudson replied: 'Thank you, Mrs Kenton. That would be very pleasant.' Gracefully he bowed himself out.

Bunny Preston was unhappy. His weekend was going wrong somewhere. He had invited James with the idea that he should partner Celia Grey while Bunny devoted himself to the siege of Diana. But James seemed totally uninterested in Miss Grey's somewhat anaemic charms, and only too interested in Diana's, deftly counter-moving all Bunny's attempts to keep him at Celia's side. Bunny's mother, the Dowager Marchioness, petite and pretty and known as "Dolly", added her charmingly tactful efforts to her son's, inveigling James into conversation with Max Weinberg. James didn't trouble to conceal his contempt for what he considered to be the financier's vulgarity, and drifted back to Diana at the first possible moment.

Kitty and Charles Gilmour sipped their sherry and watched the contest eagerly.

'It really is too deliciously amusing,' said Kitty. 'They're like two over-anxious sheep-dogs, trying to herd James in the direction of Miss Grey.'

'And he keeps slipping out of the pen and joining Diana.'

'Wouldn't it be funny,' Kitty speculated, 'if, instead of getting engaged to Bunny – which I'm sure is his express intention – she got engaged to James instead? Shall we see if we can contrive it?'

Their eyes met.

'Why not?' said Charles.

Mr Hudson, as he helped James to dress next morning, took an unobtrusive part in the conspiracy.

'Very pleasant to see Lady Diana Russell again, sir.'

'Very.' James was fastening his tie.

'She was always a great favourite of her ladyship's. I remember her ladyship saying to me once "Lady Diana is coming to dinner, Hudson. We must ask Mrs Bridges to make that raspberry pudding she is so fond of." '

'I don't remember Lady Diana dining at Eaton Place.'

'I think it was when you were in India, sir. I remember when Lady Diana arrived, she asked if you were going to be there, and seemed very disappointed when she learned that you were not.'

James's face, reflected in his shaving-mirror, was thoughtful.

His task done, Mr Hudson proceeded to the gun-room, where preparations were afoot for the day's shoot. In the butler's pantry next door he saw Breeze surveying the packed hamper and the rest of the equipment. Mr Makepiece was surreptitiously sampling the claret, and Mr Hudson deduced that he had been doing so for some time.

'I hope you're putting in some rugs and chairs, Mr Makepiece,' said Breeze. The gentlemen *will* sit on the ground, and I don't want his lordship's new suit all nasty green stains.'

Mr Makepiece's reply was blurred. 'The ground? His lordship won't sit on the ground. With his artheritis, he'd never get up again.'

Breeze sighed patiently. 'I'm talking about his *young* lordship, Mr Makepiece. His late lordship is dead.'

'I *know* he's dead!' snapped the butler. 'What're you talking about?'

Breeze gave it up, exchanging an eloquent look with Mr Hudson as they passed each other. Mr Hudson's greeting interrupted Mr Makepiece in the process of finishing yet another glass. 'Good morning, good morning,' he replied with a flustered air, peering at Mr Hudson with eyes that seemed not to focus properly. 'Who are you? Do I know you?'

'Mr Hudson. Butler to Mr Richard Bellamy and to the late Lady Marjorie Bellamy.'

'Oh, yes. Yes. That's what I thought. Just testing the claret. His lordship's very particular about his claret. Always has been. I remember, for the old Queen's Jubilee, we gave a supper for a hundred and fifty estate workers, and his lordship said "Give them claret, Makepiece," he said. "Let 'em try the real thing for once."'

'I dare say they would rather have had beer,' responded Mr Hudson.

'Thass what I said. I said, "M'lord, they'd just as soon have beer." He peered suspiciously over his glass. 'Do I know you?'

'Hudson, Mr Makepiece. I had the pleasure of taking tea with you and Mrs Kenton yesterday.'

'Oh yes. Yes. I thought I knew your face.'

Retreating, Mr Hudson shook his head sadly.

In the chilly lounge-hall Diana, Kitty and Celia sat awaiting the time when they might properly join the gentlemen for the picnic luncheon. An atmosphere of strain hung about them.

'Shooting-parties are such a dreadful bore,' complained Kitty. 'Either one's left to amuse oneself until teatime, or else one goes to have lunch in a muddy field, to the ruination of one's boots and gloves, and the men come in at four o'clock with splitting headaches, fit for nothing but dozing in front of the fire and tumbling into bed – usually their own. I really don't know why I come.'

Diana turned her head languidly and said 'Don't you?'

Kitty ignored the barb. 'At least we know why James Bellamy's come – and I don't mean for the shooting.'

'Oh?'

Kitty purred. 'But, my dear Diana, surely you know?' James said he wouldn't come at first, but then Bunny told him *you* were going to be here, so he changed his mind.'

Both Celia and Diana stared at her. Suddenly Diana rose. 'I'm going for a walk,' she said, and went briskly out. Twenty minutes later she appeared at James's side, as he took aim at a lone bird.

Luncheon was served in a capacious tent. James, entering, found himself with Max Weinberg, who had discomfited the other men by showing prowess far above theirs. Still, one must be polite. 'You shoot very well,' James said.

'Thank you. I never think it's worth doing anything, unless one does it well,' the financier replied.

They approached the long table, which bore a cloth but nothing else. Footmen milled around it uneasily, and Mr Makepiece leaned on the end of it, a glassy look in his eyes.

'Shall we get the hay-boxes out of the brake, Mr Makepiece?' asked young Henry.

'Whassat? Not yet. Don't want food to get cold.'

Henry's worried look was caught by Mr Hudson, who at the same time saw the rest of the shooting-party arriving from one direction and the ladies from another. The Dowager Marchioness, first to set foot in the tent, took in the situation with alarm concealed beneath a bright smile.

'Now, where shall we sit down?' she enquired.

It was a good question, as the folding chairs were still stacked behind the tent. She had barely spoken before Mr Hudson had whisked one inside and opened it for her. Commanded by his authoritative nod, the footmen hastened to fetch chairs for the other ladies, while Mr Hudson swiftly summed up the condition of Mr Makepiece, who was still wavering by the table and muttering that the food mustn't be allowed to get cold. Gently, Mr Hudson took his arm, led him to the brake and propelled him into it, where he immediately fell asleep. Then, with superb expertise, Mr Hudson took command of the feast.

Back at Somerby in the late afternoon, Dolly met the housekeeper in the hall.

'I hope everything went all right, m'lady,' said Mrs Kenton.

'Yes, thank you, Mrs Kenton. Poor old Makepiece was rather unwell. I think it must have been the cold.'

Mrs Kenton's sparse eyelashes flickered briefly. 'Oh yes, m'lady, it always affects him. I hope the luncheon didn't suffer?'

'Oh no. That man of Captain Bellamy's was very helpful, and everything went off splendidly. We must remember him – what's his name? Hudson? – if ever our dear old Makepiece should think of retiring. That is *exactly* the kind of man we should be looking for.'

Mrs Kenton had independently reached the same conclusion.

Dinner was over. A bridge game was in progress, from which James had neatly extricated himself in order, he said, to learn from Diana a new form of Patience. They ensconced themselves in a screened alcove, while Bunny, again landed with Celia Grey, settled unhappily in a neighbouring one. Cocky, the other non-bridge player, hovered happily near the tray of drinks.

'I'm sorry for that poor little Grey girl,' said Diana. 'Trying to do all the things her mother told her to, looking like an idiot because Mother says men detest intelligent women.'

'What does *your* mother expect you to do?'

'Oh . . . the usual thing. Marry "well". Only her idea of marrying well isn't mine.'

'What's yours?'

Diana's face clouded. 'I think it ought to be something more than agreeing to share the same house and butler.'

'Yes.'

She gazed into the fire. 'I sometimes wish I'd been born in something-or-other B.C., when people lived in caves, and men and women got married just so as to huddle together for warmth, and to stop each other being frightened of the dark.'

James looked quizzically down at her. 'Are you frightened of the dark?'

'Sometimes. Aren't you?' Her voice trembled a little.

'Sometimes. Would you like to huddle close to me for warmth?'

Her eyes laughed up at him. 'Try me!'

They kissed; a kiss that would have been long and sweet, but for the sudden apparition of Bunny. They jerked apart just in time.

The moment had passed.

Kitty, sitting out with Charles Gilmour, had seen the emergence from the alcove. 'It's really too bad,' she said, 'that we didn't have a bet on the Lady Diana stakes.'

'Right. I'll bet with you if you like.'

'On James Bellamy.'

'No, on Bunny.'

Kitty stared. 'You can't be serious! She's head-over-heels in love with James. She was head-over-heels in love with him before, but he hadn't any money. Now he has the Southwold inheritance, and she means to have him.'

'Ah,' said Charles, 'but does *he* mean to have *her*? Now Bunny does. Ten guineas?'

Kitty nodded.

Winding his watch before getting into bed, James yawned. It had been a long, strenuous day; he felt tired and curiously unsettled. He turned sharply at a noise from the door. It opened, to reveal Diana, a silk peignoir over her nightdress, her hair loose about her shoulders.

'Good heavens!' he said. 'Hello!'

'You don't mind, do you?' She slipped inside the room, leaving the door a crack open. 'It's that beast, Cocky Danby. He said if I dropped a glove outside my door, he'd pay me a visit. So I did.'

'You *did*?'

'Yes. Cecile's there – my maid. She thinks every man who comes near her is going to rape her.'

'H'm. Should be interesting.'

Diana's face was alight with mischief. 'That's what I

thought.' Both began to giggle. 'Quick, put the light out, I can hear him! Ssh.'

They crouched by the door, stifling their laughter. Outside the boards creaked beneath heavy footsteps. Then a door opened, and from within came a volley of outraged French, interrupted now and again by Cocky's attempts at explanation. 'Pardon, mademoiselle, je suis – I really am most terribly sorry – je vous assure – er – j'ai fait un – bonne nuit!'

As his footsteps passed James's door again, more swiftly this time, the two huddled together inside collapsed with laughter, shrieking and whooping, helplessly clutching each other. Recovering slightly, James found that Diana was in his arms, her face turned up invitingly to his, waiting confidently for his kiss.

But James gently released her, unkissed. He gave a slightly false laugh. 'I enjoyed that. Even if Cocky didn't. Shall I – see you back to your room?'

Her expression was blank. 'Don't bother,' she said coldly, and turned to the door. There she turned for one last appeal.

'You know Bunny wants to marry me.'

'Yes. He's not nearly good enough for you.'

The battle was lost. 'No,' she said, and left him without a goodnight.

Next morning Mr Hudson, by invitation, was taking breakfast with Mrs Kenton. Conversation had proceeded via civilities and small talk to discussion of the staff at Eaton Place, laughably small in comparison with Somerby's. Mrs Kenton appeared to muse as she toyed with a piece of sausage.

'You must sometimes feel that such a very – restricted – staff hardly exercises your abilities, Mr Hudson.'

'I have never really thought about it,' he answered with truth.

'Of course,' said Mrs Kenton, finally rejecting the sausage, 'some people might think that the responsibilities of the Somerby butler are almost *too* great. Not only this house, but the house in Grosvenor Square – fully staffed at all times – and the one in Scotland as well. Some toast, Mr Hudson? Yes, our butler has to be a man who is not afraid to take command. He needs to have a natural authority. And not everyone has.' She was observing the emotions that chased each other across Mr Hudson's face.

'No, that's very true.' He was consuming the toast with slow thoughtfulness.

'Her ladyship was remarking to me yesterday how very much she appreciated the way you – helped everything to go smoothly at the shooting luncheon.'

'I was only too glad—'

'Of course, Mr Makepiece will be retiring soon.'

'Oh, indeed?'

'If you should ever decide that you wanted a change, and felt that you would like the post of butler at Somerby – I think I can safely say that it would be yours. I don't know if the idea would be likely to appeal to you—?'

Mr Hudson was startled, interested, but cautious. 'It would certainly be a challenge,' he admitted.

Mrs Kenton began to butter her toast. 'Well, if you *should* decide to leave your present position, you have only to write a letter to me here, and the matter would be settled. Marmalade?'

Before packing for his master Mr Hudson took a stroll in the grounds. The great house, majestic in the light of an autumn morning, displayed itself before him. Well drilled in the Scriptures, his mind produced from its depths some words from the Gospel according to Saint Matthew. 'The Devil taketh him up into an exceeding high mountain, and sheweth him all the kingdoms of the world, and the glory of them.' He pictured what it would be like to hold dominion over Somerby and its related houses; and, in contrast, the saddened home in Eaton Place. Then there came to him some scraps of a conversation he had had with Mr Makepiece the evening before, when for once the old man was sober. 'It's a big responsibility, this place . . . I sometimes think going into service is like getting married. You live in the same house, back each other up, quarrel sometimes, make your lives together. And then the master dies . . . and you're expected to carry on, just as if nothing had happened . . . it's a question of loyalty, you see.'

"When the master dies . . ." Or the mistress, thought Hudson. A question of loyalty . . .

He turned back towards the house.

By mid-morning most of the guests had left. Cocky had departed disgruntled, Kitty out of temper, Celia Grey disappointed. Diana, standing at a window, saw James's little tourer receding down the drive. Mr Hudson turned to look back towards Somerby, then settled into his seat. But James didn't turn.

Bunny was hovering behind her, nervously. 'I say,' he began, 'I know you think I'm an awful bore, but—'

'But what?'

He gulped. 'Diana, will you marry me?'

She gave him a long, contemptuous look. 'Why not?' she said bitterly.

At 165 Eaton Place the study door opened and Hazel's typing stopped as she saw James. A delighted smile lit up her face. 'Oh, you're back! Did you – did you have a good time?'

He moved towards her, saying nothing for a moment. Then he said, 'Have you ever been to a party, Hazel, and thought you were enjoying yourself, and then suddenly wanted to come home?'

She was not sure what he meant; but his words made her strangely, unreasonably happy.

That same evening Mr Hudson posted a letter in the Eaton Place pillar-box. It was short and to the point, and when it arrived upon Mrs Kenton's breakfast-table its contents caused her to lapse, for once, from her ladylike dignity.

'Drat!' said Mrs Kenton.

CHAPTER FIVE

For a girl unused to night life in London, as Hazel was, the Café Royal in Piccadilly was a most exciting place. For many years it had been the meeting-place for that deliciously dangerous class, the Bohemians. Artists, actors, critics, dilettantes, came there to drink, eat, smoke and talk, talk, talk; for it had arisen in an age when the telephone was a crude and mistrusted instrument, and direct human communication still in its heyday.

Its Domino Room, with pillars of gilt and jewel-colours surmounted by voluptuous caryatids, supported a ceiling of painted grandeur; its lamps shone down on this November night of 1912 as they had shone on the pale face of young Aubrey Beardsley, sketching away, perhaps at one of his shocking depraved nudes. The red velvet bench was still there on which the portly form of Oscar Wilde had lounged, one or other of his sleazy young men at his side, his lazy voice sending sparkling showers of brilliant talk into the cigar-scented air.

Hazel looked down from the table for two on the famous Balcony at the swirl of people below, the men's dark suits, the flowery lacy dresses of the women, the white-aproned waiters scurrying about with bottles and carafes of wine. A string orchestra's rendering of the Waltz Song from Offenbach's *La Belle Heléne* served as a backing to the conversation and laughter. It was all very different from Wimbledon, or, for that matter, from the atmosphere of the Bellamy household.

Yet it was James Bellamy who sat opposite her, humming the orchestra's tune, his eyes smiling across at her. She was a very different Hazel from the discreet grey-clad typist in Richard's study. Tonight she was wearing her best costume of bottle-green, tightly hugging her figure, and a shell-pink blouse with a frilly jabot which set off her pearly complexion. James, used to drawing-rooms full of ladies in the richest of clothes and jewels, with freely displayed arms and bosoms, thought he had never seen anything so lovely.

He saw, tenderly, the wonder tinged with awe in her eyes, as she gazed down at the diners and drinkers below.

'I thought the Balcony might amuse you,' he said. 'Like being Gods on Olympus looking down at all the minor gods below.'

'Oh, yes! It's fascinating . . .'

'There's Hannen Swaffer, the theatre critic – and that's Max Beerbohm, the author. He's Beerbohm Tree's brother, of course.' He pointed out a gesticulating spectacled man in the company of a shorter one with large melancholy eyes in a face which was not unlike a bat's. 'And *that* man, with the woman in yellow . . .'

He became conscious of the patient gaze of a hovering waiter.

'Come along, let's order. Are you hungry?'

'I always have a good appetite. And I think the drive from Wimbledon's increased it.' James had driven her up (having met her by arrangement some distance from her own door) in his newly-acquired little sports car, which actually did up to forty miles an hour.

'The fresh air's certainly brought the colour to your cheeks. If – if I may be so bold as to say so, you're looking awfully beautiful tonight, Hazel.'

She laughed. 'It's probably this dim lamplight.'

'Can't be. You looked just as beautiful in Kensington Gardens last Wednesday afternoon, and I told you so.'

'Yes, you did. I must admit it.'

'In broad daylight, with the band playing *Iolanthe*.'

'Then perhaps it was the music.'

James, against the competition from the orchestra, sang softly the opening of the duet for Phyllis and Strephon.

'All in all to one another,
One in life and death are we . . .'

'Ssh!'

'Hazel, do you know that if you stood, dressed in sackcloth, with your hair in a mess, against a grey brick wall in the pouring rain, you'd still be lovelier to my eyes than all these painted Watteau shepherdesses we saw in the Wallace Collection on Sunday?'

'Oh, what nonsense.' She heard, if James did not, the faint

hinting cough of the waiter. 'Don't you think we ought to order?' she reminded him.

'By Jove, yes, we should. I think the consommé Julienne to begin with, and then the famous Café Royal Saddle of Lamb . . .'

They had reached the brandy and coffee stage, and Hazel was looking at her watch.

'I mustn't stay out too late, James. My parents worry. I've got a key, of course, but Mother always waits up, if I'm out.' She sighed.

'Would they worry if they knew you were out with me – your employer's son?'

'If they knew they might worry for a different reason.'

'What reason?'

'Well . . . they might think I was – taking advantage of my position in your father's house.'

James smiled. 'By forcing me to take you out to dinner – against my will?'

'No, silly. By allowing myself to be taken out – against my better judgment.'

'What absolute rubbish!'

'And without your father's knowledge – behind his back.'

James shook his head impatiently. 'You make it all sound so furtive. There's no particular reason why my father should be told of our meetings, is there?'

'No, nor my parents. But they're becoming curious; at least, Mother is. She's rather old-fashioned and conventional . . .' Her voice trailed off. She was looking at him with her clear direct gaze, her chin resting on her linked hands. '*Please* don't be angry with me and spoil a lovely evening. But I have to ask you something.'

'Of course I won't! Ask me what?'

'Well . . .' he could see that she found it difficult to say, whatever it was. 'You've been so very kind and attentive over the last few weeks – taking me to the theatre, to supper, to concerts, for walks in the park . . . I think I've experienced more happiness just lately than ever before in my whole life. But – I'm only an ordinary person with ordinary feelings, and like my mother I'm rather conventional. So I must ask you to make clear to me – well, your intentions.' She was looking down at the table-cloth, her cheeks deeply pink now. James reached across and touched her arm tenderly.

'Of course I know what you mean. Dearest Hazel, I believe I'm in love with you. I think you're the most beautiful girl I've ever met. And – I don't quite know how to express this – last April, when I heard – about my mother, and everything seemed so black and awful and hopeless – it was because you were with us, with my father, helping us, comforting us, keeping everything from going to pieces . . . it sort of helped me to bear it.'

Their hands were touching now, clasped together across the table, her eyes bright and brimming.

'So you see, Hazel, I've come to feel that life without you would be quite unbearable. The thought of you ever leaving us would be quite – appalling. I can only offer you my life, and love and devotion – and – well, just myself. But – will you marry me?'

The blue eyes had brimmed over now, and she had turned away her face from him, gazing unseeing over the plush rail of the Balcony. When she could speak she said:

'Please take me home. I need to think about so many things. Do you mind?'

He shook his head in puzzlement. 'If that's what you want. Hazel – what is it?'

'Please!' she answered softly. 'Please!'

Hazel put her typewriter into its case, donned her hat and gloves, and presented herself in the morning-room, where Richard sat glancing over some Parliamentary papers. He looked up with a smile.

'If I might speak to you for a moment, before I go home,' she said.

'Of course. Please sit down.'

She perched on the edge of a chair. Her expression was tense. Where was this leading? he wondered.

'I've paid all the tradesmen's books up to date, and those four letters are on your desk ready for your signature.'

'Splendid. Thank you.'

She twisted her gloved hands together. 'Mr Bellamy, I think perhaps the time has come – for me to ask to be released from my duties here . . . in this house.'

He sat up, startled. 'Miss Forrest!'

'The last thing I want is to abandon my post, while I am

. . . if I am still needed here. But I have – personal reasons for wishing not to continue as your secretary.'

Richard looked his query. She did not meet his eyes.

'I'd rather not mention them, if you don't mind. Just to ask you if you'd accept my notice to leave at the end of the week.'

Her employer got up, and began to pace restlessly.

'I see,' he said. 'Well, of course I can't force you to stay on here against your will. It just seems a pity now that things seem to be running smoothly in the house, after a bad start. The servants have come to respect you and seem willing to co-operate with you. You've been the greatest possible help over the last six months to me and my son – to all of us. Frankly, I don't know what we should have done without you.'

She looked down at her feet, in their neat grey ankle-boots.

'I'm very gratified to hear that, Mr Bellamy. But I must go. It will be best . . . in the circumstances.'

'I see,' said Richard, who could see nothing of the kind. 'Well – after Friday, then?'

After she had gone he questioned Hudson keenly. Had anyone upset Miss Forrest, in any way?

'Not to my knowledge, sir. Indeed, the staff have lately become quite attached to the young lady. She appears to be discharging the duties of – if I may so call it, a housekeeper, most competently.'

So there the puzzle was. What were Hazel's 'personal reasons'?

Hazel sat in the Wimbledon train. It was packed, reeking of tobacco-smoke and sweating humanity, but she was beyond noticing. How little Richard Bellamy knew about his employee, she reflected. About those talks with James, during their evenings together. About his questions, probing into her life, trying to solve the mystery about her which intrigued and frustrated him. She had told him that her father was an accountant with a small shipping firm – had been for forty years; that her parents disliked her working.

She hadn't told him how her mother had sniffed disapprovingly at the smell of 'strong liquor' lingering after a glass of sherry taken with James.

'Captain Bellamy? Oh, Hazel! I don't think you should

see too much of him.' And, another time, 'Why were you late tonight?'

Hazel had replied that she had been helping Mr Bellamy with the letters of condolence – 'and then there were one or two household things ...'

'Household things?' interrupted her father. 'But that wasn't what you were employed for, dear, was it? I think you have to be careful *in your situation.* I mean, a young woman going out to strange houses, doing typewriting for anyone who asks her. I know how these aristocratic families take advantage.'

Hazel, smiling within herself, wondered exactly how he knew, poor little man.

'The next thing you know, you'll be scrubbing the kitchen floor,' said her mother. 'They'll encroach and encroach. You don't have to be unpleasant about it. Just say very calmly and firmly, "I'm sorry, but that wasn't what I was engaged for." They'll think all the more of you.'

This evening she must tell her parents.

At 165 an inquest was being held on Mr Hudson's piece of news about Hazel's resignation.

Rose snorted. 'It's Mr James – who else? Can't keep his hands off of any woman, he can't. Look how he got Sarah into trouble.'

'You'd think he'd have more respect,' said Mrs Bridges, 'with her ladyship not long gone to her rest, poor soul.'

Mr Hudson fixed her with a reproving eye.

'Let us not jump to conclusions, if you please. If *Captain* James had been forcing his attentions on Miss Forrest, she would certainly have complained of it to the Master.'

'It don't follow, Mr Hudson,' Rose persisted. 'If there's been hanky-panky between the pair of them, she'd be too ashamed to mention it. Best leave and say nothing about it – *I* would.'

Mrs Bridges had an inspiration. 'Unless she's been encouraging him – you know, leading him on. And got a bit more than what she asked for.'

This was too much for Mr Hudson. 'Mrs Bridges, *please*!'

'No, Mr Hudson, I believe in calling a spade a spade. We're all grown up down here, except Ruby, and she's too young and stupid to understand.'

Mr Hudson banged on the table. 'I won't have this kind of talk at meals. Is that understood?' Rose and Mrs Bridges nodded without enthusiasm. It had been a long time since interesting gossip had come their way, and now Mr Hudson was being tiresomely Scottish about it.

'Whatever we may think of Miss Forrest, she comes of reliable, God-fearing, middle-class stock. I would not pairsonally question her respectability. She may have pairsonal family reasons for going – the illness of an ageing parent, better paid employment elsewhere – the possibilities are legion. And it is not for us to speculate.'

Ruby's eyes were like saucers. Her mind worked slowly, and she was still some way back in the discussion.

'Got a bit more of *what* than she asked for, Mrs Bridges?'

Mrs Bridges regarded her with exasperation. 'Ruby.'

'Yes, Mrs Bridges?'

'It's gone ten o'clock, my girl. Fetch the teapot, and look sharp. If that's possible,' she added to the others, as Ruby disappeared into the kitchen.

In the drawing-room at the semi-detached house in Wimbledon, Mrs Forrest was saying the same thing to her daughter that she had been saying all evening.

'But can't you see how unsuitable it is, Hazel? People like that would never accept you into the family. It's not to be expected.'

'Not in your situation,' put in her father.

Hazel was emotionally exhausted; her self-control snapped.

'Oh, damn my situation!' she shouted. 'I'm sick of hearing about my situation. What am I supposed to be, a fallen woman or something?'

'*Hazel*!' Her mother's always-upright figure was rigid, the ample sloping bosom popularised by Queen Mary quivering with outrage under her elaborately tuckered blouse. 'Don't let me hear you using words like that again. I suppose you've picked them up from your employers!'

'They're apt to be looser-tongued than us, dear,' her father said. 'You wouldn't realise, of course, not having been used—'

'Not being used?' Hazel flared back. 'Do you think I haven't heard a lot worse than that in my time, Dad? And seen things worse than you can ever imagine, living like this in a sort of box with other people living in little boxes all round you? I've learned something about life since James has been taking me out, and it's different from anything you can imagine!'

'Despising us now, then!' Mrs Forrest snorted.

'You were glad enough of your home once, Hazel,' her father reminded her gently. 'Glad of a place of refuge.'

'I know. I'm sorry.'

'If you really care for this young man,' he went on, 'if he'd make you happy – if we could be sure—'

'Be quiet!' his wife snapped at him. 'Encouraging her like that. We don't want to hear any more about this, Hazel. I'm surprised at you, coming home and upsetting us like this. It's not like you at all. That young man's a bad influence. If I were you, I'd go to bed and say your prayers.'

'I shall do that in any case, Mother.' Hazel was quieter now. 'But I must warn you that whatever you say, James is coming here to talk to you and explain how we feel. Next Sunday afternoon.'

'I see.' Mrs Forrest folded her lips tightly. 'Well, we can't stop him.' (But inwardly she was determined to change Hazel's attitude very much between then and Sunday.)

'We *ought* to see him, dear . . .' her husband ventured. She ignored him.

'Go and put on the kettle for the cocoa. And bring my smelling salts from the dressing-table!' she called after him.

It was always a bad sign when Mrs Forrest called for her smelling salts.

That evening at 165 Eaton Place James's breaking of the news to his father was not going well. Richard genuinely believed that Hazel had resigned because James had been tampering with her affections. That was bad enough, but nothing to the unbelieving shock with which he heard his son say:

'I've fallen in love with Hazel, Father, and I want to marry her.'

In the pause that followed he heard himself saying weakly: 'Hazel?'

'Hazel Forrest. It's her name. Perhaps you didn't know.' His tone was sarcastic.

'James, is this some kind of tastless joke?'

'No, it isn't. And it's almost certainly the reason for her resignation, though she hasn't mentioned it to me.'

His father rose and began to pace about. James heard him mutter: 'God help us!' and was remorseful, but the battle must go on.

'Father, I do realise Mother only died six months ago. But you said yourself that life had to go on.'

'Miss Forrest is a *typist*.'

'What does that matter nowadays? And since when has a person's class mattered to you? You're in favour of Lloyd George's Insurance Bill, aren't you?' he added unkindly.

'Yes, but – never mind about that. Of course class has never mattered to me. Of itself, that is. But there can be difficulties, James! You know damn well there can. Look what happened when you brought that wretched girl home from India.'

'Phyllis was different. And I wasn't in love with her – not really.'

'You told us you were. You *thought* you were.'

'This time I am – for certain.'

Richard stopped pacing and looked down at James, who was crushing out the second cigarette he had puffed at during the interview.

'I wonder,' Richard said. 'Phyllis was a perfectly pleasant respectable girl but she didn't fit in. You said so yourself. Do you think Miss Forrest is going to fit in?'

'*Fit in*?' James was torn between irritation and mirth. 'She's practically running this house already.'

Richard sighed impatiently. 'James, how can I take you seriously? Your record with the opposite sex is not exactly – promising.'

'You're thinking about Sarah. I'm three years older now, Father, and that much wiser, I hope. And – we've been going out together for three weeks, you know.'

'I *don't* know. And wasn't that rather deceitful of you both?'

'Hazel never liked deceiving you – it was I who insisted we should keep our meetings a secret.'

Richard sought for arguments. 'What are the servants going to make of it?'

'What they make of it is no concern of mine.'

Richard, his face drawn with worry, subsided into his chair. In the softened light of the lamp by which he had been reading he looked many years older than his age. 'It's unthinkable, James,' he said. 'For many reasons.' James was sorry for what he had to reply.

'Father, you're forcing me to remind you that I'm my own master now. I'm thirty, and I've enough money to marry on.'

'Your mother's money,' Richard retorted bitterly.

'That was unfair.'

'Yes. I'm sorry . . . Have you proposed to Miss Forrest?'

'Yes, I have.'

'And she's accepted you?'

'No, not yet. She wants time to think – it's quite natural.'

'And if she does agree to become your wife, where do you propose to live?'

'In this house, with your permission. There's plenty of room for us both. And I *am* paying most of the bills now – as you and Sir Geoffrey proposed, and I agreed, willingly.'

Richard passed his hand wearily across his forehead.

'Please leave me now, James. Go to bed, it's late.'

'Then may I take it we have your blessing, Father?'

'Your life is your own, James.'

When the door had shut he leant his head back against the head-rest of his chair, and looked across at the corner of the sofa where his wife had liked to sit, working on her embroidery or smilingly dispensing tea to her family and guests. He could see her still, vividly, in the cream lace dress he had liked best. Marjorie, Marjorie, if you could come back to me! Oh, God, turn back thy Universe, and give me yesterday . . .

It was Sunday afternoon, wet and depressing. Mrs Bridges was enjoying a peaceful snooze by the fire, a tray of tea-things beside her. The sudden opening of the door roused her with a start, to see James in the doorway.

'Oh – sorry to disturb you, Mrs Bridges. Er – I was looking for Hudson.'

She got up. 'He's out, Captain James. Gone to some afternoon service.'

James lingered. 'Oh, well, it wasn't important. Do you know, Mrs Bridges, I'd love a cup of tea.'

She beamed. 'Would you, Captain James? Well, there's a

drop left in the pot, but it's gone cold. I'll make some fresh.'

'Oh, don't worry.' He felt the side of the fat brown teapot. 'That'll be hot enough for me.'

'Well, if you're sure.' Mrs Bridges fetched a cup and saucer and poured a cup for James, who after a sip set it aside absent-mindedly. She eyed him shrewdly, remarking:

'You haven't been down here for a cup of tea, not for ever such a long time – not since you was at school.'

'No, I haven't, have I . . . Mrs Bridges, I wanted to ask you something. Well, Hudson, really, but I expect you can advise me.'

Mrs Bridges settled down proudly for a really interesting chat. 'If I can, Captain James.' She had a fair idea of what was on his mind.

'Mrs Bridges. What do you think of Miss Forrest? I'd like to know, honestly.'

She pursed her lips. 'Miss Forrest? Well, I've not seen that much of her, but from what I hear, she's a very nice, respectable young person.'

'I see. What do the other servants think of her?'

'Well, much the same, as far as I know – not that we like to talk about what concerns upstairs, not as a rule,' she added, her fingers crossed.

'But you've discussed her among yourselves, surely.'

Mrs Bridges was not giving in easily. 'Well, perhaps once or twice, Captain James. Is there any special reason why you should ask?'

'Yes, there is. If – one day in the future – Miss Forrest was to become mistress of this house, I wonder how you and Hudson and Rose and everyone would feel.'

It was the last thing Mrs Bridges had expected to hear, and she tried to understand. 'Mistress of the house?' she repeated. 'You mean – the Master and Miss—'

James shook his head impatiently. 'No, no, not my father. You see, I – I've asked Miss Forrest to marry me – and I rather wanted to find out how you'd all feel about it.'

Mrs Bridges stared at him. This was not at all according to their speculations. Then it came to her; he was actually asking her advice, this young man who'd always been so headstrong, driving even the formidable Nanny Webster to despair when he was a little boy. And here he was, coming to her almost as if she was his mother, the mother he'd lost.

The staff would have been surprised to hear the softness of her voice as she answered him.

'Well, I can only tell you this much, Master James. We've been in service here, most of us, since you and Miss Elizabeth was babies – that is, Mr Hudson and me and poor Miss Roberts – and Rose, well, she's been here a good few years, too. We've all been proud to serve your dear mother and your father, and that's a fact. Well, if you choose to get married, Master – Captain James, any lady you marries'll be "Mrs James" to us down here, and I'm sure we'll be only too happy to serve her as best we can as one of the family.'

James smiled at her, satisfied and grateful, and got up.

'That's all I wanted to know, Mrs Bridges. Thank you – thanks for my cup of tea. It was excellent.'

Her eyes followed him to the door. So was my advice, she thought proudly. And God bless them both.

Curse and confound it, thought James as he drove through the dark and the blinding rain down Wimbledon Park Side. His car was up to the speed limit and beyond, but the roads were quiet and he was in a hurry. From every quarter church bells pealed out their melancholy invitation to the evening service – it must be getting on for half-past six, and he still had the network of little roads on the south side of the High Street. He took a wrong turning and found himself in one of the grander roads leading up to the Lawn Tennis Club. He turned back, re-crossed High Street, and saw with relief the name of Hazel's street illuminated by a flickering gas-lamp.

He was wet already, for his sports model was far from proof against the elements, and by the time he had reached the Forrests' front door his hair and shoulders were soaked.

The door with its panel of secular stained glass opened. Hazel, dressed for outdoors, drew him into the small stuffy conservatory which led into the house.

'I'm sorry I'm so late,' he greeted her cheerfully. 'I lost the way in Putney and had to ask a bobby.'

She didn't lift her face to be kissed, but said formally: 'You're soaked. Let me take your coat.'

James took a seat in the small sitting-room, with its dark flowered wallpaper, brown paint, and general air of over-crowding by 'good' but heavy furniture, presided over by

Watts's picture of the blindfolded Hope perched on top of the world, Dante goggling at Beatrice on a bridge, and a large sepia photograph of Mrs Forrest's father in a Lieutenant-Colonel's uniform of the Second Afghan War. It was not the kind of room he was used to, but for all the notice he took of it it might have been any room, anywhere. He was watching Hazel's face, and conscious of an atmosphere he had never shared with her before: discomfort.

They began to talk about the weather.

'It's raining cats and dogs out there,' he ventured, as though she couldn't hear the relentless drumming of the downpour on the conservatory roof.

'Yes. I can hear it.'

'Makes driving a bit dangerous. One skids in the tramlines.'

'I suppose so.' She saw him surveying the empty chairs. 'My mother's upstairs. Getting ready for church. We – have to go soon. And Father – he's . . . I think he's gone to see somebody – to ask him to be a sidesman this evening.'

'Oh.'

There was an awful pause. James swallowed, and said 'Well?'

Hazel's face lost its strained look. She came to him and took his hands.

'James dear, please listen to me carefully and try to understand. I'm very fond of you – I've never concealed that; and I know I should have said this more definitely in the first place – but – there are reasons why I can't marry you. I've thought about it very carefully and talked to my parents – and now I have to be honest with you . . .' She was forcing back tears. 'I – just – have to say thank you for loving me and asking me to be your wife, but – I must refuse . . .' She had broken down completely now, and was sobbing on the horsehair settee, her face buried in her handkerchief.

James looked round him as though he had only just become conscious. 'I don't understand,' he said slowly. 'I thought – you seemed willing to . . .'

'Please, James, don't stay here,' she answered, muffled. 'Go back home – and forget me – just leave me, please,' as he touched her shoulder, 'it's no use – please go.'

He was trying to say 'But this is absurd,' to shake her and exert his authority, but there seemed nothing he could do against her strangled sobs and gasps. He hovered, hesitated, then, suddenly furious and humiliated, strode out of the room, swept up his wet coat and went out, slamming the door.

Mrs Forrest came downstairs quietly, and stood regarding with satisfaction the form of her daughter, crying wearily now, still face downwards on the settee. She lifted a blotched face and swollen eyes, and received a maternal pat.

'There, dear. It's all finished now. You'll get over it.'

Hazel's whisper was scarcely audible. 'Never.'

'Oh yes, you will. You'll stop here with Mother, where you belong. Where you're safe, from prying, inquisitive people. And remember all we've done for you, your father and I – and the promise you made us – remember? And forget young Bellamy. There's a good girl.'

Hazel managed to speak. 'How do you know he'd have minded – or his father? How can we ever know now – not telling them?'

'Of course they'd have minded – people like that! What about old Lady Southwold, his grandmother – what would *she* have said?'

This trump card did not seem to convince Hazel. 'It's so unfair,' she said.

'Life is sometimes unfair, dear. You stay with Mother, safe and warm.'

She went to put her arms round Hazel; but, suddenly dry-eyed, Hazel got up and moved away from her mother, icily controlled.

'The bells have stopped,' she said. 'We've only five minutes. Give me my hat, please.' Mrs Forrest, who had been holding the hat, a particularly unattractive one which she had chosen for Hazel herself, handed it over, and together the two women went out into the rain.

The first thing James did on arriving home was to make a scene with his father.

'Hazel has decided, for some reason or other, not to marry me,' he said, his brow black with anger. 'What those reasons are should be better known to you than they are to me.'

'What do you mean by that?' Richard was genuinely puzzled.

'I think you warned her off me. I think you made it pretty

clear to her that you wouldn't accept her as a daughter-in-law and that she'd better look for a husband elsewhere.'

'That is not true!'

James glared at him. 'You spoke to her about me, didn't you?'

'I advised her to think it over very carefully, the other day, and she agreed to give the matter plenty of thought. But the choice was hers, and hers alone.'

'What you were saying to her was "don't marry my son", wasn't it? And you knew damn well she was too loyal to go against your wishes.'

Richard's protest was silenced, James's anger in full flow. 'Whatever it was you said to her, Father, you've just about wrecked my chances of happiness. The one woman I've ever really loved, deeply. Now I'll never see her again, nor will any of us. It's all over, thanks to you. I'm going to bed.'

James nursed his mistake for a night and most of the next day. Returning home at teatime, hoping to find the morning-room empty and to enjoy a gloomy tea in solitude, he was annoyed to find Lady Prudence there. His mother's great friend, a handsome widow whom the staff rightly suspected of being 'after' Richard, was calling very frequently these days. This time the excuse was to collect some old clothes of dear Marjorie's for a Charity Bazaar. Resigned, he remained to make desultory conversation with her, and was glad to see Hudson entering with a visiting-card on a salver.

'A Mr Forrest to see you, sir.'

'Forrest?' James's voice sounded a note of alarm.

'A Mr Arthur Forrest, sir.'

'I see . . . you'd better show him into the study, Hudson. Would you excuse me, Lady Pru? I'd better go and see what this fellow wants.' Lady Pru nodded graciously; it would suit her admirably to have tea with Richard à deux when he returned from the House.

Hazel's father was looking out of the study window as James entered the room. He was a small man, balding, with a strange look of Hazel in the eyes set in a round baby-face. His speech was carefully refined, with occasional lapses which betrayed his background.

'I imagine you must be Hazel's father,' said James abruptly.

'Yes, sir.'

'Is she – all right? There's nothing . . .' Horrors were in his mind, a picture of the dead scullery-maid Emily, who had hanged herself for love in her tiny attic bedroom. He had not found her, thank God – it was poor Hudson who had done that; but the picture remained.

'Oh, no,' said Arthur Forrest kindly, as if he saw into James's head. 'It was just that I wanted to have a word with you in private.'

'Certainly. Please sit down. Er – this is where your daughter did her typing and helped my father with his book. What was it you want to say?'

'First of all, sir, neither Hazel nor her mother know I'm here, so I'd appreciate it if you'd keep my visit confidential.'

'Of course. And please don't call me "Sir" – it's a bit formal, don't you think?'

'Very well, I'll come to the point. There's things you don't know about our daughter – things she's never let on about – not to anybody. When she was just nineteen, training to be a teacher she was then, she met a young fellow, Patrick O'Connor. He was working as a clerk in the Post Office near our home – we lived in Putney then. Well, I won't go into all the details, but my Hazel got very friendly with this young O'Connor. He seemed a nice enough lad, clean and nicely spoken; she brought him home once or twice.'

James, listening, was tense. 'And then?'

'Well, in the spring of 1902, my daughter married O'Connor and went to live in Newcastle where he'd been sent by the Post Office. They hadn't much money but we helped a bit. Then, it seems, he started drinking. She didn't say at first, we didn't see that much of her. But she wrote to her mother most weeks, and between the lines you could see the girl wasn't happy. Well, she stuck it out for a few months but things got worse. He started beating her, Captain Bellamy, knocking her about – and calling her filthy names. He got in these tempers when he was on the drink, you see.'

'Go on.' James was very pale.

'Well, one night, very late, they had a dreadful fight. He was like a madman. Next day Hazel came home with all her things in a trunk. She'd left him and got the train. She was ill, and worn out, and frightened.'

'Oh, my God.'

'Well, my wife got her to bed. And when she undressed her, there were marks all over her body. Bruises and weals and that. He'd – he'd struck her, you see, with his belt, and the buckle'd cut in . . .'

James winced as if the past pain was his. 'Yes. Go on.'

'He'd have killed her, if she'd stopped with him. I wanted to go to the police. But Hazel refused – didn't want that kind of trouble. But she – got a divorce. It cost her mother and me nearly all our savings.'

'That's outrageous!'

'We sold our house in Putney – well, the neighbours would have got to hear of it, and we'd have been outcasts, having a daughter who'd been through the divorce courts. So we moved to Wimbledon, where nobody knew us. Hazel went out and found herself work with with her typing, and that. She went back to her maiden name, of course, and we never spoke of her marriage or of Patrick O'Connor, ever again. It was something in the past, all forgotten.'

James burst out. 'Why in God's name did she never tell *me*?'

'When you asked her to marry you, she knew it'd all have to come out. Her mother said it would – on the marriage certificate, you see – she'd have been put down as Hazel Patricia O'Connor, née Forrest. And her mother persuaded her that your family would never accept her, not the kind of people they are.' He stared in front of him. 'Last night, after church, she locked herself in her room and cried all night. She's in love with you, Captain Bellamy, my daughter is.'

The anxious little face lightened when James said: 'How soon could I see her? If I came to your house?'

'Mrs Forrest'll be at the shops tomorrow morning, just for an hour, about ten.'

She was kneeling on the sitting-room floor when James rang the bell, cutting out dress material, her hair disorderedly falling about her shoulders. When she answered the door James thought she looked like the drowning girl in his headmaster's picture, risen from her pool. She backed away with shock when she saw him, and began to stammer; her mother would be back soon – she hadn't expected to see him again . . . Firmly he pushed her before him into the room, and made her sit with him on the settee.

'Never mind all that. Hazel, darling, I know now why you refused me, but I still love you as much as ever. And I want you to know that what happened to you in the past doesn't and never would have made any difference to me.'

She seemed stunned. 'The divorce . . .'

'My dear sweet girl, divorce in Bellamy circles is becoming fashionable, and we tend to set the fashions. The day will probably come when every other couple in Putney and Wimbledon will have been through it. So you see it doesn't matter.'

Hazel nodded slowly. 'But who told you? Was it my father?'

'Never mind. Will you marry me? I want your answer, finally, before your mother comes back.'

'Oh, James, what am I to do?'

'Say you'll be my wife. We'll be happy, and we'll have lots of children.'

The front door opened and shut; footsteps were heard going into the kitchen.

'Yes,' she said. 'Oh yes, James. I want so much to marry you. Hold me close.'

And it was thus that Mrs Forrest found them when she came in.

That night, as Hudson set the bedtime grog-tray down, Richard said:

'Well, soon there will be a new master and mistress here in this house. Things won't be quite the same, Hudson.'

'No, sir.' The butler's expression gave nothing away.

'I just hope it won't prove too difficult for you – and the other servants.'

'We shall do our best, I can assure you, sir, to serve Captain and Mrs James, as we have served her ladyship and yourself in the past.'

'Thank you, Hudson. I'm most grateful.'

Hudson stooped and poured his master a stiff whisky. As Richard took the first sip the eyes of master and man met across the glass; and each saw his own thoughts in the eyes of the other.

CHAPTER SIX

Of all the staff at 165, perhaps Rose suffered most from the new order of things. She had been devoted to Lady Marjorie, even more devoted to Miss Elizabeth, and had felt deeply, without saying much, the fact that her Miss Lizzie hadn't asked her to go to the United States with her as her maid. It had not seriously occurred to her that the new Mrs Bellamy would want her in that capacity; and in any case, pleasant though the ex-Miss Forrest was, Rose had seen very little of her and couldn't help drawing certain comparisons.

Sarah, her friend, was married and gone. Baby Lucy was in America. There was nobody on whom Rose could lavish the protective affection pent up in her. Lonely, frustrated, and discontented, she began to snap at people and to sit about in corners in her spare time, her hands in her lap and her mouth drawn down at the corners.

'Moping again, Rose?' enquired Mrs Bridges. 'You want a bit of work to keep you busy. Satan finds some mischief still, you know!'

'I've got plenty of work, thank you,' returned Rose sharply. 'Got the right to sit down now and then the same as other people, haven't I?'

Mrs Bridges was offended. 'I'm sure I never said you hadn't. Only sitting down doesn't seem to do you much good, with a face like a wet Thursday.'

'Come on, Rose,' Edward coaxed. ' 'ere, I'll tell you one I 'eard at the Feathers.' Lowering his voice, even though Mr Hudson was upstairs, he began:

'There was a young lady of Tottenham,
Who—'

The stately tread of Mr Hudson descending, and a warning hiss from Mrs Bridges, stopped him abruptly. Ruby giggled, and Rose impatiently turned her shoulder on all of them.

'*I* know – it's fresh air you need, Rose,' said Edward, now all innocence. Isn't that it, Mr Hudson? I was readin' that health all depends on fresh air.'

'Indeed it does, Edward. One's very life depends on the blood gaining fresh oxygen and getting rid of stale carbonic acid unceasingly.'

Rose, unimpressed, was staring into the fire.

'You having your cocoa, Rose?' Mrs Bridges asked. 'It's getting cold.'

'No thanks, Mrs Bridges. Don't feel like it tonight.'

'Don't feel like cocoa? Whatever next?'

With a heavy sigh, Rose got up and drifted out, thereby missing an edifying discussion between Edward and Mr Hudson on the illnesses arising from uncleared drains and unhygienic dustcarts.

'What's the *matter* with that girl?' Mrs Bridges said, half to herself.

'Just sad, I reckon,' Edward replied.

'Sad? We've all been sad in our time. She's got to get herself in hand, that's what.'

Rose was, indeed, sad. Earlier she had taken a draught of castor oil to the Master – only soon he wouldn't be the Master any more, when James and his bride came back from honeymoon. Richard was feeling low and unwell, the result of an over-rich partridge dish, and of the hovering thought that in a week or two his household would be disrupted. He felt as though he belonged to and was wanted by nothing and nobody: which was much Rose's own feeling. There was a cord of sympathy between them. As he handed back the glass, he murmured a few words of thanks for her help in the last months.

'It's easy to forget or take for granted people who must feel just as deeply as oneself, Rose. Be sure I do realise how *you* feel.'

'We all miss her still very much, sir,' Rose answered, half-choked with emotion at being spoken to sympathetically. She decided to go to bed early and have a good cry.

And so, having left the others chatting about germs, she made her usual preparations in the kitchen for next morning. Passing the back door, she was surprised to hear a gentle, insistent tapping outside. Without thinking she unbolted and opened the door.

A strong arm dragged her outside into the dark area, and a large, dirty hand stifled her scream.

Through her panic she heard a hoarse whisper in a familiar voice.

'Don't scream, Rose. Please don't scream. It's only me, Alfred. You remember? I was footman here. Few years ago. Remember?'

Still stifled by his hand, she managed to nod, and he let her go.

'Alfred!' In the light from the corridor she could see his face, the eccentric, sardonic face of the footman whom nobody had liked very much, and who had left in disgraceful circumstances.

'I won't hurt you,' he whispered. 'I wouldn't hurt a fly.'

Rose backed away. 'I'll get Mr Hudson.' Alfred seized her arm and held her.

'No, don't. Is he still here? Thought he might have left by now. Please don't tell him. I need help, Rose.'

'What sort of help?'

'Look, I can't tell you out here? Can't we go in? I'm freezin'.'

She looked nervously towards the servants' hall.

'They're all *in* there.'

'When they gone to bed, then.'

Suddenly the door of the servants' hall opened, and Mr Hudson's unmistakable footsteps sounded. Rose gave Alfred a push into the shadows by the dustbins, darted back into the corridor and shut the door behind her, leaning guiltily against it as Mr Hudson approached, surprise on his face.

'What were you doing outside, Rose?'

'Er – nothing, Mr Hudson. Just thought I heard something, that's all.'

'Heard? What?'

'Noise. Cat. Nothing.'

Mr Hudson majestically locked the door with an air which would not have disgraced the Keeper of the King's Keys. 'You want to be careful, poking your nose outside at this time of night. There's no end of ruffians and scoundrels on the streets. Call me, in future.'

'Yes, Mr Hudson.' She hovered uncertainly as the others passed her on their way to bed, at last retreating into the servants' hall, only to find Mr Hudson looming up behind her.

'Aren't you going to bed, Rose?'

Hastily she picked up a piece of darning. 'Just got to finish this, Mr Hudson.' He gave her a curious look.

'Don't be too long about it, then. You've been looking tired lately. Goodnight.'

She bade him goodnight and listened tensely for him to go out of earshot. Then, stealthily, she crept out into the passage, unfastened the back door, jumping at every squeak of the key and bolt, and let in the bedraggled Alfred, muttering, as she re-locked the door, 'I must be going daft doing this. Go on, get in there and keep quiet.'

By the light of the servants' hall fire Alfred looked a pathetic figure indeed. His shabby clothes were sodden with rain, his limp black hair straggled like the feathers of a dead bird, his face was unshaven. Rose's heart was softened by his appearance: she began to mother him.

'You're soaked! Take them wet things off and go by the fire. Go on. You'll get pneumonia.' Pushing him forward, she ran to fetch a blanket from the kitchen airing-cupboard, while Alfred dazedly stripped to his vest and long pants. Returning, Rose wrapped him in the blanket, sat him down, and bustled about collecting food for him. While he greedily ate the meal, Rose told him of the events of the past year. He knew of none of them, not even of Lady Marjorie's death. When she had told him all he remarked, with his mouth full:

'Lots of changes, then.'

'Yes. But some things don't change.'

'Mr Hudson. Mrs Bridges. Rose.' Suddenly they smiled at one another, for the moment in sympathy.

'And what about you?' she enquired. Alfred's eyes slewed away from her before he spoke.

'Well – I went to Germany – as valet to Baron von Rimmer. Remember?'

Rose suppressed a shudder. Remember? How could she ever forget? It had been she who'd gone blithely up to Klaus von Rimmer's room with clean towels, and caught the young Baron and Alfred engaged in an activity unmistakable to anyone brought up in the country, as Rose had been. Horrified and sickened, she'd rushed down to tell Mr Hudson, and the consequence had been that the Baron had vanished, taking Alfred with him. It had been an episode they all preferred to forget.

'Not a bad life, really,' Alfred went on, unaware of her distaste. Schloss in the mountains, we lived in. Beautiful scenery.'

'But you couldn't speak German. How did you get on?'

'Learnt it. Enough to get by. Might have stayed, only . . . Baron got married. He did, Rose. To a Beautiful Princess – ugly cow. She didn't like me. Fat, stinking . . .'

He began to shake with recollected emotion.

'Her Highness made changes in her household. Got rid of me – all very civil, polite, very cordial. Fare paid back. And a position arranged with a gentleman friend of the Baron.'

'English, was he?'

'Lithuanian. English-speaking Lithuanian Jew.'

Suddenly Alfred's blanketed shoulders began to heave with dreadful gasping sobs. Rose put her arms round him and rocked him like a baby, murmuring comfort, until the sobs dwindled to sniffles.

'You won't give me away, Rose?'

' 'Course I won't. Why should I?'

Alfred seemed cheered. 'After all, it's not a crime, is it?'

'What isn't?'

'Falling in love.' Alfred's expression was comically sentimental.

'Falling in love? *You*? Who with?' Alfred turned what she could only think of as a soppy look on her. 'It should of been you, Rose.'

'Don't be daft!' she snapped. Then, afraid to hear the answer.

'Was it – a man?'

Alfred's expression changed to one of shocked propriety.

'Oh, no, I'm past all that. That was – religious mania, or something. It's girls, girls I love now. Their lithe bodies, their silken hair—'

Rose's sympathy began to evaporate a little. It all sounded so unconvincing, coming from Alfred, whose only use for girls in the past had been to tease and frighten them; and he was talking in a most peculiar way, like somebody quoting something they'd once read.

'Yes, well, never mind,' she said. 'Who is it?'

'The niece.'

'Whose niece? The Lithuanian's?'

'That's right. Arabella. She come to stay. From – from Herefordshire. Vision of loveliness. Mutual, it was. 'Course, we had to keep it secret from him, from the crusty old bachelor. We wrote poetry and left it for each other in flower vases.'

Rose couldn't restrain a giggle, and Alfred gave her a suspicious glare.

'What's the matter? You mocking me?'

'No, no, sorry, Alfred,' she said hastily. 'Go on.'

'Well, he found out. Found one of our letters.'

'In the flower vase?'

' 'Course. It was a hobby of his, flower arrangin'. He took it up, after his wife died.'

'Thought you said he was a bachelor.'

'He was, after she died.'

'No he wasn't. He was a widower.'

'Hadn't got a woman, that's what I meant, Clever! Don't you believe me? Look, look, I'll prove it to you, Doubting Thomas.' He dragged out of the blanket-folds a small charm suspended from a thread round his neck.

'She gave me this, and I swore it would never leave my neck, till the day I die.'

Rose glanced at it quickly. 'Yes, it's lovely, but put it back on. It's bad luck.' Mystery again. Somewhere she'd read about someone saying just those words. In fact, she'd often read them, in the magazines she was fond of – people giving each other half-sixpences and that sort of thing, and promising never to take them off. And all this about the beautiful niece and the letters. She wanted to believe Alfred, but it was getting more and more difficult.

'What happened, when he found the letter.'

'Oh.' Alfred seemed to have forgotten what he was talking about. 'Oh yes. He turned me out and sent her back to Herefordshire. He was jealous, you see, jealous of her, promises to her mother, or something – make a good marriage. Not me, not the valet, I wasn't good enough. I was dirt, filth, vile, putrid—'

'Yes, well,' Rose interrupted hastily. Alfred's language had often been embarrassing. 'When did he turn you out?'

'What? Oh. Two days – two days ago.'

'And you've been wandering about ever since, in this weather? Didn't you have no friends to go to?'

'I had friends, yes, but they were employed by his friends. I was banished, exiled, I was desperate, trying to think – what to do. Then – I thought of you, Rose.'

'Me? Why?'

He smiled, again with that sickly look. 'Friendly face – spanning the years – angel of mercy.'

Rose could have kicked herself for taking him at all seriously, but in spite of her better judgment his flattery was too much for her.

'Come on,' she said, 'and bring your togs with you. I'm going to put you in the little store room where the wringer's kept.'

It so happened that Edward had partaken rather freely of the dish which had affected Mr Bellamy's digestion, Mrs Bridges's exotic *Perdrix aux Graines de Genièvre*. Though the Master had eaten quite enough to make him ill, more had come downstairs untouched than Mrs Bridges liked to see, and as nobody else fancied it much at that time of night the ever-hungry Edward was for once able to eat his fill of one of 'Mrs B's Specials.'

But the combination of well-hung partridge, fat salt pork and ham, rich stock, juniper berries, wine and onion, was too much even for his young stomach. Just as Rose had got Alfred as far as the store-room Edward appeared, night-shirted and pale.

'What do *you* want?' snapped Rose, rather unnecessarily to one who was clutching his middle and groaning pathetically.

'I've been poisoned by Mrs Bridges, Rose. Got any of that medicine?'

Rose sighed with exasperation and gave him a sharp push in the direction of the servants' hall. There, as he postponed drinking the castor oil she had poured, he looked curiously round and saw the two cups still on the table.

'You been entertainin', then? *You're* a sly one. Cavalry officer, is he?'

'That's right. Here. Swallow.'

As he was forcing down the medicine, with cries and grimaces, she remembered something.

'You still got that old coat of yours? That heavy grey

one you had, before Mr Hudson went to Somerby and you got given that new one?'

Edward nodded. 'On my bed, keepin' me warm at nights. Why?'

'It's for an old tramp who came round this morning. Freezing.'

Edward grinned, surveying the telltale cups. 'Here now, isn't he? All right, I won't tell Mr Hudson. Where is he?'

'Get the coat,' Rose ordered.

'What, now?'

'Now. Go on,' and she pushed him towards the door. When he came back all traces of the cups and of Alfred's presence in the servants' hall had vanished.

At breakfast Edward couldn't resist teasing Rose about her visitor.

'Morning', Rose – sweet dreams, eh?'

Rose was intent on capturing an end of new loaf to carry to Alfred, and answered abstractedly, 'Yes, thank you, Edward.' He dug her in the ribs.

'Cavalry charges and all that?'

Mrs Bridges caught this, as she brought the porridge-bowl in from the kitchen.

'And why should she dream of cavalry charges, Edward, pray?'

He giggled. 'Rose knows – don't you, Rose?'

'Dunno what you're talking about,' said Rose, tossing her head. The loaf-end tucked under her apron, she left hurriedly. It was bad luck that just as she had almost reached the store-room door Mr Hudson should appear. His sharp eyes at once lit on the bread.

'What do you want with that, Rose? Can you not wait for your breakfast?'

A faint blush mantled in Rose's usually pale cheeks. 'It's not for me, Mr Hudson. It's for – for a pigeon.'

'Pigeon?'

'Yes, I been feeding it. I think it's hurt its wing.'

Mr Hudson sniffed as though the pigeon's presence might be tainting the air. 'It's not inside the house, I hope?'

'Oh no, Mr Hudson.' Rose's voice was all injured innocence. 'It's outside the back door, on a window-ledge. In a box.'

His sandy eyebrows arched. 'A box?'

'A hat box,' Rose elaborated desperately. What was he going to ask next – the colour of the pigeon's eyes, or how many stripes were there on the hat-box? Suspiciously he looked at the bread in her hand.

'But that's fresh bread you're feeding it. That's extravagant, and these are difficult times.'

Near the back door stood a garbage-pail waiting to be taken out to the dust-bins. Neatly he removed a mouldy crust from it, gave it to Rose and took the bread she held, to her dismay, for it was green with mildew. She pointed out its condition, and he smiled.

'Go on now, Rose – you're too sentimental. It's quite good enough for a pigeon. There are human beings in need of this.' He passed on majestically to the kitchen, with the fresh bread.

'Little you know' Rose muttered after him, and hurried to the store-room.

In the dark little apartment, used for storing cleaning materials, a wringer and clothes-horse, and some humble furniture, Alfred was sleeping on the floor, huddled in the coat. His snores were punctuated by moans and broken phrases, sometimes so loud that Rose shook him.

'Sssh. Quiet, Alfred, quiet!'

He began to toss about. 'No, no . . . keep away from me. Keep away, you . . . bastard. I'll smash – smash . . .' Suddenly his eyes opened. He stared at her blankly until she whispered 'It's me. Rose.'

'Rose!' He broke into jerky, frightening sobs, and, clutching her, buried his face against her shoulder.

'There, there,' she said mechanically. 'There, there.'

When he was quieter she offered him the crust. He took a bite from it and spat it out.

'What you trying to do? Kill me?'

'I'm sorry, Alfred – it was Mr Hudson gave it me. I had to say you was a pigeon.'

'A pigeon?' He began to make realistic cooing noises until Rose had to smile, for all her impatience.

'Now,' she said, 'get your clothes on fast, and I'll see if the coast is clear.' Just as she put her head out of the door someone turned the corner. It was, of course, Mr Hudson, who should have been at breakfast.

'Is this where you keep your pigeon, Rose?' he enquired

with a benevolent smile which faded when he saw the cringing Alfred.

Every man has his private dreams. Mr Hudson's was that of being a great criminal lawyer. Now was his chance to realise it in part. He sat in state at the head of the kitchen table, stern-eyed, the Hanging Judge in person, though a baize apron and not a legal wig adorned him, for while haranguing Alfred he was polishing the silver. The other members of the Court were also carrying on with their duties: Mrs Bridges kneading bread, Rose ironing, and Ruby peeling potatoes, while Edward brought up new supplies of silver to be cleaned.

At the opposite end of the table Alfred perched on a tall, uncomfortable stool, looking miserably from one to another. Rose looked hardly any happier.

'I take a very serious view of this, Rose,' Mr Hudson was saying. 'This young man brought shame and disgrace on the house which it took a long time to recover from. I'd rather see the Forty Thieves in here than him back.'

Edward nudged Rose, whispering. 'Here, what did he do?' Mrs Bridges silenced him with a look, but not before he added to the awe-stricken Ruby 'Must have been somethin' terrible.'

Rose looked up from the ironing table. 'I always thought you was a forgiving man, Mr Hudson.'

'I am, Rose. But there are some things that can never be excused.' (Including, he added mentally, aiding and abetting a German spy and introducing nameless perversions into a Christian household). He squashed Alfred's attempt at self-defence, but Rose interrupted him.

'We don't even consider he might be here for a reason,' she said. 'He might be in trouble through no fault of his. We just kick him out with no money and nowhere to go, 'cause we've judged him on his past. Well, a man can change, can't he? And one thing we've always done is look after our own, isn't it? Remember Sarah? How Mr James and Miss Lizzy found her starving in Whitechapel and brought her back – if they could show some decent Christian feelings, why can't we?'

Mr Hudson held up a hand. 'All right, Rose, that's enough.'

'At least let Alfred tell his story,' she pleaded. The others murmured agreement, and Mr Hudson graciously consented. The culprit was silent.

'Go on, tell them, Alfred,' Rose prompted.

'Tell them – what, Rose?' It was not a promising beginning, to Rose's surprise.

'Well, about falling in love!'

Mrs Bridges snorted. 'Him? Who with?'

'With the niece of my employer who came to stay with him,' Alfred said slowly and carefully.

'From Herefordshire,' added Rose.

'What was her name?' asked Edward.

Alfred looked towards Rose as if for a reminder, and, as she gave none, stammered that it was Arabella. Edward gave a hoot of laughter.

'That's a cow's name – Herefordshire cow!' He mooed.

Mr Hudson could see that none of this was getting them anywhere. Summarily he dismissed the two young ones and continued the trial with only Rose and Mrs Bridges present.

Alfred seemed strangely reluctant to give evidence in his own defence; could it be, Mr Hudson pondered, that he'd forgotten what he'd told Rose? It was she who helped him out, telling the story of the love-letters in the flower-vases and the cruel uncle who had turned Alfred from his doors. Mrs Bridges looked sceptical.

'That's a very fine story, Rose, but how do we know it's true?'

With an exasperated noise, Rose said 'Won't you believe anything? Here, look – she gave him this.' She fished out the charm from Alfred's vest, and led him up to them by it, like a dog on a lead. 'He promised her, Arabella, he'd never take it off as long as he lived.' Mr Hudson inspected it critically.

'He could have stolen that from anywhere.'

Alfred dragged the charm out of Rose's hand and turned on his judge.

'That's not true, Mr Hudson. I may have been a lot of things, but I never been a thief!' Mr Hudson exploded in anger.

'I'm not putting up with any more of this! Has it never occurred to you, Rose, there could be another, more sinister side to this whole business? That he's been gulling you with this cock-and-bull love story simply in order to get his foot inside this house again?'

'Why should he want to do that, Mr Hudson?' asked Mrs Bridges.

'I'll tell you why, Mrs Bridges – and anybody else who cares to hear!' He glared at Rose. 'Because there are people who want to do mischief to this great country, and his former employer, the notorious Baron von Rimmer, was proved to be one of them.'

Mrs Bridges put her hand to her heart. 'Oh my God – a spy, he means!'

'That's right, Mrs Bridges, a foreign spy. And now he has the effrontery to send his servant, a man of loathsome perverted habits, to seek re-employment.'

Alfred cowered, and Rose rushed to his defence.

'You got foreigners on the brain, Mr Hudson! You always did have. You used to think they'd landed, the whole German Army, and they was waiters and hairdressers on the South Coast, and they was going to rise up and murder us in our beds. Well, they didn't. We're still here, aren't we? Oh, I may not be clever, but at least I can tell real people and I don't judge them on what I read in newspapers and books.' Alfred was now making keening sounds of fear. Rose gathered him to her like a child. 'There now, it's all right.'

Mr Hudson stroked his chin. This was not going at all like a model trial. He decided to break the atmosphere of hysteria which had crept into the Court.

'Perhaps Alfred will kindly tell us the name of his former employer, the Lithuanian, so that we can verify his touching story.'

Alfred raised his head sharply. 'No – I can't.'

The Judge smiled. 'I thought not.'

'Why can't you?' Rose asked Alfred.

'Because he doesn't exist,' put in Mr Hudson.

'He does!' Alfred protested. 'I can't tell you – for Arabella's sake. I promised. Faithfully.'

'I suggest your last employer was a German, living in this country,' Mr Hudson put to Alfred.

'No, he wasn't.'

'Isn't – a German. He's a Lithuanian – Jewish – gentleman. I told you. Not even a German name, Zabadoff, it's—' He stopped, a look of shock on his face.

'Zabadoff,' repeated Mr Hudson softly.

'No! I didn't say that...'

Mr Hudson had got what he wanted. Now, straightening up, he asked Mrs Bridges 'Well, what would *you* do with him?'

'Well, he's been a bad boy – but let him stay for dinner. Can't do no harm. And think about it, shall we?' Rose smiled gratitude at her.

'Very well, but for dinner only,' Mr Hudson pronounced. 'Then he leaves.'

They all watched his departing back with relief. Alfred turned to Mrs Bridges, his saviour.

'Thank you, Mrs Bridges. You always was very considerate to me. Very understanding.'

She preened herself. 'Was I, Alfred? Yes, I suppose I was.'

Rose had beckoned him to the door, but Mrs Bridges motioned her back and whispered conspiratorially: 'You're very fond of him, aren't you?'

Rose seemed taken aback. 'Fond?'

'Well, you took a big chance hiding him. You must be fond of him.'

Rose considered. She wouldn't have put it as strong as that, herself. Perhaps the truth was that she had nobody else to be fond of. Mrs Bridges was saying:

'I don't believe all that stuff Mr Hudson was saying about spies. Alfred hasn't got the brains. The point is – what's going to become of him? If we turn him out after dinner, where's he going to go?'

'That's what I've been wondering,' Rose confessed.

'This man, Zabadoff, this Lithuanian gentlemen. I wonder who's cook there?'

'What you mean is – we might help Alfred get his job back again.'

Alfred's face, as he hovered in the lobby within earshot, was one grimace of fear. He swiftly returned to Mrs Bridges's side, making her jump.

'Sorry, Mrs Bridges, but couldn't help overhearing, just then. Very kind of you to think of me like that, Mrs Bridges. But you see, Mr Zabadoff, my employer, it's – not his real name.'

'Not real?'

'No. I – made it up. Keep Mr Hudson off the scent. Keep

my promise to Arabella.' His face twitched into a nervous grin.

'Then what's his real name?' asked Mrs Bridges.

'It's no use – anyway. My going back there. He's going to live abroad.'

'In Lithuania?'

'That's it.'

'And you wouldn't consider going with him?'

'Can't speak the lingo. And anyway – heart belongs to England.' He threw a sentimental glance towards Rose, who seemed not displeased by it.

Upstairs in the study, Mr Hudson was talking to Richard Bellamy, who was in conference with Sir Geoffrey Dillon. Richard had not been unduly worried to hear of the return of Alfred; but Sir Geoffrey was of a more suspicious nature.

'The man's been mixed up with at least one bad character before, Richard. I think you should take Hudson seriously.'

'I agree with Sir Geoffrey, sir,' said Mr Hudson. 'It's the security of the house that I'm worried about.'

'Let me see, now.' Sir Geoffrey was thinking. 'Did he tell you the name of his last employer?'

'Yes, Sir Geoffrey. A Mr Zabadoff.'

In the kitchen Alfred was being treated like an honoured guest. He took Edward's ribbing good-naturedly enough, all the jokes about his being hidden by Rose. 'Thought you might have been her cavalry officer paramour – deserter, perhaps.'

With a sudden gesture Alfred pulled Edward towards him, almost nose to nose, and barked in an exaggerated 'officer' voice, gritty and harsh:

'Deserter, eh? 'Gad, sir, desertin' me post and hidin' behind the skirts of a lady? I wouldn't be such a blaggard.'

Edward was more than a little scared; his laugh was tremulous.

'Here, he's good with the imitations, i'nt he?' Then, nervously pulling, 'Here, let go.'

Alfred let him go very slowly, and with a fiendish grin.

'Don't look so worried, Edward,' said Rose, who was cutting bread. 'He always was a bit funny.'

The study bell summoned Mr Hudson upstairs. The Master and Sir Geoffrey awaited him.

'Is that man still downstairs, Hudson?' asked Richard.

'Yes, sir. He's about to have dinner.'

'Make sure he doesn't leave.' He read surprise on Hudson's face. 'You were quite right to inform us about him.'

'Yes,' put in Sir Geoffrey, 'when we telephoned, the instrument at Mr Zabadoff's residence was answered by a Police Inspector. Mr Zabadoff was found early this morning on the floor of his bedroom – butchered to death with a meat-axe. The police are on their way here.'

Alfred had enjoyed an excellent meal of roast beef, meanwhile instructing the others about the preparation of Sauerkraut, Commissbrod, brown bread pudding, and flour-fattened snails, when the front door bell rang insistently. Mr Hudson went to answer it, and did not return. Apprehensively, Alfred waited.

'We're not certain of anything, yet, sir,' Detective-Inspector Bowles was telling Richard Bellamy, 'beyond the fact that Alfred Harris was seen in his master's company on the evening of the fifth – that's three days ago – and has been missing, till now, sir.'

'Was anything taken? Money? Valuables?' Richard asked.

'It seems not, sir. Er – I wonder if you could throw some light on Harris's personal life – the sexual nature of it. The Lithuanian, you see, was an unmarried man, of some age. Effeminate, if you know what I mean, sir.'

Richard's eyes met his butler's. 'I think we do,' he said.

Edward and Ruby were clearing the kitchen table, while Rose took up the 'bits' with a carpet-sweeper.

'Will Mr Hudson come back for his pudding?' Ruby asked, eyeing it hungrily.

'Oh, put it to keep warm. It's a favourite of his,' said Mrs Bridges. 'Ooh, my back! This weather plays the very dickens with it.' She eased herself into the fireside chair.

Edward had stopped clearing and was peering out of the window. 'Here, there's a copper up there!' he exclaimed. The noise of Rose's sweeper drowned his remark for all ears but Alfred's. His face sickly-pale, he stole to the dresser and took the carving-knife from the dish that held the end of the beef, hiding it swiftly in his jacket. Above, the pass-door opened and he could hear measured footsteps descending. With a movement like a tiger pouncing, he grabbed Edward round the neck and pushed him out into the passage, just as Mr Hudson, Detective-Inspector Bowles and his sergeant appeared downstairs.

For a moment everything was confusion. Rose started back in terror, her hands to her face, while Mrs Bridges stared unbelievingly at the presence of policemen in her domain. Then Bowles cried: 'After him!' and with the Sergeant on his heels rushed down the passage after the fleeing Alfred. They had almost caught up when he reached the door of the little store-room, shoved Edward roughly in before him and slammed the door.

Bowles opened it and started back a pace. In a corner of the tiny room Alfred, an animal at bay, held Edward against the wall with the point of the carving-knife against his throat. His wild eyes took in the faces of the policeman, Richard and Sir Geoffrey behind them.

'One step, any of you, and—!' The knife was beginning to bite and Edward screamed. Rose's face appeared among the others at the door.

'Alfred!' she cried, trying to force her way to him.

'Don't come near! Don't you move, Rose!'

There was a muttering of voices outside the door, the policemen, Hudson, Richard; Mrs Bridges begging someone to tell her what was going on, Rose refusing to budge, pleading for Alfred.

'He's scared, that's all, sir. He doesn't really mean harm, I'm sure of it.'

'Well, I'm not,' Bowles said. 'He's killed once.'

'Killed?'

Then Richard was talking to Alfred, trying to reason with him. 'But what are you going to do, Alfred? You can't stay here for ever, and they'll wait.'

'Want – to see – Rose,' Alfred gasped. 'Alone – door closed – private.'

'Oh, let me talk to him, sir!' Rose begged. 'I'm sure he'll listen to me.'

Richard protested, but Bowles agreed with Rose. 'All right. But you must make no attempt to disarm him. Just talk – right?'

She was in the store-room, the terrified eyes of Edward on her. His captor turned slowly towards her, keeping the knife where it was.

'What are they saying, Alfred?' she asked gently. 'Who did you kill? Tell 'em they're wrong.'

'Can't' he said. 'Evidence – there. Bedroom carpet, blood.'

'Whose blood?'

'My – Lithuanian. Baron's friend. Baron's vile, disgusting . . . Not like here, decent people always, here. Wanted to be decent. Wouldn't let me, always asking – pushing me to grovel like – serpent. Laughed at me. Stop, stop, stop it. Wouldn't. So I took the cleaver. Sleeping. As he slept – and finished it.'

'So – no Arabella,' said Rose.

'Pure – free,' Alfred rambled on. 'New life. Ship's cook. Just need – to get past *them*. Help me, Rose.'

'I can't, Alfred.'

'You promised!' He was glaring now.

'I didn't promise. Please—'

He began to shriek hysterically. 'Get out! You filthy whore – woman, scum, like all women! Delilah, Jezebel . . .'

They had withdrawn and left him alone with Edward. It was Sir Geoffrey's idea to lead him into a false sense of security, and it worked. Within a few minutes they heard his voice, low and coaxing. He was telling Edward that they would go away together, down to the Docks, escape, start a new life. Then Edward's voice, faintly answering. So the knife had been withdrawn. Suddenly there was an outburst of cries, the sounds of a scuffle and of objects crashing down. When the policeman went in the roles of victim and captor had been reversed, Edward holding Alfred at knife-point and calling them to help him.

A short struggle, and he gave in. The handcuffs were on, and the Sergeant was dragging him, a limp bundle, towards the area door where the Black Maria waited.

On a cold, cheerless morning, five weeks later, Rose opened the window and looked up through the area railings at the leaden sky. Somewhere nearby a church clock slowly began to chime the hour of eight. Edward, shirt-sleeved, began to lay the breakfast-table, cheerfully whistling.

'Quiet, Edward,' said Mr Hudson.

Edward stopped whistling. 'Why?'

The clock chimed its last stroke, and Rose turned away from the window.

'They've hanged him,' she said.

Mechanically she took the tray from Edward and began to lay out cups and saucers.

CHAPTER SEVEN

Hazel Bellamy sighed over the pile of correspondence before her on the desk which had been Lady Marjorie's. Personal bills, a draper's account for the new curtains, an invitation or two (not many, for it was August and anybody who mattered was out of town). Perhaps it would have been better to have gone to Southwold until London awoke again; but she and James hardly knew the Talbot-Carey cousins, and the Dowager Lady Southwold was really a very trying old lady. She had never, Hazel knew, really approved of James's marriage to his father's secretary, of the fact that it took place in a 'hole-and-corner' registry office, or of anything at all, indeed.

She pushed the heap of paper from her, irritated with herself. Perhaps this was the boredom she had heard so much about as the curse of High Society. If so, she was ashamed of herself for feeling it. But her life was just a little like that of a fish out of water. Life at 165 Eaton Place was far from being a mad whirl of pleasure, with so little money to manage on; visits to her parents at Wimbledon were uncomfortable, with her mother's manner ranging from sarcasm to the prickliness of inverted snobbery, and her poor little father half-afraid of her, it seemed. The few acquaintances she had made in Wimbledon had vanished from her life with her marriage, and had not been replaced by any from James's army set. Downstairs, the staff accepted her, she knew, and respected her domestic efficiency and lack of 'side'; yet they would never put her in Lady Marjorie's place.

She looked up at Guthrie Scone's portrait of Lady Marjorie over the mantelpiece – the poise, the grace, the aristocrat's unmatchable look, the crown of coppery hair. 'I wonder if your son would have married me if I hadn't had the same colour of hair as you?' she asked the portrait. After the best part of a year of marriage to James, she knew that he no longer saw her as the romantic damsel he had rescued from a narrow-minded suburban world. She was a shade plumper, a shade heavier than when she had worked for her living and travelled by Tube. Her beautiful hair had been improved by grooming, and her skin by better diet, but she knew that the Millais princess who had enchanted James was gone for ever.

At least there was still Richard. Dear Richard! Gentle and honest, so lonely in his widowerhood, he and he alone of those in her household had put aside all prejudice and accepted her, glad of her feminine company. There was real affection between them; he seemed to Hazel more like a brother-in-law than a father-in-law. She smiled as she thought of him.

The clock-face caught her eye. Almost lunchtime, and she had to speak to Hudson. She rang the bell. Almost at once, like a Genie, he appeared calmly awaiting her commands.

'You wished to see me, Madam?'

'Oh yes, Hudson. I'm a little worried about Rose. She looks tired.'

'Madam.'

'I've asked her if she has too much to do, but she assures me she can manage. I wondered what you thought about it.'

They both knew that the other's mind was dwelling on the distressing episode of the reappearance of Alfred, that poor deranged creature who had been executed. Rose had been terribly upset by it, given to nightmares and sudden attacks of crying, and the doctor had prescribed her Parrish's Chemical Food for her nerves. It would never do for Rose to be overtaxed again.

'I think,' said Mr Hudson, 'it depends on how much entertaining Captain James and yourself plan for the coming Autumn, Madam.'

'Well,' Hazel's tone was guarded, 'I think Mr Bellamy will continue to lead a quiet life.' (He could hardly afford to lead anything else, poor dear, she thought.) 'As to Captain James and myself, well, I think we shall probably do the same. So I expect it will be a fairly quiet Autumn.'

'Quite, Madam. Then I presume you would wish the question of an under-housemaid to be deferred for the time being.'

'Yes, I would.'

Mr Hudson was about to leave the morning-room when the telephone rang. He answered it, frowning faintly at the unfamiliar voice at the other end.

'Mr Bellamy's residence. Yes. Would you be requiring Mr

Richard or Captain James? Oh, Mrs James Bellamy? I'll enquire. Hold the line one moment, please.' His hand over the receiver, he turned to Hazel. 'The Countess de Vernay wishes to speak to you, Madam.'

'*Who?*'

'The Countess de Vernay, Madam. From the Savoy Hotel.'

With a little shrug, embarrassed at having to deal with a stranger under the keen eye of Mr Hudson, she took the telephone.

'Hullo? Yes, it is. No, I don't think we have. How do you do? My father-in-law. Yes, he does live here, that's right. Where have you just arrived from. Well, I – I'm sure he would be delighted to see you, Countess. Perhaps you could spare the time to dine with us during your stay in London. Er – who did you . . .? Oh, your brother. I see. Well, please do both come. May I suggest Wednesday evening – at half-past eight? Until then, Goodbye.'

'How extraordinary,' she said, putting the telephone back.

'Madam?'

'I've never heard of the Countess de Vernay, have you, Hudson?'

'Never, Madam.'

'Well, she says she met my father-in-law years ago at the Hoffmansthals in Vienna, and as she was passing through London on her way to New York she felt she must renew her acquaintance. I have asked her and her brother to dinner on Wednesday evening.'

'Very good, Madam. I'll tell Mrs Bridges.'

Mrs Bridges was glad to hear it.'

'About time we had a bit of company in this house,' she said. '*And* a bit of nice cooking for me to do. Look at the Upstairs luncheon today – Cottage Pie! Cottage Pie, when it used to be Game Pie with potato straws. Might as well let Ruby do the meals and me take a holiday. Cottage Pie! In a house where King Edward once come to dinner!'

'Aye . . .' Mr Hudson, too, felt a nostalgia for the good old days.

'Royalty don't come to this house now.'

'That may be, but we have a solid worth, Mrs Bridges, and provided we keep up our standards – at least below stairs –

we shall survive. In any case, I doubt whether Their Majesties lead as gay a social life as the late King Edward.'

Mrs Bridges sniffed. 'Don't look as if they do. Not but what the King's got enough on his mind with all that's been happening, first poor Captain Scott and his friends frozen to death at that South Pole – beats me what they wanted to find the nasty thing for – and then the Greek King getting murdered, and Colonel Cody smashed up in that flying machine, only the other day.'

'He looked right nice,' he did,' said Ruby wistfully. 'Lovely moustaches he had, better than Thomas's was.'

'Never you mind about moustaches, my girl,' Mrs Bridges admonished her. 'Them as goes against nature taking wings to themselves can't escape the consequences, be their whiskers never so fine.'

Mr Hudson was thinking of that year's disastrous Derby. He was fond of a little flutter on the horses, usually at second-hand, through a bookmaker friend, but for once he had taken a long-overdue day's leave to go down to Epsom and see the classic race for himself. The thrill of actually setting eyes on the horse he had backed, and of hearing the approaching thunder of hooves as the noble creatures pounded down from Tattenham Corner was all too sadly offset by the incident which was to make the race unforgettable. As the King's horse came in sight (Mr Hudson had an excellent position at the barrier) a woman had suddenly detached herself from the spectators and rushed at the animal's head, apparently in a mad attempt to stop it. Horse, jockey and woman were a writhing confusion on the ground amid the screams of the crowd. Miss Emily Wilding Davidson, the Suffragette, had made her last attempt for her cause.

Not only that, but the winner, which Mr Hudson chanced to have backed, was disqualified.

There was no sign of nostalgia or regret about the lady who had just telephoned Hazel Bellamy. Lili de Vernay turned a beaming face towards her brother, as he hung up in the large wardrobe of her Savoy hotel room a selection of the dresses which, after her own looks, were the chief weapons in her armoury. Frothy, frilly and flowered, hand-embroidered and fur-trimmed, they were as irresistible as the lovely Lili herself. She was, as one of her many lovers had put it, All Woman. She would never see twenty-five again, or even thirty; but only the piercing scrutiny of another woman would have guessed it.

Kurt Schnabel, her equally handsome and elegant younger brother, surveyed her with satisfaction.

'There,' he said. 'Did I not tell you it was quite simple? You have achieved for us a good dinner – if not a weekend – if not more. Richard Bellamy's wife was a Southwold. A lot of money there. Let me see –' (he was turning over the pages of Burke's Peerage) ' "Southwold, Earl of . . . sister living", alas, she is not and neither is he, "Lady Marjorie Sybil Helen Talbot-Carey, born July 12th 1864, married Richard Bellamy . . ." '

'And yet the son's wife invited us.'

'She will be mistress of that house now.'

'Please remind me once more,' said Lili, '*where* did I meet Richard Bellamy?'

'At the Hoffmansthals in Vienna, very briefly, some fifteen years ago.'

She pretended to bridle. 'And how old does that make me?'

Kurt smiled. 'Oh, very well. A few years ago.' He picked up a sketching-block and pencils, and began to draw the river-scene which Lili's window overlooked, leaving her to do the rest of the unpacking. She made a cross face at his back.

'I wish you would draw and paint in your own room, Kurt.'

'But I have no Thames, only ugly chimneys. Would you care to change with me?'

Lili had forgotten her annoyance in the inspection of her wardrobe, and was holding up one dress after another against her cheek, studying the effect in a mirror.

'The apricot chiffon or the yellow tulle, do you think?' she asked him. Kurt, the experienced, pondered.

'For a middle-aged English gentleman the yellow tulle – so innocent.'

Lili was looking critically at another dress. 'Everything creased. I seem to spend my whole life packing and unpacking. Why is that?'

'Because you are never satisfied.'

'I have had to pay seventy pounds for this dress. If that silly woman in Monte Carlo had not interfered, her husband would have paid.' She made a moue of displeasure, and allowed her miraculously smooth brow to wear a furrow. Her brother laughed.

'When you look like that you are irresistible. I'm sure the seventy pounds will prove an excellent investment. Don't distress yourself.'

'It had better be.' She sighed. 'It's the last of what we have.'

He took his eyes from the Thames to approve her, the yellow tulle held against her magnificent body.

'No wonder you inspire passion, wherever you go.'

'While you sketch and paint!'

He had returned to the sketching-block. 'Ah well. If one has a pretty sister, why not make use of her? I have a talent with my brush – you have . . . other gifts. The one must subsidise the other.'

She slipped her travelling-dress off and tried on the yellow chiffon, Kurt taking not the slightest notice of her state of charming undress.

'I wish you were not so afflicted by integrity, Kurt,' she said. 'Then you could take a rich bride, and I would not be obliged to look for a rich husband. Mrs James Bellamy – what is she like, do they say? Young, beautiful?'

'A pleasant lady, I have heard, but without style.'

'And her husband?'

'An eye for a pretty face, and was once the subject of much gossip.'

'H'm. Respectable women put up with anything rather than make a fuss. They always lose their husbands in the end. At least I lost mine by my own bad behaviour. There is some dignity in that. And this Richard, the father, he is very rich, you say, and not too old?'

'He lives in a bon quartier, Belgravia; a butler opens the door; he belongs to the best clubs. Of course he is rich. Such Englishmen always are, and the more philistine they are, the richer they remain, having nothing to spend their money on but horses, fishing-rods and guns. And there must be a limit to that.'

Lili was striking an attitude before the cheval mirror. 'Should I become the Mrs Richard Bellamy, all that would have to change,' she pronounced. 'I think I would like to have a salon, to patronise the Arts. I would make landscape painting fashionable, my dear.'

'Admirable indeed, little sister. But tonight we must find a cheap little café somewhere, and buy our own dinner. Yes?'

'Yes!'

They both laughed, two children engaged in a delightful adventure.

Could they have seen into the dining-room at 165 Eaton Place their exhilaration might have been modified. Round the table, reduced to its smallest capacity, for nowadays it never required to extend for a multitude of guests, sat James, Hazel and Richard. Richard's mind was elsewhere; he was quite unaware of the rather plain meal before him, though he ate it readily enough. James gave his father a bad-tempered look, then laid down his knife and fork to ask:

'What's this we're eating?'

'Cottage pie,' replied Hazel.

James pushed away his plate. 'I thought so.'

'Well, *I* think it's delicious, and Mrs Bridges has excelled herself. Do you like it, Richard?'

'What?' Richard brought his mind down with an effort. 'Oh, the food. Delicious.'

'Very economical, too. The remains of Sunday lunch. There's no sense in needless extravagance.'

James beckoned Edward, who with Mr Hudson was in attendance.

'Please take this away, Edward. I'm not hungry.'

'I'm not surprised you have no appetite, James,' Hazel said, addressing her plate rather than her husband. He took the bait.

'Oh, I see it all now! I am being punished with cottage pie for being home late from the Regimental Dinner last night. Well, James will take his punishment like a man. Bring back the cottage pie, Edward.'

Edward obeyed, and James proceeded to pick round the edges.

'All the same, Hazel, I hope when the Comtesse de Vernay and her brother dine here on Wednesday we shall not be served with cottage pie.'

Hazel's mouth twitched in a smile, though she knew James hated being laughed at. 'Well, I had considered it. Oh,

Richard – by the way, is it not customary to curtsey to an older woman of title in France?'

'Not that I know of.'

'Is she very grand?'

Richard thought. 'Frankly, I can't remember meeting her. Still, it's a large family. It wouldn't be that dreadful Louise de Vernay – no, of course not, couldn't be. She was over seventy when I was in the Foreign Office. So which one is it? Ah well, we shall find out on Wednesday.'

Mrs Bridges was warming up to a sparkling exhibition of her talents, as she pored over her menu for the evening. Rose was happy at the prospect of company; even if it did mean a bit of work, it would cheer things up a bit. In any case, she would soon be relieved of her harder duties. for Mrs Bellamy had decided at the weekend that it would after all be better to engage an under-house-parlourmaid than to wear out the invaluable Rose. Mrs Bridges was happy that Mr Bellamy was going to have guests of his own in a house which was becoming increasingly merely a place in which he was allowed to live.

'Consomme,' murmured Mrs Bridges. 'Poulet François Premier with scarlet tongue garnish. That's easy. Roast Grouse. Pommes Anna. Cheese straws. Always use cheddar myself, Parmesan's got a nasty foreign taste. Lovely doing a French menu again, even though it *is* only for five . . .'

Her musings were interrupted by the voice of Mr Hudson. 'Ah, Mrs Bridges. If you can spare a moment—'

At Mr Hudson's side, descending the stairs, was a stranger; a neatly dressed young woman – and not so young either, Mrs Bridges noted. In one cloth-gloved hand she held a little bunch of flowers. Before speculation could run rife in the kitchen Mr Hudson was introducing her.

'Mrs Bridges, this is Gwyneth Davies, the new house-parlourmaid, come to help Rose.'

'Oh, I see,' was all Mrs Bridges could think of to say. In the ecstasy of haute cusine she had forgotten the imminent arrival of this new member of the staff. Before she could collect her thoughts Miss Davies had burst into a flood of speech, delivered in a rich Welsh accent.

'These are for you, Mrs Bridges, just a small bunch of wild

flowers. They are very modest, but I spent Sunday in the country, and I would like to bring a little of that pleasure to you.'

'How very kind,' murmured Mrs Bridges, taking the unaccustomed floral tribute and looking about for somewhere to put them. Seeing Ruby hovering, she handed them over. 'Put these in a jug, Ruby. That blue one.'

Meanwhile Miss Davies was addressing Mr Hudson. 'Oh, my references. I trust you find them in order. The agency have checked them and Madam has taken them up over the telephone with my last lady. Nonetheless you may prefer to see them in writing.'

'Come along then, Gwyneth,' said Mr Hudson, a shade overwhelmed. In the servants' hall they encountered Rose; but before Mr Hudson had a chance to introduce them, the newcomer had extended a gracious hand.

'Ah, you must be Rose. I will do my best to learn the ways of the household quickly, Rose. And I look forward to working happily and well under your direction.'

Rose's jaw dropped. 'Yes,' she said.

Mr Hudson was a patient man, but he was not to be deprived of something like his usual little homily on the arrival of a new servant. Running his eye swiftly through the references, he said, before she could start again:

'You are welcome here, Gwyneth; since I see you are stated, in the most glowing terms, to be honest, sober, clean, industrious, neat, tidy in person and in work, regular and systematic; precise in the care of stoves and ornaments, a clever dressmaker and as a hairdresser both discreet and watchful, conversant with haute cuisine, and able to wait well at table and to carve.'

'Carve? *I* can't carve,' put in Rose. Smiling sweetly, Gwyneth returned:

'The master in my last place gave me lessons.'

His gaze still on the references, Mr Hudson said with a tinge of severity: 'I think we will excuse the reason given for your leaving your last place.'

Mrs Bridges peered over his shoulder. 'What was that, then?'

' "Desirous of change." '

'Well, she's young. Haute cuisine, eh? All right, Gwyneth. What do you do if a mayonnaise curdles?'

'Add a spoonful of iced water and beat it until it emulsifies once more,' Gwyneth replied almost in one breath.

Deflated, Mrs Bridges could only gasp: 'Well, I must say . . .'

Her bright eyes darting from one to another, Gwyneth said 'If I could be shown to my room, I could change at once and begin afternoon work. Idleness is abhorrent to me. My hands quite dance about from lack of occupation.' And indeed, they were moving restlessly, twined in one another.

Mr Hudson prepared to lead her off. 'If you will follow me to the pantry, Gwyneth, I will give you your written terms of service. We follow many of the old ways here . . .'

When they had gone, Rose said with a hint of malevolence: 'Perhaps she snores. There must be *something* wrong with her.'

The dining-room had not witnessed such a cheerful scene since the night James had entertained a party of friends to meet his bride. Hazel had arranged a charming centrepiece of summer flowers, and was playing the hostess with more ease than usual. It was not difficult, with a guest as vivacious as Lili, who managed to combine lively continuous chatter and a wealth of theatrical gesture with the consumption of a hearty meal.

James, for once, was enjoying himself in his own house, enchanted by Lili; while Richard watched and listened to her with quiet amusement. He was perfectly certain by now that they had never met before. How could he have forgotten?

Kurt was watching her too, admiring the skilled charm with which she caught men's fancy and held it. He was ready with details which her dramatically told life-story left in the air.

'Since poor André was taken from me—' she was saying, her voice already in widow's weeds. She caught Richard's look of enquiry, and so did Kurt.

'Lili's last husband, the late Comte de Vernay,' he clarified.

'Yes. He is dead, five years last autumn.' Lili dropped her beautiful head.

'Oh dear. I'm sorry,' Richard said with real sympathy.

'Without André I am unhappy in Vienna, so I travel with Kurt each year around Europe. To Paris for a little, Monte Carlo, Budapest, Berlin, Rome, and here I am – in London.'

'On your way to New York.'

Lili looked surprised, and got a frown of reprimand from Kurt.

'Isn't that what you told my daughter-in-law?' queried Richard.

'Of course,' said Kurt. 'My sister is confused. We go to New York next month.'

Lili turned a soulful gaze on him. 'But London is so beautiful, Kurt. I think I shall stay here for a while.'

Nicely fielded, Richard thought. Obviously she'd quite forgotten what excuse she'd given Hazel for telephoning. 'I hope you will stay here,' he said. 'And you must let me show you round a little.'

'That would be delightful!' She fluttered long lashes at him. James saw his opportunity to cut out his father.

'And when Parliament reassembles,' he said eagerly, 'and my father's busy in the House of Commons, you can call on me. Perhaps a ride in the Park – a punt on the river . . .'

Hazel gently interrupted him. 'I should explain that my husband works in an office all day.' James gave her a look sour enough to curdle any mayonnaise on the table. The conversation continued with an undercurrent of rivalry between father and son, Lili sparkling with triumph, Hazel and Kurt watching the game from the sidelines.

Behind the screen which hid the machinery of service from the diners, Rose and Gwyneth were piling the plates from the first course into the lift which would convey them down to the kitchen. Then Gwyneth pulled on the rope that operated the hoist, but found it hard work.

'Not smooth running, is it,' she said, when the thing finally began to move. 'I'll fetch a can of oil to it in the morning. The master in my last position taught me how to oil the pulleys.'

'The master taught you quite a lot, seems to me,' commented Rose drily.

'Oh, he did.' Gwyneth warmed to her subject. 'And I became the object of his unlawful and unbridled lust. His eyes would strip the clothes from my poor female body . . .' The arrival of the lift, laden with roast grouse, interrupted her, and the staring Rose helped her to hand the hot-plate over to Mr Hudson and Edward. Then Gwyneth continued in a dramatic whisper: 'That was why I had to leave, you see. And the parlour-maid had followers in the kitchen on the cook's night out. It was our local bobby, too. They would be quite unchaperoned for at least twenty minutes. I would not dare go in, for fear of what I might see.'

Rose could only say: 'Well!'

The grouse, though excellent, might as well have been boiler chickens for all that Richard tasted of them. His attention and his eyes were on Lili, and she unashamedly plied him with irresistible flattery.

'Kurt says you are a most important personage. You make the laws, yes? I like a man who makes laws. Strong Men make laws!'

Richard repressed a smile. He knew perfectly well what she was doing, and he liked it. 'Unfortunately,' he returned, 'my party is not in office at the moment. I merely oppose the laws which the present Government tries to pass.'

'Ah, how sad for you.' She all but reached out a white hand to him.

'You're interested in politics?' he enquired, knowing what kind of answer he would get.

'Oh yes! Our Prime Minister is an old friend.'

'Count Sturgkh?'

There was the tinest pause before she said 'Yes.'

'I was sorry to read in *The Times* that he's abandoned the Bohemian Diet.'

Lili shook her head sadly. 'Ah, I also. He is too fat.'

Richard had to concentrate closely on his plate before he could say straight-faced: 'I mean the Czech Provincial Assembly.' Quite undeterred, she replied: 'Yes, of course you did.'

The conversation turned on game, the grouse being the first of the season. Kurt volunteered the information that in the previous year he and Lili had spent a month in Hampshire with Lord Borrowmere. 'I painted. Lili joined the grouse shoots.'

James's eyebrows went up. 'Hampshire? Pheasants, surely.'

'Pheasant, yes, of course. Lili shot many, did you not, my dear. She is very deadly with a gun.'

Just how deadly, Edward revealed to his open-mouthed colleagues when dinner had been cleared away.

'Yes, shot her husband, she did, five years ago. It's common gossip at the Crown and Anchor. He came after her with a gun, and there was a fight and he got killed. Lord Ellerdale's valet told me – he was there when it happened.'

'And did Lord Ellerdale's valet say why he was after her with a gun?' asked Gwyneth.

'Not for your ears, Gwyneth. Or yours, Ruby.'

'Oh, go on, tell us, please!' Ruby begged. Edward beckoned them close.

'He found her in flagranty with a baron.'

'In *what*?' Ruby gasped.

'In bed, of course!'

'What they call a crime of passion, isn't it,' mused Gwyneth.

'They hushed it up, of course,' Edward said. 'The de Vernay family contested the will so she didn't get a penny. Only the clothes she stood up in. Well, laid down in, ha ha!'

'How does she live, then?'

'On her wits – and worse. Now she's after Mr Bellamy. Plain as a pikestaff.'

'How can you be sure?' Gwyneth asked.

Edward grinned. 'I know a rogue when I see one. I'm a bit of one myself, aren't I?'

He gave a playful pinch to Ruby's bottom, just as Mr Hudson appeared in the doorway with the news that the silver corkscrew was missing.

'I'll go and look for it now, Mr Hudson,' Gwyneth proffered eagerly. 'Everything must be accounted for at the end of every working day.' Before Mr Hudson could endorse this pious sentiment, she was gone.

Richard gave a slight start as the door opened. He had been alone in the darkened dining-room after the departure of the others, standing by the flower-filled hearth, gazing up at Marjorie's portrait, silently talking to her. 'Would you mind, my dear? Would you blame me? It's been so long . . .'

Gwyneth's 'Excuse me, sir', broke into his reverie. Seeing his surprise, she said 'I'm the new maid. Gwyneth, sir.'

He smiled. He had smiled a good deal that evening, as Mr Hudson had noted with approval. 'Good evening, Gwyneth,' he said.

'I hope I'm not disturbing you, sir, but Mr Hudson sent me to look for the corkscrew.'

He picked one up. 'Is this it? It was under the table.'

'Oh yes, sir. *Thank* you, sir.' She gazed on him with limpid eyes, moving him to say for no reason that he understood: 'I hope you're going to be happy with us, Gwyneth?'

'Oh, I think so, sir!' This time there was no mistaking her expression, if he had been studying her face; but he had turned to leave the room.

'Poor man!' said Gwyneth with an enormous sigh. Tenderly she stroked the corkscrew he had handed to her.

The family, upstairs and downstairs, watched the progress of Richard's romance with varying emotions. Hazel was frankly sceptical. She told James that Lili was an obvious adventuress, after his father for some imaginary fortune, and years older than she appeared; while James openly admired her and was equally open in his lack of interest in his father's future. Mr Hudson and Rose were pleased to see the Master, as they still out of habit called him, taking some healthy exercise in walks by the river, in the Park, through the Galleries, with the Comtesse de Vernay; while Gwyneth jealously observed the lady's comings and goings and resented the number of times she was a luncheon and dinner guest.

Richard began to suffer a series of small losses – a cuff-link, a cravat pin, personal articles of no particular value. Mr Hudson put his staff through a cross-examination, but in vain. If anybody held a clue to the mystery, it was Hazel, after a telling little encounter with Gwyneth.

She came swiftly into the morning-room to see the girl standing by the desk, reading a crumpled letter. At Hazel's entry Gwyneth jumped and threw the letter back into the waste-paper basket.

'What are you doing, Gwyneth? Afternoon work is over, isn't it?' Hazel asked, not over-pleased.

'Oh, I'm not at all tired. I was tidying up your desk, Madam.'

'Thank you, Gwyneth, but there was no need.'

As if scenting a stronger reproof, Gwyneth hurried on: 'I am quite fascinated by the difference in the colour seen through the patina on this side of your desk, Madam. It has been exposed to rather more sunshine than the other, has it not, Madam?'

Hazel couldn't restrain a smile. 'You're very observant, Gwyneth, and very knowledgable,' she said.

'Oh, thank you, Madam. May I confide in you, please?'

Hazel sat down at the desk. 'Of course,' she said, wondering what could be coming now from this extraordinary girl. Gwyneth put down her duster and struck a dramatic stance.

'Madam, why is everyone so blind? They see only what they want to see. Edward is quite right – the Comtesse de Vernay is a wicked woman. She killed her husband in Vienna and had her face slapped by Lady Digby-Cave in a hat-shop. She is quite penniless, you know, and her brother lives off what gentlemen give her, yet she is here nearly every day, and poor Mr Bellamy is quite taken in.'

It was fortunate for Gwyneth that Hazel was not a Lady Marjorie, who would have dismissed her on the spot for insolence. Instead Hazel asked mildly: 'How do you know all this, Gwyneth?'

The girl looked down, twisting the corner of her apron.

'Since you've been gracious enough to engage me in your household, I feel I owe it to you to be honest – about my true identity . . .'

Hazel was by now utterly mystified. 'Yes?'

'I am the natural daughter of Viscountess Ellerdale, you see, Madam, by her husband's estate agent. His Lordship had me well cared for and educated, but I chose domestic service. You see, although I cannot be accepted in Society, as a servant I can live among those who are.' Her expression was that of a virgin martyr justifying her faith before Caesar, while surrounded by starving lions. Hazel studied her with understanding and compassion, tinged with a spice of amusement. The girl was a pathological liar, but such a good one. In other circumstances she might have become a highly successful lady novelist, writing lurid romances after the style of the late Ouida.

Gwyneth glanced at her nervously. 'You're not angry, Madam.'

'No, Gwyneth, I'm not. And I will respect your confidence.'

'Thank you, Madam.' As Gwyneth left the room her hand went to the breast-pocket of her pinafore, where reposed a gold cuff-link monogrammed with the initials R.B.

'Poor Mr Bellamy is quite taken in.'

Gwyneth had not been entirely right there. Mr Bellamy was not at heart taken in at all, though as yet the full circumstances of Lili's position were not known to him, nor did he realise just how rich they supposed him to be. It seemed hardly to matter. On one of their delightful afternoons together they had stood before the great Turner in the National Gallery, talking about Art and Life, and he had asked her:

'What is your true nature, Lili?'

She smiled up at him.

'I think it is to be happy. And yours?'

Richard astonished himself by his answer. 'Perhaps – the same.'

They were surrounded by pictures again; this time in the room at the Savoy where Lili slept, and where Kurt painted. Sketchbooks and canvases were everywhere, some on the bed itself, which, however, was the object which dominated the room. Lili was sitting on it, inviting, irresistibly lovely in the apricot dress which set off her white shoulders.

Richard looked down at her, smiling. 'You know, this is really rather scandalous, Lili.'

She tilted her head provocatively. 'For one to be here, unchaperoned? Well, this is an artist's studio, and to artists all things are allowed.'

'Do you think so?'

'Yes. I have devoted much of my life, not so much to my brother, perhaps, as to his talent. Since our parents died, I have been a mother to it.'

Richard studied one of the landscapes. 'I like his work, though I suspect he would not wish me to. It has a deliberate – perversity, I think.'

'Yes.' She seemed to be making up her mind to say something more significant than their light exchanges. 'Richard?'

'Yes?'

'My brother depends upon – me – for money.'

'Lili!' He sat down beside her on the bed.

'I get so tired of hiding things,' she said.

'My poor Lili.' For the first time they were both facing the truth.

'I am very fond of you, Richard,' she said without a hint of her usual coquetry.

'And I of you, Lili. You have beautiful shoulders.'

He turned her towards him and kissed them. She neither repelled nor encouraged him. 'I'm sorry,' he said. 'But you're so beautiful.'

They had never been so close before, in body or in spirit. She was telling him of the death of her husband, shot by her hand with his own gun. 'He was twenty-five years older than me. But I married him so that Kurt could have his paints and canvases. I didn't love him. He didn't expect me to. Then I met a man I did love – the Baron d'Arras. I could not help myself – that is my nature, to love. But so few are worth the loving, Richard.'

'Am I?' he whispered into her scented hair.

'If you kissed me again, I might know for sure.'

He kissed her again. They were lying on the bed, the canvases pushed aside.

'You will be compromised, Lili.' He heard her little laugh.

'Yes, please. I am a scandalous lady, Richard.'

But before things could go further she was telling him about Lady Digby-Cave slapping her face in a hat-shop, because Lord Digby-Cave was buying her a hat, and Richard was laughing immoderately and telling her she was adorable.

'I love you,' he said. 'I'll buy you a dozen hats to join the three thousand you have already.' She gave him a little push, saying: 'I don't want gifts from you. I want more. I want your soul.'

'If you can find it, you can have it,' he told her. 'Do you have any more confessions?'

It was thus, as she lay in Richard's arms with his mouth on hers, that Kurt found them. At his exclamation they hurriedly sat up, Lili patting her disordered hair and Richard straightening his tie. Kurt stood before them in judgment.

'Mr Bellamy,' he barked, 'I am appalled. You, an English gentleman, take advantage of my absence in this way? When I have eaten at your table!' Lili protested.

'Kurt, what is the matter with you? This is our good friend—'

'What is the matter with *you*, sister? Do you wish me to kick you out, sir, or will you go?'

'Oh, I will go. I remember this kind of occurrence from my extreme youth. Only then it was husbands, not brothers.'

As he went unhurriedly to collect his hat, gloves and stick from the little hallway, Lili ran after him.

'Richard – dearest—'

'Lunch with me tomorrow, please. I'll fetch you from the foyer downstairs at one o'clock.'

Kurt, when she faced him angrily, was calm and unrepentant.

'We were mistaken,' he told her. 'That man is not wealthy. Lady Marjorie left the bulk of her estate to the son and daughter. We have wasted our time. Kindly order me some tea.'

At the quiet little restaurant Richard had chosen, luncheon was over. They sat opposite each other at the small table, and talked, softly and frankly, of their situation.

'It won't do, of course,' Richard said.

'Of course not.'

'We are each as bad as the other.'

Her eyes searched his. 'I know.'

'But we are both much nicer than the people around us. All the same, we love them, and have our duties to them, and cannot hurt them.'

Lili sighed. 'I suppose not.'

He touched her hand. 'Will you be very grieved?'

'A little,' she said. 'You?'

His look was sufficient answer, but he said: 'I am a man for marriage or nothing, and I don't think either of us can afford to marry without money.'

Her 'No' was hardly audible, and she turned her head aside so that the waiter advancing with the brandy should not see her tears. After the brandy was gone, they walked together down to the Victoria Embankment, and by way of the little streets behind the Abbey down Millbank to Chelsea Village. The river dimpled in the afternoon sunshine; from the trees, beginning to turn russet, came a faint delicious scent of Autumn, for September was near. By the little church they paused to rest; and Richard looked back to where the Victoria Tower rose towards the clouds. Soon the light would be burning above Big Ben, showing that the House was sitting; and he would be back on his Opposition bench, with nothing else before him in life, perhaps. He turned to the woman beside him, and looked and looked, as though to imprint the sight of her into his mind for ever.

When they told him that the new maid, Gwyneth, had been taking small possessions of his, and after confessing her fault had suddenly departed without notice, merely telling Mrs Bridges that she was "desirous of change," he was puzzled.

'But what could she have wanted with – what was it? a single cuff-link and a tie-pin?' he asked Hazel.

'She had conceived a fondness for you, Richard,' Hazel said.

'Oh. No – really?'

'It's true, poor creature.'

'She'll get over it,' said Richard. 'She'll get over it.'

CHAPTER EIGHT

Summer was determined to linger late that year of 1913. In the kitchen of 165 Eaton Place the heat was overpowering, although it was early September, and the staff were suffering accordingly. Edward, complaining bitterly, was turning the stiff handle of the ice-cream machine, while Ruby languidly picked over a dish of late strawberries, and Mrs Bridges sliced cucumber to decorate a salmon which, as she said, if left any longer in the larder might be expected to walk out on its own two feet.

As for Mr Hudson, he had actually abandoned formal dress for the comfort of an open-necked collarless shirt, and was wearily wiping the sweat from his brow as he placed a bottle of hock on ice in the sink.

'Oh, Edward,' he said, 'go and remove one place from the dining-room. There'll only be two for dinner tonight.'

'Oh fudge!' cried Mrs Bridges, slamming down her knife on the salmon-plate. 'I'm sick of only two for dinner, or only one for dinner, or nobody at all for dinner. Who is it this time?'

'Mr Bellamy will be dining out at his club,' replied Mr Hudson, in a tone which implied that he, too, missed the old days of great dinner-parties.

'What's more,' Mrs Bridges went on, 'I'm sick of not cooking. "Something cold, Mrs Bridges," *she* says. How I long to get my hands on a nice leg of mutton!"

Richard Bellamy, a whisky-and-soda at his side, was slumped in an arm-chair in the cathedral quiet of the smoking-room at Boodle's. The only other occupant of the room was one of those old gentlemen whose remarkable air of repose, beneath a copy of *The Times*, may well be due to his having died some days earlier, unnoticed by the waiters. Richard studied him with disfavour, imagining himself, all too clearly, looking much the same in thirty years' time.

Without much interest, he noticed that another member had come in, obviously for a quiet read, with a batch of newspapers under his arm. He looked again, and recognised the face.

'Jack Challen?'

The other glanced up, puzzled. 'Yes. But I'm sorry – Dick Bellamy!' He crossed the room to Richard's side. 'Well, well – I don't believe it.'

'I didn't even know you were a member here,' said Richard, his mood lightening at the sight of a familiar face.

Challen sat down. 'Only just. I'm hardly ever in the place – live in the country now.'

'Then it's an ill wind! It's been donkey's years since we met.'

Challen smiled. 'That's right. Not since Paris – when you were grand Second Secretary and I was humble Fourth.'

'United in our loathing of the First Secretary.'

'Not to mention the Ambassador!' Both laughed.

'You left the Foreign Office?' Richard asked. Challen had a certain look about him of belonging to a different world. He nodded.

'Married into commerce. I loved the girl and needed the money. I prefer it now . . .' He remembered Richard's situation and said with an Englishman's embarrassment: 'I was sorry to read about your wife.'

'Thank you.' They both knew that no more would be said on the subject. Richard caught sight of Bunting, the manservant, hovering some distance off, and beckoned him. 'Ah, Bunting. Another for me. And – whisky for you, Challen?'

'Thank you. But it'll have to be a quick one – I've got a train to catch.' He looked round the smoking-room with a grimace. 'This place is like a morgue.'

Richard agreed. 'London's always tedious, this time of year. The House in recess, everyone away.'

'You should get away yourself, Dick.'

Richard shrugged. 'Nowhere to go.'

'No country seat?' asked Challen in surprise. It seemed a come-down for one who had been Second Secretary. Richard shook his head. 'Heavens, no. There's only our London house, which belongs to my son now. I just – board there.'

Bunting returned with the drinks, as Challen digested this surprising information about a man he had thought of as comfortably situated. Bunting was adding soda to Richard's glass as Challen asked:

'Ever go down to Southwold?'

'Never. Marjorie's cousin's not quite my—'

An inept movement by Bunting sent a cascade of soda-water over Challen's trousers. He leapt up with an exclamation of annoyance, as the old man stammered apologies. 'I'll get a cloth, sir. It's a new siphon, that's why—' Richard produced a clean handkerchief and dabbed at the stains, but Challen was already mopping them with his own.

'It's all right, no harm done. They'll dry out. Just put a drop more in my glass, if you would – carefully, though!'

The debacle over, conversation was resumed; Richard admitted wryly to being an impoverished widower with a small income and precious little capital. Not usually fond of talking about his troubles, something about the boredom of the evening and the sight of a sympathetic face from the past encouraged him to dwell on them. Challen was silent and thoughtful as he listened. Then he said:

'Tell me, Dick. Do you ever gamble on the Stock Exchange? Shares? Consols?'

'Never. It's a mystery to me.'

For a moment it seemed as though Challen had something else to say. Then, downing his drink, he got to his feet, saying that he must go and catch his train. Richard, disappointed of company, said:

'You can't dine and go later? I'm on my own.'

'Alas, no. I've got my Chairman coming for the week-end, and, since he's also my father-in-law, I really must get back.'

Richard sighed. 'Well. It was good to see you again.'

With a promise of looking him up next time he was in town, Challen went to the door. As he reached it he hesitated, and turned back.

'Dick. Just a thought . . .' Richard raised his head enquiringly.

Challen sat down again, and lowered his voice, though there was no one else in the room except the recumbent old gentleman.

'I'd like to give you a tip, if I may,' he said.

'Thanks, Jack, but I never back horses.'

'It's not a horse. Listen. Any spare cash you *do* have –

anything you can raise – buy Cartwrights' Engineering. It's a motor-car firm. Might just ease your situation.'

'That's very kind of you, Jack,' said Richard, meaning it, 'but surely all motor-car firms are as dead as the Dodo. Even I know that. Too much competition for too small a market. Isn't that what they say? Sorry.'

'You *will* be sorry if you don't,' Challen said with a conviction that impressed Richard.

'Do you really mean that?'

'I promise you. But' and he looked Richard directly in the eyes, 'one thing you must promise me. For certain reasons which I can't disclose, you must not mention to anyone that *I* told you to buy them. It's got to be absolutely confidential.'

'Of course.' Richard was a shade irritated when Challen pressed him. 'Word of Honour, Dick!'

'Word of Honour.'

'Right. I must be off.'

He was at the door before it occurred to Richard that he had no address where he could communicate with Challen. He called after him, but it was too late.

On the principle of sleeping on every decision, Richard did nothing about Challen's tip until mid-morning the next day. Then, after a final struggle with his natural caution, he picked up the telephone on his desk. He was just on the point of winding the handle when, the receiver to his ear, he heard Hudson speaking on the downstairs instrument, in low and confidential tones.

'. . . that's right, Jock,' he was saying, 'a shilling each way Apple Cider in the 2.30 and five shillings to win White Magic for the St Leger – and, Jock, I'll have a saver on the big race – Seremond – aye, two bob each way. Thank you, Jock.'

Smiling, Richard waited for a decent interval after Hudson had hung up, then wound the handle and asked to be connected to a Chancery number. As their switchboard operator answered, Hazel entered the room with James's cigarette box in her hand. She paused at the door, but Richard beckoned her in and handed her a tin of Abdullas from the desk drawer. As she filled the box, paying no attention to the telephone conversation, her attention was arrested by hearing him say:

'Now would you do something for me, Mr Main? I'd like

you to buy for my account some Cartwright Engineering shares – the motor-car firm. Yes, I know they are. All the same, I'd like . . . yes. Five thousand pounds worth. The what? Ordinary Shares? Yes, I suppose so. What do I have to do? I see. No, I am quite certain. Thank you very much.'

Hazel ventured timidly: 'I couldn't help hearing – isn't that rather a lot of money to risk?'

Richard shrugged and smiled. 'What have I got to lose?'

What indeed, he thought when she had gone. Perhaps the venture would gain him nothing or lose him his small capital, or perhaps it would make him rich. How ironical it would be if it did make him rich! Less than a month ago a lucky gamble would have made it possible to defy convention and marry Lili. How gladly he would have taken her, lurid past and all! Ah well, nothing could be altered now, and all the probabilities were that Challen had been talking through his hat.

It was three weeks later, when Richard, about to leave for the House, glad to be at the end of the dreary summer recess, was sorting out correspondence with Hazel, James appeared at the study door, a newspaper in his hand.

'Didn't you buy Cartwright's Engineering Shares?' he asked his father.

'In a moment of aberration. I should have taken old Main's advice. Why?'

James waved the newspaper. 'Something about them in here.'

'Oh? They went up a ha'penny a month ago. I suppose they've lost it again.'

James grinned. 'Not exactly. You bought them at what?'

'Three-and-sixpence. It's engraved on my heart.'

James allowed a dramatic pause to elapse before he said: 'Well, today they're fourteen shillings.'

Richard and Hazel looked at him, astounded. Richard, normally at home with figures, found his mind a blank. 'But that's – incredible. How much am I worth? Quickly, you're the mathematician.'

James counted on his fingers, and Hazel quickly said: 'It's four times as much.'

'That's right,' said James. 'Your five thousand's worth twenty.'

Richard sat down suddenly. 'My God. But why have they gone up so much? There must be a reason.'

'There is. They've just pulled off a whopping great contract with the War Office, to make trucks for the Army.'

Something stirred, a little uncomfortably, in Richard's mind.

'What made you buy them?' James asked. 'Someone put you on to it?'

Richard's reply was guarded. 'An old friend.'

The clock caught his eye, and he realised that it was time he left. James, already late for the office, followed him into the hall, where Hudson was waiting with Richard's hat, gloves and stick.

'Don't go and spend it all, will you, Father,' James advised jocularly. 'I mean, it's only on paper, unless you sell the shares again.'

'Oh, I won't do that,' Richard promised. Hazel put her hand on his arm.

'I'm so glad for you,' she said.

'You've backed a winner all right – must be your lucky day,' James said. 'Perhaps you ought to have a flutter on the Big Race too. It *is* the Cambridgeshire today, isn't it, Hudson?'

Hudson's face was as expressionless as his voice. 'I believe so, sir.'

Downstairs, however, his normally composed face was beaming. Mrs Bridges eyed him curiously. 'Here,' she said, 'what are you looking so full of cream about?'

'The Master's had good news. Though naturally I can't say what.' (To both of them, Richard would always be The Master, even though the title technically belonged to James.)

'Yes you can, and yes you will,' Mrs Bridges declared; and of course he could and he did.

In the Commons Lobby, that afternoon, Richard strolled about, greeting colleagues, pondering on the Home Rule debate in which he intended to speak; happy to be back again in that Gothic temple of paint, gilding and marble, great murals of kings and queens, brooding statesmen in effigy, Victoria and Albert serenely unconscious that there had been a change in monarchy. It was, Richard thought, very beautiful and reassuring, and there was an added charm in returning to it the possessor of a fortune. He found himself humming an old song his clergyman father had been fond of and had quoted often, though by now Richard could only remember the refrain:

> 'How pleasant it is to have money, heigh-ho!
> How pleasant it is to have money.'

He was brought back to earth by bumping into a short, sharp-faced man who exclaimed: 'Bellamy! Just the fellow.'

Richard responded coolly. He was not fond of Henry Pritchett.

He would have left it at that, but Pritchett and his companion, a man unknown to Richard, stood in front of him. 'Good summer?' Pritchett enquired.

'Tolerable, thank you.'

Pritchett produced from his sheaf of Order Papers a green page bearing a single line of typing. 'Got your extra sheet?'

There was no such page among Richard's papers. 'Something interesting?'

Pritchett's manner was curious, with a hint of mischief in it. He introduced his companion, Arthur Naws, Lobby Correspondent of the *Evening Gazette*. Richard did not take warmly to Arthur Naws, but shook hands civilly.

'Naws was asking me about this Cartwright business,' said Pritchett. 'You've heard? They've a contract to re-equip the Army with motor-trucks.'

Richard addressed Naws. 'Why ask Mr Pritchett? He's not War Office, just a backbencher like myself. The Government benches, of course. You should talk to Deeping or Maycliff. Would you like me to see if they're around?'

'Oh, don't go to any trouble, I beg,' said Naws. Richard disliked his 'off' voice and the swift sly glance he exchanged with Pritchett as he said 'Mr Pritchett has been most helpful.'

Pritchett put in: 'I thought perhaps he should have a word with *you*. I believe you know something about it.'

Richard had no time to protest before Pritchett had vanished in search of some real or imaginary acquaintance, leaving him alone with the little man from Fleet Street. He tried to move away, but Naws was at his side, saying: 'It's this motor-truck I'm curious about. The one the Army favours so much they're spending a fortune on it. Cartwright

Engineering have been working on the machine for some years. With encouragement, I've heard.'

By now anxious to get rid of Naws, Richard turned his back on him, saying 'I really can't help you.' Naws followed him, raising his voice enough to attract the attention of passing Members.

'It's an interesting Question Mr Pritchett has put down for tomorrow. Don't you agree?'

Richard swung round and faced him. 'I get the impression you're trying to say something,' he snapped.

'Not me. It's your friend Mr Pritchett's question.' As Richard was saying that Pritchett was not his friend, that he knew nothing of the Question, Naws unfurled his copy of the green sheet and began reading with theatrical emphasis.

' "Mr Henry Pritchett, the Liberal Member for Stutworth North, to ask the Prime Minister if he will set up an Inquiry to investigate the circumstances in which allegations have been made that certain Hon. Members have made use of information improperly acquired, when dealing in the shares of Cartwright Engineering Ltd." '

He shot a look of malicious enquiry at Richard from under his brows.

It was a tiresome little incident, but Richard had almost forgotten it by the time he got home. The aspect of the shares which interested him was their value. 'I may as well sell them while they're high,' he told Hazel. 'Now will I be a bull or a bear? I never know.'

'Bull, I think. Suppose they go even higher?'

'I almost hope they don't.'

Hazel laughed. 'Spoken like a Socialist!'

'Why? Some idiot has put down a damfool Question about them. It even worried me for a minute, but it's nonsense. Still, may as well get rid of them and be done with it.'

He was looking in his address-book for the stockbroker's number when Mr Hudson entered, with the expression of one announcing a death in the family. There was a newspaper in his hand. Gravely he murmured:

'I think perhaps you ought to see the evening paper, Sir.'

Hazel took it from him, as Richard said: 'Do we take an evening paper?'

'No, sir. It is my own copy, sir. But—'

Even then Richard did not realise that Hudson was trying to break bad news. 'That's very kind of you. Now, would you get me Chancery 2214 on the telephone?'

'Very good, sir.' Hudson left as funereally as he had entered. Richard looked after him, amused. 'Extraordinary man. Must think I'm not up to date enough with the news.'

Hazel, scanning the paper, gave a shocked cry. Oh, Richard!'

She held the paper out to him, and he saw the headlines. "M.P. IN SHARES ENQUIRY." "TORY EX-MINISTER AND MOTOR FIRM."

"QUESTION TO BE ASKED IN HOUSE." BY ARTHUR NAWS.

Underneath was an unflattering photograph of himself.

'God Almighty,' he said.

The telephone bell rang. Hudson's voice, on the downstairs instrument, said 'Your number, Sir.'

'Cancel it, please, Hudson,' said Richard.

A few hours later, Sir Geoffrey Dillon was shown in, fretting and fuming. Wearily Richard answered his questions. Yes, it was the five thousand pounds James had given him for the house, and it was all the money he had. No, he had not thought of how it would affect the Dowager Countess, and he had no idea why the Question should have been put to the Prime Minister rather than to the War Secretary. The argument had hardly begun when Hudson announced Mr Johnson Munby.

'I thought your Chief Whip would be round here before you could say the word "Scandal", said Dillon, with relish.

Mr Johnson Munby was seriously concerned. 'My dear Bellamy, you have purchased shares in a firm, possibly knowing – I will allow you possibly – that the firm in question would benefit from a government contract. That was a dangerous thing to do.'

'*Did* you know, Richard?' Dillon asked.

'No! I did not.'

Steadfastly he refused to give the name of his adviser; he had promised to keep it secret, on his word of honour.

'Let Pritchett ask his Question and be damned!' he said, defiantly.

Next day, Munby, coolly unfriendly, showed him the Prime Minister's reply to Pritchett's Question.

It was a curt statement that the Prime Minister knew nothing of dealings by Members in the shares of Cartwright Engineering, but that he proposed to appoint a Select Committee to look into the matter. Richard would be required to appear before it and give evidence under oath.

165 Eaton Place was besieged by Pressmen, milling round the door, crowding the pavement which they shared with curious passers-by, taking pictures of the house.

'Gawkers and newspaper-people!' fumed Mr Hudson. 'Mrs Bellamy should let me call the police.'

'They won't throw a bomb, will they?' Ruby whispered.

'Get on with your work, Ruby!' shouted Mrs Bridges. 'God in Heaven! *Will* they, Mr Hudson?'

'I think it unlikely, Mrs Bridges. Let us be calm.'

'Calm! It's like one of them sieges with the enemy all around.'

The back door slammed, and to their astonishment Richard appeared in the kitchen, hatted, coated, and gloomy-faced.

'It's all right, Hudson. I came in through the Mews. There's rather a crowd by the front door.' He went up the stairs, Mrs Bridges shaking her head like a prophet of doom.

Sir Geoffrey Dillon was not at all satisfied. The motive behind Pritchett's attack on Richard eluded him. As he said, the indiscretion of one Tory Member would not bring down a Liberal Government, and it was impossible to bring down an Opposition. What, then, was his reason.

'I hardly know the man!' Richard protested. 'We're only nodding acquaintances in the House.'

'Well, it's not good enough. That's why I'm having him looked into to see where his interests may lie. Now look here, Richard. For the last time, because we *have* no more time, who was this man you claim advised you to buy those shares? Are you going to disclose his name?'

'For the last time, Geoffrey, I am not. I've already told you, the advice was given to me in absolute confidence. I happen to believe that a gentleman should keep his word.'

In the Commons Committee Room the Select Committee

was assembled. In the chair was the Attorney General, Sir William Trevanion, whose eye was guaranteed to make the brashest witness quail. He and Geoffrey Dillon had read law together at Oxford, and cordially detested each other, but Dillon had graciously been given permission to be present. At his right hand sat Sir Percy Devenish, Tory and North Country brewer, a Buddha-like figure, while on the left Reuben Chantry, pale and delicate of feature, represented the Liberal party. A shorthand-writer prepared to take notes.

After a tetchy beginning, in which Trevanion was enabled to show his claws, much to his own satisfaction, Chantry read out the affidavit of Robert Main, senior partner of Richard's firm of stockbrokers. Mr Main attested to the purchase by Mr Bellamy of Ordinary Shares to the value of five thousand pounds in Cartwright Engineering. Although he had advised against the purchase, Mr Bellamy had insisted, and to Mr Main's astonishment promptly the shares had soared in value.

From that moment the grilling began. Steadfastly Richard protested that he had seen no reason to sell the shares when news of the Army contract appeared in the Press. Was he a regular speculator? asked Chantry.

'Up until I bought the Cartwright shares, I had never bought a share in my life,' he answered.

It was Trevanion who fired a salvo calculated to destroy the impression of innocence Richard had made on the Committee. Glaring above lowered spectacles, he announced: 'I have in my hand a Minute of the Proceedings of the Imperial Defence Committee for Friday, June 27th, 1905, a well-attended meeting of that most important body. Among the names of Members present is listed that of Mr Richard Bellamy M.P., who was at the time Parliamentary and Financial Secretary of State at the Admiralty in Mr Balfour's Government.

Richard was bound to admit it.

'*Thank* you. On that day there were two matters on the agenda. Reports on the manoeuvres of the German Grand Fleet, and a report on the development of a promising new truck for the Army in its first stages of design by Cartwright Engineering Company Limited. To be known as the *Bulldog*. From the minutes, it is quite clear that the further development of that vehicle was encouraged by, among others, Mr

Richard Bellamy.' He raised his spectacles. 'Would you care to comment on that?'

Richard could only stare at him, bereft of words.

Hazel was pleading with him. 'Surely, Richard, all you need do is tell them the name of this man you met in your club.'

Richard banged on the table. 'I will *not* betray a confidence, Hazel. Not for a whole army of lawyers and politicians. If they choose to put a scurrilous and insulting interpretation on what I did in perfect innocence, then be damned to them!'

James sneered. 'Yes, and allow the whole Press and public, to say nothing of your friends and family – *and* the servants – to go on believing you acted in a dishonourable manner, using your privileged position—'

'I did nothing of the sort!'

'Then prove it!'

Father and son glared at each other. Hazel put down her needlework.

'James, please. Your father's been through a lot today.'

'And more to come tomorrow,' Richard muttered.

The morning paper on the kitchen table bore an ominous headline.

"BELLAMY ENQUIRY: SECOND DAY."

'Will they put him in prison, d'you think?' Edward enquired.

Mrs Bridges stared into her empty cup, as if the tealeaves could forecast Richard's fate. 'I don't think. I daren't think.'

Mr Hudson interrupted her musings, a letter in his hand held at arm's length. 'Where is Ruby?' he asked.

'Ruby? In the scullery.'

Edward was despatched to fetch her, while Mrs Bridges enquired:

'What do you want her for?'

Mr Hudson permitted himself to be amused. 'She's going up in the world. She has "correspondence".'

'*Ruby*?' Mrs Bridges took the envelope and calmly opened it, to Mr Hudson's pained surprise.

'Mrs Bridges! A letter is private, even a kitchen-maid's.'

She read it, undeterred. 'I've the right. If it's from some man, I'll give her one she won't forget.'

By this time Ruby had been fetched, and was blankly regarding the envelope. It seemed too good to be true. '"Ruby Finch", that's my name . . .' Mrs Bridges handed the letter to her. 'Here, girl. It's from Bradford – your mother.'

Ruby handed it back. 'Tell me what it says! It'll take me all day and I've got the pots to scour. Is she all right? It's not her leg? Not my sister Ethel?'

Mrs Bridges, conscious that all eyes and ears were at her service, read importantly.

'"Dear Ruby. You're to come home at once. Your Dad and me don't want you serving in no house what gets in the papers. Second we don't want you working for someone who like as not will soon be in prison your Dad's sure of it. Third I've got you a place as kitchenmaid with Doctor Reardon round the corner. It's live-in and all found so you won't be under my feet. Enclose money for train. P.S. Spot died run over by the brewer's dray. Your Dad and Ethel send their love.

Mother."'

Ruby burst into noisy tears.

In the Commons Committee Room, Henry Pritchett was being questioned by Sir Geoffrey Dillon, and was manifestly enjoying it, quite sure of his ground, undeterred by the fearsome glare of the Attorney General and the fathomless dark gaze of Reuben Chantry.

'Will you tell the Committee,' Dillon was saying, 'how you first came by the knowledge that Richard Bellamy was on the register of shareholders in Cartwright Engineering Limited?'

'I went to the Company's Office and looked up the share registers.'

'Did you find the names of any other Members of Parliament in the register of shareholders? Anyone at all whose holding of shares might have discomfited you?'

'I did not.'

Dillon looked round him. 'So there is no great Tory plot.

One begins to wonder why you made the expedition to the Company's office in the first place.'

Pritchett assumed his canvassing expression. 'I am interested in the good name of this House and rectitude in public life. I am vigilant against corruption on behalf of my constituents.'

Dillon smiled the smile of a boa-constrictor. 'Ah yes, I quite forgot your constituents in Stutworth North, I believe. Now. Until 1904, you, Mr Pritchett, were, I believe, a shareholder in a company called Rankin Mechanicals Limited.'

A stir of interest went through the others, like a ripple on a pool. Pritchett's equanimity was visibly shaken. 'I did have a few shares, yes. What of it?'

'Were not Rankin Mechanicals the only possible competition for that War Office contract?' Dillon purred. 'Rankin Mechanicals, whose factory is in Stutworth North – your constituency?'

Pritchett hesitated fractionally before saying 'That is so.'

Dillon sailed into action with all guns firing.

'I put it to the Honourable Member for Stutworth North that *Rankins* found out that Richard Bellamy was a shareholder in Cartwrights, their successful rivals, that *Rankins* pressured him – how I do not know, – and Heaven forfend I should find out – to start this calumny; not to destroy Richard Bellamy, a mere victim standing in the way, but to negate Cartwright's contract by painting a picture of corruption so that the War Office and the Treasury would be forced to cancel it.'

Pritchett leaped in on his cue.

'I agree the contract should be cancelled! The whole thing should be re-examined!'

'And go to Rankins next time?' Dillon made it sound like a polite suggestion. Richard, however, heard only the words without the irony, and broke out impetuously:

'That, if I may say so, would be disastrous. To place such a contract with another firm – when Cartwrights have already developed a truck, which can serve as ambulance, troop-carrier, supply wagon, even light artillery . . .' Too late he realised what he had said. Chantry surveyed him sadly.

'So you do remember the details, Mr Bellamy. Quite clearly, it seems.' He sighed regretfully.

The case had attracted attention from the moment its details were released by the Press. Unpleasant letters had at once begun to come in, including one to Richard from the Chairman of the local Conservative Association, and righteous missives from the public. Less than three months before Mr Lloyd George and Mr Rufus Isaacs had caused a nationwide scandal by the revelation that they had speculated in American wireless shares in the Marconi Company, and had been duly examined. Both had cleared themselves satisfactorily of the charge of corrupt motives. But, as Sir Geoffrey Dillon glumly reflected, they were exceedingly shrewd gentlemen, and his client, demonstrably, was not.

'Has it struck you that in this day and age your attitude may be a little old-fashioned?' he demanded as they left the House after Richard's damning admission.

'I should have thought the keeping of a man's word of honour was unlikely to become dated,' Richard snapped. 'And if they choose to judge a perfectly innocent action by their own corrupt standards, then be damned to them.'

He had to face a similar attitude at home. James, concerned with his own feelings as much of those of the rest of the family, their friends and the servants, accused him of being 'guilty by implication', while Hazel pleaded with him to tell the Committee the name of his informant. Steadfastly he refused, until James stormed out in a temper and Hazel was left wondering what, if anything, could be done.

Next day she had a painful scene with the tearful Ruby, who protested that she didn't want to go, she was happy; while Mrs Bridges indignantly pointed out the difficulty of getting another kitchen-maid at a moment's notice, and Mr Hudson tactfully averted Mrs Bridges's wrath away from the blubbering Ruby. Hazel promised to write to Ruby's mother.

'I'll see if I can persuade her to change her mind, Ruby. But – well, that's all I can do.'

'Blow your nose and come with me, Ruby,' said Mrs Bridges, conducting her charge from the room. Mr Hudson remained, sensing that Mrs Bellamy had some other business with him. They exchanged a few more words about Ruby before she came to the point.

'I want to ask you a favour, Hudson.'

'Anything I can do, Madam.'

'Please keep this to yourself – I mean, from the other servants, and indeed Mr Richard or Captain James.'

'Madam?'

Hazel played nervously with the fringe of a cushion.

'The night before Mr Richard telephoned the stockbroker and bought those wretched shares—'

'I do recall, Madam.'

'Oh, do you? Well, can you remember the date? Because, you see, he dined at his Club that night and someone he met there advised him . . . I won't go into all the details, but for various reasons Mr Richard can't *himself* reveal this man's name to the Committee – but I, that is, I and Captain James—'

'You would be hoping to persuade the gentleman to come forward, Madam,' proferred Hudson.

'Exactly. Well, I can't walk into Boodles and ask the Hall Porter—'

'Quite, Madam. I well remember it was the night of September 2nd, because the following day was the 3rd, St Leger Day at Doncaster; and when Mr Richard telephoned that morning it crossed my mind that he might be wishing to place a wager on the big race.'

'Then if someone at the Club could remember—'

'Quite, Madam. I will slip over to Boodles this afternoon, Madam.'

Nothing could have been more convincing than Mr Hudson's enquiry after a pair of spectacles his employer was supposed to have left in the Club smoking-room, which had possibly been picked up by another member. Bunting scratched his head thoughtfully.

'When was that, then?'

'Evening of the second of September.'

'Now . . . would that have been the night he nearly got a wetting from my soda-siphon?'

Mr Hudson raised his eyebrows. 'I've no idea.'

Bunting pointed to a group of chairs. 'He was sat just over there with Mr Challen, was Mr Bellamy, having a whisky and soda, only this siphon squirted a bit too sharp, you see, all over Mr Challen's trousers.'

Mr Hudson looked innocent. 'Mr Challen?'

'Country member. Doesn't come in much.'

'Ah. Would that have been the night before the St Leger, September 2nd?'

Bunting stroked his chin. 'Yes, I reckon it was. 'Cause when I took the siphon back to Jack in the dispense, and told him as Mr Challen had wet his trousers, he laughed and said it must be a good omen, 'cause he was backing a horse called April Shower at Doncaster next day.'

'I see. Could you tell me this Mr Challen's address?'

'Oh, no.' Bunting's tone was shocked. 'Against Club Rules to give members' addresses to strangers. Sorry. More'n my job's worth.'

A five-pound note had somehow appeared in Mr Hudson's hand.

'But you have a members' address-book.'

'In the Hall Porter's cubby-hole,' said Bunting, eyeing the note. 'I suppose when he slips down for his tea . . .' He glanced at the clock. 'Wait here,' he said.

At the last-but-one day of the Committee's enquiry, Richard reiterated wearily his refusal to disclose the name of his informant. Chantry, the most sympathetic of his questioners, made a last friendly appeal.

'The Committee would very much like to believe in the existence of this mysterious and knowledgeable friend, but we can't and you can't expect us to.'

Trevanion boomed from the head of the table. 'Were we to believe in this man's existence, which we must question, another question would have to be answered. How much did this individual know, and how did *he* know it?'

'Then at least,' Richard answered, 'I am right to protect his name.' He looked at Chantry, who said 'Yes, Bellamy.'

'Though at what a cost,' added Devenish.

Sir Geoffrey Dillon had arrived at 165 in response to Hazel's summons, after Hudson had returned with his news. Together he and Hazel searched through *Who's Who.*

'Chadwick, Chaffey, Challen, Alfred . . . Challen, John Stuart. That's the man.'

'And his address is Hillgreen Hall, near Taunton,' said Hazel.

Dillon was running his eye down the entry. Then, triumphantly, he shut the book with a slam. 'I've got him. And what's more I've got his reasons for keeping Richard's mouth shut all this time. Give me that telephone, quickly! I'm going to ask Trevanion to delay tomorrow's findings, until I can put one more question to Richard in front of that Select Committee. It's our last chance.'

The atmosphere in the Committee Room was electric; Trevanion, Devenish and Chantry with their eyes intent on Richard like cats at a mousehole, while Dillon, another cat, toyed with the mouse.

'You told the Committee,' he said urbanely, 'that it never occurred to you to ask this man his reasons for advising you to buy the Cartwright Engineering shares. I'm going to suggest to you that this man is a senior director of Cartwright Engineering: that he is married to the daughter of the Company's chairman, Mr William Cartwright, and that his reason for demanding your discretion was that he knew of the War Office contract about to be signed with his firm, and that he could be in breach of City ethics by tipping his company's shares at that time to anyone.'

In the silence, Richard stared back at Dillon like a hypnotised animal, his face white with shock. At last he managed to speak.

'What am I supposed to say to that?' His voice was shaking.

'You are under oath to answer the questions put to you here truthfully, so I must, as your legal adviser, ask you one final question, and you must answer it – truthfully.'

Richard's reply was scarcely audible. 'What is your question?'

'Was the man who advised you to buy those shares a Mr John Stuart Challen?'

They hung on his answer, as he looked wildly round, inescapably caught and struggling. Then he let out a sigh, beaten at last.

'Yes, it was. And may God – and Challen – forgive me.'

When he returned home Hazel was waiting in the hall, summoned by the sound of his key in the door; while Hudson hovered nearby. Richard, stony-faced, ignored them completely, as utterly as though the hall had been empty. Without even taking off his coat he strode into the study and slammed the door.

Hazel, with an apprehensive glance back at Hudson, tapped and entered. He was standing by the window, his back to her.

'Richard . . .?'

He did not turn round. 'There is to be no Report,' he said icily. 'At least, not one that will cause any scandal. I am declared innocent, if foolish, and my lack of forethought is to be deplored.'

'Deplored? How dare they?'

He swung round now, his eyes blazing. She had never seen him look so before.

'How dare they?' he shouted. 'They could have dared a great deal worse! How dare *you*?'

Hazel shrank back like a threatened child. 'Richard . . .' she stammered. Carried away with rage, he came nearer. 'Going to my club!'

'I didn't, I—'

'Sending my servant! Involving my servant in my affairs!'

She was almost weeping. 'But I had to – someone had to!'

'Clubs *exist* so that women and servants can't meddle! As a result, I've been forced to break my word. *You* make me a man whose word is worthless. I'd rather prison than that!'

Frightened and shocked as she was, there was enough pride in her to dry the tears before they fell. All the resentment which had built up in her since the first gloss of her marriage had worn off came out in a burst.

'Then you're a fool! You think I care a damn about your word? Your word-of-honour, hand on your heart, never tell a lie, precious public school code?' She could hear her voice getting coarser, losing the 'gentry' quality she had imposed on it, becoming more like her father's when once in a while he had a row with her mother.

'Such things matter to a man,' he retorted.

'Well, they don't matter to a woman – any woman!' Her face was crimson with temper. 'We fight for things that *do* matter – our families. You're *my* family, like it or not!'

'Women should keep out of men's affairs – always.' His tone said 'My wife did' though it was not strictly true.

'Keep out? Newspapers? Servants leaving? Those that do stay in turmoil?' Suddenly she tried an appeal. 'Oh, Richard, please. Don't be angry – just because you needed help.'

'I'm angry,' he said deliberately, 'because you behaved so

wilfully and improperly. Clearly your ways are not yet our ways.'

It was the cruellest thing he had ever said to her. A few moments earlier it would have broken her, but rage still kept her colours flying, on the defence. With a good imitation of calm, she said:

'I'm not sorry about that. I quite frequently think you and James are insane.'

'Thank you,' he said. 'You may be interested to hear that I shall instruct Main to sell my shares at once, make sure my original investment and brokerage costs are covered, donate the remainder of my profit to Marjorie's favourite charity, and never buy a share again as long as I sit in the House of Commons. And now, get out of my study!'

She turned and left him. Mr Hudson, still lingering in the hall, looked after her with pity as she went slowly upstairs.

CHAPTER NINE

Richard Bellamy smiled, as he entered the morning-room, to find his daughter-in-law pacing the floor, a frown of worry on her usually smooth brow, muttering to herself.

'Pad, not paw . . . mask, not head . . . brush, not tail . . .'

'Why not?' Richard enquired, though he knew the answer.

Hazel flopped into a chair with an exasperated laugh. 'Oh, it's this awful list of words one must and mustn't use in hunting society. James says I've got to know it by heart before we go for this wretched weekend. Tea?'

'Please.' Hazel rang the bell.

'It's *quite* mad, Richard. Nothing has a tail – foxes have brushes and hounds have sterns, and a crop isn't a crop, it's a whip, and as for horses—'

Richard laughed. 'I know exactly how you feel. I can still remember, vividly, the first time I went to stay at Southwold. I made little lists for weeks. If I hadn't been engaged to Marjorie I think I'd have funked it.'

'But you were different,' Hazel said. 'You'd been to public school and Oxford. You were used to it.'

'Oh, you'd be surprised how naïve I was. After all, I was the son of a poor country parson – quite clever, I admit, but Latin and Greek don't go down very well in the hunting field.'

Rose and Edward came in with the tea-things and quietly arranged them, Edward listening keenly to the scraps of conversation he could hear over the tinkling of cups and teaspoons.

'But you did know *their* habits,' Hazel was saying.

'Not a bit of it. I couldn't play bridge; when we went shooting I could feel Lord Southwold's eyes on my back, counting every bird I missed – and my man in London hadn't put in a white waistcoat.'

Hazel looked depressed. 'Poor her,' thought Rose as she and Edward left.

'I'm dreading it more and more, the nearer it gets,' she said with a sigh.

'Oh, it's all different now. And the Newburys are very

easy – anyway, you know them, don't you?'

'Well – we've dined with them once in London.' The recollection didn't seem to elate Hazel. 'I liked Bunny. But I wasn't so sure about his wife.' She was picturing the young Marchioness of Newbury, who had been Lady Diana Russell, pointed-faced and russet-haired, with big mischievous eyes and a sharp wit, which Hazel had fancied was sometimes directed against her.

'Diana? She's all right,' said Richard. 'I mean, she and James have known each other for years – they were practically brought up together. In fact, Marjorie thought at one time—' He pulled himself up short. Hazel finished the centence for him.

'—that she'd make a suitable wife for your son.'

'Oh, no, not exactly that. I mean . . .'

'Never mind.' Hazel sighed again. 'I'm sure I shall make the most ghastly faux pas, and James will be dreadfully shamed.'

Richard patted her arm. 'Just be yourself.'

'I haven't even any idea what to wear.'

'You'll need a maid.'

'I know.' She shuddered. 'The thought of a strange woman doing my hair horrifies me!'

'Why not take Rose? She always used to look after Elizabeth.'

'Rose? Hudson would have a fit!'

'Nonsense. We've got that temporary girl and the cleaning women. I think we'll just about survive a weekend without Rose. And James is taking Edward.'

Hazel smiled. 'You're a comfort, Richard. I'm sorry, I'm being a bore. Have some more tea.'

Downstairs, a few days later, Edward and Rose were engaged in packing James's hunting gear, Edward putting each item in the case as Rose ticked it off on a list.

'Hat brush – velvet pad – gloves. Two pairs spurs complete with straps.'

'Right.'

'Boot jockeys – hunting whip – top hat – boots. That's all. And remember, Edward, when we're there I am Miss Buck, and you are Mr Barnes.'

'Yes, Rose. Will I have to help wait and all that?'

Rose fixed him with a stern glare. 'You will not demean yourself by such a thing. You're Captain Bellamy's valet, and you'll not lift a finger to touch nothing that isn't his. Like as not we'll be invited to take our meals in the steward's room, and you'll be asked to take in someone else's maid.'

Edward grinned. 'Hope she's a good-looker.'

'None of that, either! There's temptations in those big houses.'

Edward looked innocent. 'I thought that's what weekends in the country was for – a little bit of what you fancy on the side.'

Rose answered his wink with a frown.

'Beg pardon, Miss Buck, I can see I've offended your delicate sensibilities. Well, that's it, then. We're off.'

In the kitchen passage at Somerby, newly-arrived, they regarded with awe the long row of service-bells and the cards attached to them, showing where each guest would be sleeping.

'Here, look, Rose.' Edward pointed. ' "Lord Charles Gilmour. The Queen's Room." "Captain and Mrs Bellamy. The Chinese Room." "Major and Mrs Cochrane-Danby. The Rose Room." '

A face peered round the doorway of the valets' room; the round cheerful face of Mr Breeze. 'Good evening. Would you be the Bellamys?'

Rose was about to stammer a denial when she remembered that visiting servants took their employers' names. 'Yes,' she answered. 'Er – Mr Hudson sent his kind regards, Mr – Makepiece?'

'Breeze. Lord Newbury's man. Mr Makepiece is unfortunately indisposed.'

Down the passage a female figure was approaching. Edward rapidly sized it up and mentally lablled it Very Tasty. Cecile, Lady Newbury's French maid, was petite, with a provocative sway to her walk, a head of frivolous curls, and a come-hither in her eye. Graciously she greeted Rose as Breeze introduced them, but favoured Edward with a long, appraising look which brought a flush to his cheeks.

'Too young for a valet de chambre,' she said coyly, in a pretty accent which was rather more French than it need have been. Her smile included Rose rather perfunctorily. 'We wish you to have a very nice stay. Miss Buck, may I show you your room?' and she led Rose away.

Two footmen, gorgeously apparelled, appeared and while one bore off the Bellamys' luggage the other took from Edward the suitcase and hat-case he was carrying, and took them into the valets' room, into which Edward followed him.

It was a room primarily designed for the care of garments, with ample cupboards, ironing-tables and irons, trouser-presses and the like. At separate tables, working on their masters' hunting-kit were Mr Breeze and an elegant, languid man whom Mr Breeze introduced to him as Joseph, though officially known by his master's name as Mr Gilmour. He eyed Edward from head to foot almost as comprehensively as Cecile had done, and favoured him with a benevolent leer. Embarrassed, Edward said 'Well, I'll just – er – just go up and unpack, then.'

'First floor,' Mr Breeze said. 'You'll see the card on the door.'

Joseph followed Edward out of the room with his eyes, then said appreciatively: 'Nice-looking boy. Nice fresh complexion.'

Mr Breeze sniffed disapprovingly.

'Well,' said Joseph, if *I* don't have him, Cecile will!'

James and Hazel arrived in the great Hall of Somerby as the hunting-party were finishing a hearty tea. The men had exchanged their pink coats for tweed ones, and Mrs Tewkesbury had changed into a drifting teagown. Hazel, still wearing the hat she had thought looked smart in London, felt as though she would have looked conspicuous and vulgar in any hat, or in no hat at all. As she entered, all eyes were fixed on her like muskets on a condemned military offender. She shrank towards James, but he was being warmly kissed by Diana, who then extended three cool fingers to Hazel; Bunny shook hands with them both.

'Lovely to see you – come over and get warm and have some tea.' Hazel was briefly greeted by everybody with the exception of Cochrane-Danby, whose smile of welcome was more of a leer, and who pressed her gloved hand with uncomfortable tightness. 'I say, jolly nice to meet you,' he enthused, and managed to insert himself between her and Kitty, regaling her with plates of buns and cakes which she felt would choke her if she tried to swallow. She was relieved when a buzz of hunting-talk began, a mélange of the names of places and people and horses, falls at ditches and jumps over fences; all incomprehensible, but at least it meant that there was no need for her to talk.

But the indefatigable Cocky was leaning over her with yet another plate.

'Do you hunt, Mrs Bellamy?' he enquired tenderly.

'N-no – but I've ridden quite a lot – in London.'

Cocky looked delighted. 'I say, what fun! Nothing's more boring than other people's hunting stories – except their children and other ailments.'

'Oh, I'm rather enjoying it – I've never heard so many nice people I didn't know talking about so many nice horses I didn't know . . .' It sounded feeble enough to her but Cocky laughed loudly.

'I say, that's jolly funny – I must remember that! I bet you look damn handsome on a horse.'

Hazel became even more embarrassed, and managed to change the subject by asking him if he lived near Newbury.

'Good Lord, no,' Cocky chortled, or that was what Hazel imagined it was, 'no one actually *lives* up here. Just come up to Leicestershire, don't you know, for the hunting.'

'Do you mean, just to hunt foxes?'

Cocky flung a world of meaning into his sidelong glance. 'No, dear lady – not just to hunt foxes.'

Diana's appearance to conduct her to her room rescued Hazel for the moment. Cocky swiftly laid down his cup of cold tea and poured himself a very large whisky. The others followed Hazel's retreating back with speculative glances. 'Not bad looking in a farouche sort of way,' was Charles Gilmour's comment. She was not his type.

'Really quite presentable,' said Kitty, 'if only she wouldn't open her mouth.'

Cocky defied her. 'Damned attractive girl, that.'

'Girl!' Kitty sneered.

'She's as old as I am, if she's a day,' Natalie contributed. In fact, she was right.

Edward was rapidly having his eyes opened. During the preparation of their respective masters' evening clothes Breeze and Mr Gilmour were discussing the 'odds and ends' who made up the weekend party. Edward bridled.

'Excuse me, if you're referring to Captain Bellamy and—'

Breeze quenched him. 'Mr Gilmour was referring to Major and Mrs Danby, who, as you might say, are on the fringe of society, not having personal servants of their own.'

Mr Gilmour broke the ensuing silence with the fascinating news that his master, Lord Charles, had come to Somerby in order to pursue a lady with an unenthusiastic husband.

'Oh, I see,' said Edward, who didn't. His eye fell on the waistcoat the valet was brushing.

'Lord Charles has some nice things,' he ventured.

Mr Gilmour affixed another diamond stud to the waistcoat and smirked at Edward. 'We have even nicer things upstairs. You must allow me to show them to you sometime.'

Edward beamed. 'Oh, I'd like that!'

He was alone, finishing off James's tailcoat, when Cecile arrived and enquired solicitously whether he was finding everything to his liking. He had barely replied before she was standing close to him, fingering his lapels and peeping coquettishly into his face. 'You are a nice-looking boy, Edward. Not like some of them – *you* know . . .' She mimicked Mr Gilmour's languid walk.

'Not likely,' said Edward, with only the most shadowy idea what she meant.

She came back to him. 'You are sleeping down here?'

'Just along the passage.'

'By yourself?'

'Oh yes, I hope so,' replied the innocent youth.

Cecile giggled. '*I* hope *not*.'

Edward blushed, and she kissed him full on the lips, at which he blushed even deeper, and was glad to be interrupted by Rose.

After a few terse words with Edward, Rose went upstairs to maid Hazel. The Chinese Room was large and luxurious, with a handsome Sheraton four-poster, a chaise-longue, and a desk for writing letters to less fortunate people in London. Hazel had reached the stage of having her hair done. Rose heated the curling-tongs in the flame of a methylated spirit burner, and carefully transformed the naturally waving hair into a mass of artificial waves and curls. Still in negligée, Hazel was holding Lady Marjorie's diamond necklace against her white throat.

Rose coughed. 'If you'll excuse my mentioning it, madam,

Lady Marjorie always used to say "No diamonds in the country." '

Hazel looked with genuine gratitude. 'Thank you, Rose.'

'Not unless it was a big formal party, or a ball, of course.'

'I see.' She took from her jewel-box a simpler ornament of which Rose quite approved. So did James, who entered at that moment, fully dressed for the evening. He kissed the back of her neck, with its appealing tendrils of hair.

'You're looking very beautiful tonight, my darling. I'm very proud of you.'

With a smile, she rose and gave him her arm. Compliments from James were not so frequent as they had been, and she valued them accordingly.

For a group of grown-up people, the house party were behaving very oddly. Cocky, wearing two ears made of scarves and a false snout, was grovelling on the floor, grunting and snuffling, while the rest sat about guessing what he might represent; for he was enacting the first syllable in a charade.

'I know!' squeaked Natalie. 'He's a piggywig!'

'A wild boar,' Hazel ventured. 'Too fierce for a pig.'

'A boar, of course!' Kitty echoed. 'Cocky doesn't even need to act that.'

The boar snarled at her, rose on two feet and disappeared, reappearing to say 'Second syllable.'

James strode on, a white skin rug over his shoulders, flourishing a club, beating his breast and roaring. Diana crouched behind him. Suddenly he picked her up, flung her over his shoulder and carried her round the room amid cheers, finally depositing her on the floor and devouring her face and throat with kisses. Hazel did not cheer. Ever so slightly, she bridled, and refrained from joining in the guesses. They both appeared to be enjoying their acting. Kitty turned to her with a malicious cat-smile. 'Hazel, my dear, what a life you must lead at home,' she purred.

The third syllable brought James on again, this time on all fours with a large bone across his teeth. He progressed across the carpet even more savagely than Cocky had done, growling and tearing at objects, including the ladies' dresses. 'Tiger!' someone called. 'Lion!' suggested another.

'What a fierce lot they are,' commented Charles.

Cocky, James and Diana proclaimed in chorus 'The whole

word!' and went behind the screen, from which James and Diana emerged, she with one shoulder of her dress pulled down temptingly, James in a smock with a chisel in his hand. He posed Diana in a rapt attitude on a stool, where she stood immovable, and began to work on her with the chisel, stepping back occasionally in devout admiration. Suddenly Cocky bounded on in a ballet-skirt with a tinsel wand in his hand and touched the fair 'statue', who smiled, stretched, stepped down from her pedestal and embraced the sculptor warmly.

'My dear,' Kitty hissed to Hazel in an aside, 'has this been passed by the Lord Chamberlain?' The shot went home, though Hazel tried hard not to show it. Everybody got the answer to the charade simultaneously. 'Pig – male – lion. Pygmalion!' To a round of applause the actors appeared hand in hand, and bowed.

'Bunny,' said Kitty as their host entered at that moment, 'you just missed your wife practically seducing James in public.'

Bunny Newbury laughed, but the laugh was not hearty. 'Wouldn't be the first time,' he said.

'Or the last,' Charles whispered to Kitty.

Bunny had brought with him the details of the next day's hunt.

'They're meeting here. Sam Hames is bringing over a horse for you, James – swears it can jump. What about Hazel?'

'Hazel doesn't hunt.' It was a flat statement.

'You ride, don't you, Hazel?' Diana asked. She had been listening to Hazel's earlier conversation with Cocky. Hazel stammered 'Well . . .'

'We'll only be messing about in the wood all morning, no jumping or anything. Bunny, Hazel could have that old mare of your mother's.'

'Oh yes! Old Blueberry, she's as quiet as a lamb.'

Hazel was beginning to get enthusiastic, but James repeated firmly: 'I'm sorry. Hazel isn't going to hunt.'

Natalie drifted off to an early bed, with a meaning look at Charles Gilmour, Bunny and James went to play billiards. Diana poured drinks for the remaining guests. Cocky downed his at one gulp, and said 'I think it's jolly bad luck if Hazel does want to hunt.'

'I wouldn't stand for my husband ordering me about like that,' Kitty declared, while Diana told Hazel 'If you'd like to hunt you jolly well hunt.'

Hazel hesitated. 'Well, I . . . James doesn't want me to.'

Diana snorted. 'Don't you let James rot you. He's getting very bossy and it's time he was taught a lesson.'

Hazel tilted her head like a considering robin. James certainly *was* bossy – quite overbearing, sometimes. But still she felt obliged to protest. 'I haven't any proper clothes.'

They all moved in on her with argument and suggestion. Diana said there were enough clothes at Somerby to equip a female squadron of yeomanry; Charles suggested that she might wait until the hunt had moved off. Their enthusiasm was infectious. When Diana said 'It would be rather fun, wouldn't it?' Hazel answered wonderingly 'Yes. It *would* be rather fun.'

Night had fallen. In the rooms behind the strong doors of the bedrooms, the guests and hosts slept, or did not sleep, as the case might be. In the shadowed corridor Edward appeared, stepping with needless caution. A pair of dainty shoes arranged outside Lady Newbury's bedroom would be a sign that Cecile was waiting for him. The anticipation was thrilling.

But before he could reach the door another door opened. Edward shrank back behind a potted palm, and stood there silent as the imposing figure of Lord Charles emerged stealthily from what Edward knew to be Mrs Tewkesbury's. Resplendent in a scarlet and gold dressing-gown he passed within a few inches of Edward's nose, on the way to his own room. Edward couldn't be sure whether he had been seen or not. It wasn't worth the risk. With cautious tread he went back the way he had come, and hurried down the backstairs.

Next morning, as Edward, having passed a disappointingly chaste night, was returning to the house after seeing James safely on to his horse, he stopped in his tracks and stared. In the Orangery, on a garden seat, were Mrs Tewkesbury and Lord Charles, wrapped in an unmistakably intimate embrace. Edward shook his head and walked on.

He joined Rose at the Bellamy's bedroom window to

watch the hounds and the huntsmen moving off, a brilliant procession.

'Pity the mistress doesn't hunt,' he said, 'she'd look nice.'

'I'm sure she would,' agreed Rose.

'Still, I suppose she's not been brought up to it, not like the other ladies. Here – talking of ladies, do you know what I just seen?'

'No, and I don't want to neither,' Rose snapped.

Cecile entered, with garments draped over her arm. Pointedly she addressed Rose, ignoring Edward.

'Lady Newbury 'as asked me to bring these to you. They are for Mrs Bellamy.'

Rose stared at the riding-habit, stock, boots and top-hat. 'But those are for hunting in. My lady isn't going hunting.'

'Ah, but yes! It has been arranged as a little surprise.'

'I see. Now, Edward, you hop it and get on with your work.'

Cecile backed her up with a snarl that might have come from a cross kitten. 'Yes, you go away, we don't want you.'

'Look,' he began, hoping for a chance to convey to her what had happened the previous night. She flounced. 'Some men are never in the right place when they are wanted.'

Edward realised that he was not to be forgiven, and dejectedly left.

Half an hour later Hazel was dressed and ready. Rose and Cecile stood back to admire their handiwork. Hazel's Rossettian beauty was set off admirably by the severe dark habit, more becoming to her than the slightly fussy clothes she chose for herself. Behind the veil which kept the topper anchored to her head she was smiling happily. She felt confident, important. When James saw how splendid she looked and how well she rode he would stop bossing her around. Diana was quite right. She picked up her whip. Followed by Rose, she went down to the stable-yard, where her groom was waiting at the horse's head. Nearby Cocky lurked, drinking in with his eyes the handsome sight she made.

She paused before mounting. 'But this looks quite a young horse. I thought I was to have Lady Newbury's old mare.'

'Ladyship's orders to give you Donovan, madam,' said the groom. 'Seems Blueberry wasn't too well this morning.'

'I say,' Cocky bustled forward, 'you sure he's safe? Looks a bit wild in the eye to me.'

'Couldn't tell you much about him, sir. Her ladyship only brought him over from Ireland the other week – I've not rode him yet.'

Hazel was patting Donovan's nose, an attention which he seemed to accept with more resignation than pleasure. 'He's beautiful,' she said, 'I'm sure I'll be all right on him.' Cocky assiduously helped her to mount, caressing her waist as he did so. From the distance came the terrible music of the hounds.

'They've found a fox,' Cocky said. 'You might have some fun.'

In a clearing in Somerby Woods the field waited for the Fieldmaster's orders. Diana's ears picked up hoofbeats; she looked over her shoulder with a malicious smile as Hazel on Donovan emerged from the woods. James followed her glance, and was struck with admiration for the slender upright figure he didn't recognise. 'Who's that good-looking woman on the bay?' he enquired.

Diana looked innocent. 'Never seen her before in my life.'

But something in the carriage of the rider's head and the distinctive colour of her hair roused James's suspicions. The Fieldmaster began to canter, followed by the rest of the field. From a canter Hazel's horse broke into a gallop and outpaced them, running like a lightning-streak.

'Get after her!' James shouted, setting his own horse to a gallop, and followed by Bunny and Hazel's groom. Hazel tried desperately to pull up, dragging the reins tight, but the jerk of the bit in his foaming mouth only urged Donovan to a faster pace. Her wide horrified eyes saw that they were going down a hill with a fence at the bottom, and heading straight for a farm gate. Over the thud of hooves James, behind her, heard her scream as she was carried towards the inevitable crash.

Then the miracle happened. Donovan made for the gate and soared over it like a bird – and Hazel stayed on his back.

On the other side the horse relaxed his pace. Hazel managed to pull up as James came up beside her. She was white-faced, sweating and shaking. James's shock had turned to violent anger.

'Well,' he ground at her, 'I hope that's taught you a lesson you'll never forget.' She shook her head, gasping and speechless. James beckoned to the groom. 'Please take my wife home,' he said. As the groom led Donovan away Bunny approached.

'I say, is Hazel all right?'

'Yes,' snapped James.

'Look, James, I'm awfully sorry—'

'I'd better apologise to the Master for my wife's behaviour,' said James between his teeth.

Hazel was sitting by the fire in the hall, shivering. Cocky put a stiff brandy and soda into her hand, and poured an even stiffer one for himself. Hazel sipped it slowly.

'Oh, I made such a fool of myself,' she said.

'Doesn't sound to me as if you did. Very nasty thing to be run away with, happens to us all – but jumping the Avenue gate and staying on, that's a very fine thing. I think you're a damned plucky girl.'

Hazel smiled faintly. When one feels utterly degraded any admiration is welcome. 'You're very kind, but I really couldn't help it.' Cocky patted her hand and poured two more drinks.

She felt a little better after the hot bath Rose prepared for her, and for the report that they were saying downstairs they'd seen nothing like it since Lady Warwick had hunted at Somerby. But she knew there would be more trouble to come when James got back.

Bunny and Diana preceded him, Diana pouting. 'Really,' she said, the way James behaved was quite too ridiculous – going off in a sulk like a spoiled child! No harm came to his precious wife.'

'Could have been very nasty, though.' Bunny handed his pink coat to Breeze and was helped into his tweed one. A thought struck him.

'Why wasn't Hazel riding mother's old mare? I thought that was the idea.'

Diana didn't meet his eyes. 'Oh, she was lame, so I let Hazel ride the new Irish horse.'

Bunny stared. 'The one you can hardly stop yourself – even in a gag?'

Diana shrugged. 'She said she could ride, didn't she?'

Even now Bunny failed to understand completely just what his wife had done. 'I do think that's a bit hard. She might have fallen off and been killed!'

'You try falling off a sidesaddle. Don't be a bore, darling,' and she drifted away. She had not forgotten a certain night when, as she stood warm and tempting within the circle of James's arms, in his bedroom, he had put her away, and gone back to marry that white-faced carroty nobody from Wimbledon. Lovingly Diana recalled Hazel's ordeal in every detail. If she *had* fallen off and been killed . . . well, accidents will happen . . .

Hazel was sitting at her dressing-table, pretending to brush her hair, strung-up with tension, when James came in. He had carefully prepared what he was going to say, and there was a steely glint in his eye.

'Well? Did – did you have a nice hunt?' was all she could think of to start the conversation, or trial-scene, as it well might become.

James took a deep breath for his set piece.

'I gather from all the sniggering that went on behind my back that your little exhibition was meant to be some sort of a joke. If so, I hope you enjoyed it. One thing is quite certain – everyone round here will be laughing their heads off about it for the rest of the winter.'

Tears were in Hazel's reply. 'James, I'm sorry. Now please go away and leave me.'

'I certainly shan't go away until I've had some sort of explanation of why you deliberately disobeyed me. I thought I'd made myself perfectly clear.'

'Oh well, it – it wasn't my idea, really—'

'Don't start trying to blame it on other people! You knew very well—'

Hazel spun round in sudden fury, shouting at him.

'Don't go on about it! They all said you were getting stuffy and arrogant and needed teaching a lesson, and my goodness, they were right!'

James stepped back, astonished at the turning of the worm.

'So – you agreed to collaborate. Very loyal of you.'

'I was only trying to do what you've been telling me to do, day after day, for weeks – to get on with your silly friends!'

'They may be silly but they can ride – which is more than you can, so stop boasting about it.'

'*Some* people say I did rather well.'

He sneered. 'Cocky, I suppose.'

'Yes.'

'What the hell does he know about it? The Master told me to see if I could interest my wife in paperchasing in the future!'

With a slam of the door he was gone.

As James came down the stairs everybody in the hall reacted, visibly or not.

'All right?' asked Diana.

'Yes, thank you.' His tone was cool. She took his hand. 'Come and have a drink and stop looking like a cross old sheepdog.'

As they approached the drinks table Cocky finished his whisky and made a neat, unobserved exit up the staircase.

James took the drink Diana had poured for him without thanks.

'*You* were behind all this, weren't you?'

She made saucer-eyes. 'Me?'

'You're a very wicked girl.'

'Darling James.' She cooed. 'You've known that for years. Now haven't you?'

He didn't join in her laughter.

Upstairs Hazel was lying on the bed, in negligée. A book was in her hand, which she looked at from time to time, but her eyes were sore and swollen with crying. Her head went up hopefully as the door opened. But it was not James returning to apologise; it was only Cocky, giving a melodious 'Cockadoodledo!' To her surprised look he responded, not very lucidly, 'My dressing-room door was open, so . . . I say, you do look beautiful.' He came closer, and she drew her filmy wrapper closer round her shoulders.

'Major Danby, do you usually come into a lady's room without an invitation?'

'Didn't I read an invitation in your eyes?' He saw, with real concern, that her cheeks were wet. 'My dear lady is sad.'

'I'm quite all right, thank you,' she said, with an attempt at coolness; but her voice was still out of control. Cocky took her hand and sat down beside her. The role of comforter was one he thoroughly enjoyed. 'What's the matter? You can tell me.'

The kind tone broke her down again, and Cocky gave her his large clean handkerchief to wipe her eyes. 'It's that husband of yours, isn't it.'

She nodded dumbly; but with the thought of James came another thought. Suppose he came in suddenly? 'There'd be a terrible row if James—' she began. Cocky stroked her leg reassuringly. 'But he won't, will he, my dear? Otherwise engaged, what?'

Hazel's tears dried. 'Doing what?'

'Now you're teasing me.' He put his arm round her shoulders. 'You mustn't be upset about it – not serious, only games.'

'Games?'

'Bedgames. He's been playing bedgames with Diana for years. Everybody does it, such fun, you know – and country-house weekends would be pretty dull if everyone – er . . .' He seemed to be losing the thread. 'I say, you have the most stunning shoulders.' He aimed a kiss at one of them but Hazel edged away and pressed the bell. Cocky, unseeing, was trying out the bed.

'What about a little game of our own, eh? I say, what a lovely bouncy bed . . .'

'Major Danby, I really think it would be better if you went back to your own room,' Hazel said. Before Cocky could protest a sharp knock on the door sent him scuttling headlong for his own room through the other exit.

'Yes, madam?' Rose was in the doorway.

'We're going back to London, Rose.'

'What – tonight, madam?'

'Yes. Now. Immediately.'

A quarter of an hour later the two women were being let out by the back door, Edward carrying a suitcase. As Hazel went up the steps Rose pressed a piece of paper into Edward's hand.

'You're to give this to Captain James, but not for half an hour. Got it?' Edward nodded.

James and Lord Charles were playing backgammon when the note was delivered. James's face was thoughtful, for Lord Charles had just remarked that Diana had gone a bit too far, switching horses and putting Hazel on an animal that pulled like a train. It was news to James, and disturbing news at that. The note appeared at his side, on a salver held by Henry the footman. He read the words 'Gone home. Sorry, I've had enough,' and re-read them.

'Who gave you this?' he asked.

'Your man, sir.'

Edward, promptly sent for, was sheepish and unhappy. Yes, he had known Mrs Bellamy had left.

'How long ago?'

''Bout half an hour, sir. They was going to catch the seven-twenty, sir.'

'Why didn't you tell me before?'

'I was told not, sir.'

'By *whom*?'

'By Rose, sir. On behalf of the mistress, of course.'

'I see. You put Mrs Bellamy before myself.'

Edward rallied. 'No, sir. Of course not, sir. But – well, Mr Hudson told me I must do as Rose said while he was away.'

The argument, as James well knew, was unanswerable. 'You've no idea why she left?'

'No, sir. Er – Mrs Bellamy seemed a bit upset. She just told me to telephone up for the cab from the station, and then gave me the letter when they went.'

'I see.' James picked up the telephone.

'Excuse me, sir, it's not connected now. The local exchange closes at seven o'clock.'

James scanned the timetable by the telephone. 'There's a train at eight-fifty – we'll catch it. Please pack everything ready.'

There was delicious fodder for gossip among the party dressed for dinner and enjoying their cocktails. Charles had just told them the latest.

'I say, have you heard – Hazel Bellamy's bolted!'

'Not again – not twice in one day! But how, darling?'

'Just upped sticks and dashed off to London.'

'What drama! and there's Bunny furious with Diana, and James—'

'Sssh!'

James, dressed for outdoors, was coming down the stairs,

followed by Diana and Bunny, Henry carrying his luggage. He ignored the watchers by the fire. To Bunny's 'Do let us know if we can do anything . . .' he returned no reply, but made for the front door. Bunny joined the others, his face without its usual smile. 'I suppose none of you can throw any light on Hazel's departure?'

Diana, who had been sulking, brightened up at a new opportunity for mischief. 'Apparently somebody was in her room talking to her after tea.'

'Probably her maid,' put in Cocky hurriedly.

'A man's voice, according to *my* maid.'

Charles was quick to exonerate himself. 'Well, I was playing backgammon with James.'

All eyes were turned on Cocky, who became flustered and fiddled with his tie. Lord Charles shook a finger at him.

'Cocky, you dirty old stoat – at it again!'

Cocky whipped round to Kitty. 'I never touched her, Kitty darling, I swear it – I just went in to see if she was all right, you know – the shock . . .'

Nobody believed him.

The morning-room of 165 Eaton Place looked like paradise to Hazel. She had had a drink and some hot soup, and was sitting with Richard by the fire, trying to calm down, while Richard's temper correspondingly rose.

'What is quite unforgivable is James's behaviour. I've never heard of anything so deliberately cruel and thoughtless! That son of mine—'

Hazel glanced at the clock, and got up. 'I'm going to bed. I don't think I could face him, Richard.'

'He won't come here tonight.' Richard was fierce. 'When he does show his face here again, leave him to me.'

As if on cue, the front door opened and James's voice was heard in the hall. A second later, and he was in the room. Hazel recoiled, trembling.

James looked from one to another. 'I'd like to talk to Hazel alone, please, father.' Hazel threw Richard a glance of entreaty, and he said 'I think that Hazel would prefer me to stay, so that you can explain your behaviour to both of us.'

'My behaviour?' James was obviously not conscious of any guilt. 'What on earth made you bolt like that?' he asked Hazel.

'Can't you think of one good reason?' said Richard.

'No. I've been trying to, for the last three hours. I mean, Hazel, why didn't you tell me you wanted to leave—?'

Hazel's reply was icy. 'For once, I don't think your darling Diana would have been very amused if I had walked into her bedroom and asked to be allowed to talk to my husband.'

James subsided on the sofa, utterly baffled. Then, collecting his thoughts, he said: 'First let me say that I have never been in Diana Newbury's bed either before or after her marriage. Second, let me say that after tea I never left the hall for one minute. I played backgammon with Charles Gilmour, and until the man brought your note the only movement I made was to get myself a drink. Now who told you all this nonsense?'

'Major Danby.'

James exploded. 'Cocky! The man should be shot. He *would*. I suppose he pussyfooted his way into your room.'

She nodded, beginning to smile. 'I wish you'd been there, James. He was so funny!' She started to laugh, half in genuine amusement, half in hysterical relief. James caught the infection and joined in. Their arms round each other, they rolled and shrieked on the sofa, quite unable to stop.

Richard surveyed them, smiling ruefully. The fire was very tempting, and he would have enjoyed taking his nightcap beside it. But instead he would ring for Hudson to bring it to him in his bedroom. He was quite used to such things.

CHAPTER TEN

The Crown and Anchor in Elizabeth Street, Belgravia, was the time-honoured meeting-place for the local butlers, footmen, valets and chauffeurs – even of the occasional coachman. A cosy Victorian pub, the shape of its bar-room was convenient for the division of the sheep from the goats; the sheep being represented by the stately senior butlers, distinguished by the wearing of bowler hats, and the goats by the frivolous footmen and valets.

On a November night in 1913 Edward pushed open the door of the Crown and savoured the pipe-smoke and chatter which made him feel very adult and sophisticated, though in fact he was still self-conscious among his fellows until ale had mellowed him.

He pressed through the throng to reach the bar, and his friend Robert, who was waiting for him with a glass of ale at the ready.

'Thought you was never comin',' said Robert. 'Here.'

'Ta.' Edward took a copious draught. 'That's better. What's been going on at your place today?'

Robert grinned, beckoned Edward nearer, and whispered something.

Edward registered surprise. 'Lady Charlotte did? Go on. Really?'

They proceeded to gossip like a couple of old ladies at a sewing party. As glass succeeded glass they grew merrier and merrier. Another footman, John, joined them, and Robert urged Edward to tell one of his stories again.

'Tell him what happened at Somerby. Go on.'

Edward, slightly guilty, drew patterns on the bar with his glass. 'Don't know as I should, really.'

'Come on,' John urged him, 'we won't tell nobody.'

'Well, you see, my master – I was valeting him down at Somerby Park, last weekend. Well, there's this French girl was there, Cecile, Lady Newbury's maid – I got friendly with her, you see, in the servants' hall; and she said if I came by her lady's bedroom door at midnight, she'd give me a sign—'

John nodded. 'Pair of her lady's shoes pointing towards the female servants' quarters.'

Edward gaped. 'How did you know?' The others exchanged an amused look.

'We all know that French maid of Lady Newbury's,' said Robert. 'Got plenty of footmen in trouble around the country houses, *she* has.'

Edward looked deflated. 'Well, I never got to Cecile's room that night, anyway. Someone come out of one of the bedrooms just as I got to the top of the stairs.'

'Whose bedroom?' John asked.

'It was a Mrs Tewkesbury.'

'What, a man, was it?'

'Well, what do *you* think?'

'Bet it wasn't her husband!'

Edward lowered his voice. 'It was Lord Charles Gilmour. One of the gentlemen of the house-party.'

'Tory politician,' said John. 'Brother of the Duke of Bolton.'

'That's right. And he hops back into his room – which is conveniently situated across the corridor, right opposite hers.'

'How d'you know it was him – was his name-card on the door?'

'Didn't look.'

John asked 'Did his lordship slip you anything next day, to keep quiet about it?'

'Oh no! He never saw me. But I saw *them* together next day. Cuddlin' in the Orangery. Cor, they weren't 'alf . . . Here, look, it's late. I've got to get back.'

'Don't matter what time *I* get back,' said John. 'Our butler's drunk by ten.'

As Edward turned away from the counter a neat undistinguished-looking man who had been drinking by himself a little distance away accosted him.

'Evening,' he greeted Edward, who looked at him in some surprise.

'Evening.'

'Not seen you in here before, have I?'

'Don't come in all that much.'

'Heard you mention Somerby – nice place, Marquess of Newbury's.'

'That's right.'
'Been there meself, in the old days.'
'Go on. In service, were you?'
'Yeh. You Captain Bellamy's valet, you say?'
'Well, footman really. Went up to valet the Captain last weekend. He was up there, hunting.'
'Oh, ah?'
'I work for him and his father and Mrs Bellamy – Eaton Place.'
The little man looked thoughtful. 'Bit of luck, you bumping into the gentleman coming out of Mrs Tewkesbury's room. Seeing what you did.'
Even now Edward had no suspicion that he was being pumped. 'Why?'
'And them, next day, in the Orangery. Holding hands, were they?'
'Bit more than that. They were kissing, bold as brass, and he had his hand – well, on her leg.'
The man gave him a sharp look. 'You better be sure of what you saw, my lad.'
Edward was still without a clue. 'Why?'
'Because you're quite likely to find yourself called up as witness in a divorce case, that's why.'
Edward stared. 'Who are you, then?'
'Never you mind.' A half-sovereign had appeared in his palm. 'Just take this, keep your mouth shut, and if they should happen to call you up in court, you tell the judge what you just told your friends. All of it.' He turned and walked away, but paused. 'One more thing. How was Lord Charles dressed when you saw him come out of that bedroom? Might be important.'
'Oh, he was in his dressing-gown. Scarlet it was, with gold braid and that. Posh. Here – are you somebody's valet?'
'Private Detective. Name of Clough. Good night.'

Edward spent an uneasy night; and with reason. On the afternoon following his encounter with Clough, Richard Bellamy was having a furious quarrel with his solicitor, Sir Geoffrey Dillon. It was not like Richard to shout, but he was shouting now.
'How dare you, Geoffrey! You of all people. A trusted,

respectable solicitor! To put spies on to my servants in public-houses!'

Dillon retained the poker-faced calm for which he was famous.

'Don't overdramatize matters, Richard. An enquiry agent acting for me, on behalf of my client Colonel Tewkesbury, merely established your footman as the probable key witness in a divorce action. As such the man is bound to appear in court and give evidence. Whether he's your servant or King George himself.'

'And you are ready,' Richard fumed, 'to stand by and see young Charles Gilmour – just the kind of dynamic young man the Tory party needs today – politically destroyed by a harmless flirtation with somebody else's wife at a weekend house-party?'

Dillon looked over the top of his spectacles like a tortoise inspecting and then rejecting a piece of lettuce. 'I am a solicitor, Richard. I act for Colonel Tewkesbury. Divorce is a part of my business. I also happen to believe that the truth is more important than promising careers. Now, if you'll excuse me, I have work to do.'

He had barely left when Hudson showed Lady Prudence Fairfax in to the still seething Richard. Graceful and elegant as ever, the lady who had been Marjorie's best friend swam into the room and bestowed a sisterly kiss on Richard's cheek. He seemed, she thought, a little distrait as he returned the kiss and welcomed her.

'You're alone?' she asked.

'Yes, I am. James took Hazel off to Florence for a week to see some picture-galleries.'

'Leaving you to fend for yourself? Once more?'

'Yes. *And* they're off to Paris for Christmas.'

'Poor Richard!' Her pity was genuine, and a little of it was for herself, for she would dearly have loved to step into Marjorie's vacant place; and Marjorie would have been the last to mind. It seemed so ridiculous, Richard a lonely widower and she a lonely widow – of considerable attractions . . . But there, one can hint but one can't very well propose.

'I'll be all right,' he said. 'Old Mabel Southwold's coming to keep me company.' Lady Pru made a face. Then 'Why all this rushing off abroad?' she asked.

'Hazel didn't enjoy her weekend at Somerby.'

'So I heard. A little out of her depth, no doubt, in Diana Newbury's world.'

'Who wouldn't be? The things that go on in that house . . .'

'Yes, and that's precisely why I've called, Richard. Apropos one of those things that went on – alas! at Somerby, last weekend.'

Richard sighed. 'And what might that be?' He knew the answer in advance.

'Harry Tewkesbury is divorcing Natalie, citing your young protégé, Charles Gilmour. Did you know?'

'Yes, I did know, as a matter of fact.'

'I've got Natalie staying with me now. Harry's kicked her out, and she can't stop crying.'

'Do you happen to know if she's in love with Charles?' Richard asked.

'Not in *love* . . . she just enjoys sleeping with him. Really, Harry's suddenly behaving like a madman. Raging at her, calling her a faithless wanton, as if she'd never looked at another man before.'

Richard sighed again. He was beginning to hear rather too much of the Tewkesbury affair. 'And what am I expected to do?'

'Well, take some steps to protect Charles Gilmour's name. If he's cited—'

'—his political career will be in ruins. Do you think I don't know that?'

'Then stop the case!' she said with the triumph of a woman who has proposed a brilliant solution. Richard stared at her.

'How can I?'

'Speak to Sir Geoffrey Dillon. I gather he acts for Harry as well as for you, and he's a good Tory. He won't want Charlie Gilmour broken on the wheel. Then stop Edward giving evidence.'

Richard looked thunderstruck. '*Edward*?'

'Your footman. I gather he's to be the chief witness.'

'How the devil did you know that?'

'It's all over London, Richard. Natalie's maid heard it from one of the servants at Lady Vereker's.'

Lady Pru had never seen the mild Richard look so angry. He sprang up and began pacing up and down the room with a brow like a thundercloud. She thought it advisable to retreat while he was in this mood, and rose to leave.

'You won't stay for tea?' He stopped his pacing.

'No, thanks. I must get back to console poor Natalie. I really can't have her weeping all over my furniture.' In the hall she encountered Edward and gave him a frosty look. When the door had closed on her Richard beckoned him into the morning-room. He followed, apprehensively.

'I'd like a word with you, Edward.' He rang the service bell. 'I'm ringing for Hudson; I want him to hear what I have to say to you.'

'Sir.'

Mr Hudson appeared with genie-like swiftness.

'Come in, Hudson,' said Richard. 'I want you to listen to what I have to say to Edward.'

'Sir.' Hudson had obviously heard nothing on the servants' grapevine.

'Now then, Edward. It has come to my ears that, as a result of boasting about your employment in front of other servants in a public-house, you are to be called as witness in a divorce case.'

'Yes, sir. I believe so, sir.'

'Some story about Lord Charles Gilmour and Mrs Tewkesbury. Something you claim you saw one night at Somerby. Perhaps you'd care to repeat that story to me now.'

Wretched, Edward looked from Richard to Mr Hudson, who said 'Do as you're told, boy.'

'Well, I said – I'd seen Lord Charles and Mrs Tewkesbury together, sir.'

'Where? In what circumstances?'

'Well . . . just sitting in the Orangery, together.'

Mr Hudson had a nose for prevarication. 'Tell the truth, Edward,' he said.

'It *is* the truth.'

Richard frowned. 'That can't be all, Edward. What else?'

Patiently, bit by bit, he got Edward's story out of him, examining every statement like a practised Counsel. How did he know it was Mrs Tewkesbury's bedroom? How did he recognise Lord Charles Gilmour? He made Edward show him exactly how far away the figure had been, and describe the amount of light. Finally he threw doubts into Edward's mind about the famous dressing-gown.

'And what was it like, this dressing-gown?'

'Scarlet and gold braid, like. His valet showed it me, when

he was laying out his lordship's dress-clothes before dinner.'

'You're certain of that?'

'Well, sir . . . I couldn't be that certain, sir. I couldn't be positive . . .'

'You'll be under oath in Court to tell the truth. As I trust you've told it to me, just now. That's all for the moment, Edward. Thank you, Hudson.'

Downstairs, Edward shamefacedly endured a homily from Mr Hudson about tact, loyalty, the embarrassment his conduct would bring upon all concerned – not least the Bellamy household. It was not an interview he would ever care to recall in later life.

Richard had little appetite for dinner that evening, to Mrs Bridges's disappointment. He felt he could not stand by and see an excellent young man, and his own protégé, ruined for the sake of a foolish weekend frolic with a woman who was known to be not merely generous but lavish with her favours. Harry Tewkesbury had known of her other affairs, and ignored them, Geoffrey Dillon had told him. Why should Charles Gilmour be picked out for reprisals? Dillon had reported that Tewkesbury's resentment was based partly on the fact that Gilmour had bought a house in his constituency, Wolverton North – an action which he was sure meant that the young politician intended to ingratiate himself with Tewkesbury's constituents, as well as having easy access to Natalie.

'Nonsense,' said Richard to himself. He picked up the telephone and asked the exchange for Gilmour's number.

Punctually at eleven o'clock the next morning Lord Charles was shown into the morning-room. Accepting a small glass of madeira by way of refreshment, he sat down and contemplated Richard with every appearance of relaxed ease, the very picture of a man *not* in imminent danger of having his career smashed.

'It's very kind of you to see me,' he said, sipping appreciatively.

'I thought it was a good idea.'

'In fact, I was on the point of calling on you. But I didn't see why you should be involved in my scrape.'

'Well, it seems I *am* involved, indirectly. What's the latest?'

'The latest is that Harry Tewkesbury is going ahead with a divorce, naming me.'

'Yes, I did know that.'

'All he can possibly gain is my ruin, both social and political. And it's all really based on a misunderstanding. When I took that house outside Wolverton I confess it was partly to be near Natalie, and I did have certain political motives, as well.'

Richard's eyebrows went up. 'I'd be careful about admitting that.'

'But it was all in good faith. You see, I thought Harry was retiring. He'd given that impression to Natalie. Hadn't *you* heard about it at Westminster?'

'I must confess I hadn't. People like Harry don't retire, do they – they hang on to the bitter end.'

Lord Charles frowned. 'Then it was a devilish ruse on his part. He let it be known to Natalie, so that I'd show my hand. Then he pounced, and closed the trap on me.'

'Well,' said Richard, 'it's quite simple – you must set your sights elsewhere.'

'You mean – politically?' He smiled wryly.

'There will be other seats vacant.'

'Yes . . . Richard, what I really need is your advice.'

'Well. There's only one way to prevent a scandal, Charles, and that, I'm afraid, is too late. Give up seeing Natalie. Could you?'

Charles smiled and shrugged. 'I don't know. She's beautiful, enormous fun to be with, but not indispensable. Nor am I to her, I should imagine. She – disconcerts me.'

'She's one of those people of whom a lot is assumed, and not much verified, isn't she?'

'Yes. One must be wary of visiting footmen passing in the night.'

'I'm sorry about that, Charles. It would damn well have to be one of *my* servants.'

'Would the fellow's story stand up in court?'

'It might. But we must try to prevent it getting to that . . . get Harry to see the error of his ways. I don't know him very well, but I'll do my best for you.'

In the late afternoon Mr Hudson ushered into Richard's presence the person of Colonel Harry Tewkesbury. Middle-aged, bluff and sporting in appearance, he had a face which gave little away. His expression was as guarded now as his manner was cool. Richard waved him to a chair.

'How good of you this is, Tewkesbury. I do appreciate it.'

'I'm not normally in the habit of discussing my domestic affairs with acquaintances, Bellamy. However, since we *are* old colleagues in the Tory Party, and Geoffrey Dillon sees no objections, here I am.'

'Well.' Richard was nervous, disliking the part he was playing, but Parliamentary professionalism prevented him from showing anything it. 'My interest in your forthcoming divorce action is two-fold. First of all, the footman in this house has got himself involved as an important witness, and I'm bound to consider his interests as an employee of my son and myself.'

'I take it the man is capable of telling the truth in court.'

'I think you can depend on that – should the case come to court.'

'There's no question of that. The writ has already been issued.'

There was a tiny pause before Richard said: 'The other matter, of course, hinges on our common membership of the Conservative Party. Whatever you may think of Charles Gilmour as a man, his political promise will not have escaped you.'

Tewkesbury stiffened. 'I know nothing of his political ability beyond what I read in the Society gossip-columns.'

'He has more to offer than that sort of thing, Tewkesbury, and you know it. He's most highly regarded in the Party.'

'H'm. You're asking me to drop the case – for the good of the Party?'

'Frankly, yes. And if you're worried about the future of your Parliamentary seat, I can assure you here and now that Gilmour is going to put his house on the market at once.'

Tewkesbury couldn't help showing surprise. 'Oh, is he?'

'Any idea that he was after your constituency was a complete misunderstanding. That I do know.'

'He's my wife's lover. Bellamy, and for that he must pay the price.'

'The price of getting caught, eh? Tewkesbury, for God's sake – for the last time – this is 1913. Queen Victoria's dead. And the country needs all the able young men it can muster.'

Tewkesbury's mouth was set in a hard line. 'Gilmour knows the rules. He gambled and lost. He must pay the price.'

'To hell with the rules!' Richard burst out.

Tewkesbury hauled himself out of his chair, leaning on the stick he needed nowadays. 'I don't think we have anything more to say to each other, Bellamy,' he said.

After supper that night the servants' hall was deserted but for Edward, busy getting a stain out of one of this white gloves, and Daisy, the new under-house parlour-maid. She was small, plump and pretty; very different from the austere Rose and the gormless Ruby. Edward found her attractive, and talked to her when Rose or Mr Hudson was not by to break them up.

'Got any brothers and sisters, Daisy?'

'Four brothers and three sisters.'

'Cor! That's a lot. You the youngest?'

'Youngest but three. Least, I was . . .'

'How do you mean?'

'I was last time I was home. Don't go home that often.'

'Where's home?'

'Hoxton. Where's yours?'

'Walthamstow. My dad's a carpenter. He's a real card. You must come and meet him when I go visitin'.'

Daisy's eyes were wide. 'Would you take me?'

'Yeh. 'Course I would. I mean, if you want to come.'

'Yeh. Be nice.'

Ruby appeared at the door carrying a letter. She looked askance at the two heads close together. Edward had never spent much time in cosy chat with *her*. 'Man outside give me this for you, Edward,' she said. 'Said his name was Joseph, and you'd remember from Somerby.'

Edward took the note and read it.

'What's it about?' asked Daisy.

'Nothing,' he said. 'Ta, Ruby.'

The bar-parlour of the Crown and Anchor was unusually quiet when Edward entered it after supper. Edward had no difficulty in spotting Joseph, known in country-house parlance as 'Mr Gilmour.' He was leaning gracefully on the bar, two drinks poured out in front of him. He smiled winningy as Edward approached.

'Here we are again, Eddy. I've got one waiting for you.'

'Thanks, Joseph. Got your note.' He took up his ale.

Joseph favoured him with a long, languishing look. Such fresh cheeks and crisp hair, such a charmingly innocent air. He ought to be as easy as falling off a log; but that was not the immediate matter in hand.

'Glad you haven't forgotten me,' he said. 'We didn't see enough of each other at Somerby.'

'No, you was always too busy. Except that time when you called me into your master's room.'

A wary look came into Joseph's eye. 'Did I?' he said vaguely.

'Yeh, that evening before dinner, when you were laying out Lord Charles's dress clothes. Don't you remember? You wanted to show me his solid gold cuff-links and his expensive new dressing-gown from Rome.'

Joseph stroked his perfectly-shaven chin. 'Yes. I did. You're quite right. That's what I want to see you about. I want you to forget about that dressing-gown, Eddie. You never saw it, did you.'

It was a statement, not a question. Edward stared. He saw mentally the splendid garment spread across the bed, a blaze of regimental scarlet and heavy gold braid, dazzling to view and rich to feel. 'Why d'you want me to forget it?'

'Never mind.' Joseph drew from his pocket a thick envelope, unaddressed.

'Here. Don't open it now. I can tell you what's in it, though. Money. Quite a bit of money. For mumming your dubber.'

Edward's blank face, uncomprehending of the thieves' slang as of the notion of bribery, irritated the worldly Joseph. 'Don't wave it about! Stick it in your jacket. That's right.'

In a corner, veiled by a large, healthy aspidistra, an inconspicuous-looking man smiled to himself.

Edward was an innocent, but he was not a fool. Having downed his pint he made his excuses to Joseph, who had made another suggestion for passing the evening, and went straight back to Eaton Place and to Mr Hudson's pantry. There he told his story and handed over the envelope. In it were ten pounds, with no accompanying letter. Mr Hudson studied them.

'And he handed this over in full view?'

'Yes. But it doesn't matter, because I'm not going to keep it. I'm going to give it back. And stand up in that witness box, if I've got to, and tell the truth. It's my duty, whatever he says. I've been offered a bribe, and I'm rejectin' it.'

'Don't be too hasty, Edward,' said Mr Hudson thoughtfully. There are times when the truth, the literal truth, has to give way to higher things – like discretion and loyalty.'

Edward's brow was wrinkled. 'I don't understand that, Mr Hudson. I couldn't keep that money.'

'Nobody's asking you to put it in your pocket, boy. But you might have to consider giving it to some charity. Now leave it with me and get yourself off to bed.'

A few minutes later Mr Hudson was telling the story to Richard, who was drinking his nightcap by the fire.

'You'd better tell him to forget about it, Hudson. Tell him that I shall be dealing with the matter myself.'

'Very good, sir. Good night, sir.'

They understood each other perfectly.

It had, of course, been Lord Charles who had sent the bribe by Joseph. Taxed with it next day by Richard, he tried to laugh it off.

'I'm sorry, Richard. It was done with the best of intentions, to save *you* embarrassment. I thought the boy would keep quiet, conveniently forget the colour of my dressing-gown, and that would be the end of it. I couldn't know he'd trot off to your butler who in turn would trot off to you. They're making servants uncommonly scrupulous these days.'

Richard was not amused. 'And aren't you relieved to hear it? The alternative might have been blackmail.'

Lord Charles shrugged. 'Sometimes easier to deal with.'

'I don't know anything about that. All I do know is that you've outraged his sense of honour. I think he might have total recall of the colour of your dressing-gown and the whole incident. So what happens now?'

'We'll see. My solicitors have retained McCorquodale for my defence. He'll tear your footman to shreds.'

Escorting him out, Richard asked 'How is Natalie bearing up? More settled now she's living with Prudence?'

Lord Charles looked faintly surprised. 'Oh. Yes, I believe she is. To be truthful, I haven't had a moment to see her. I'll let myself out, thanks.'

Daisy should not have been in Edward's bedroom, but she was, perching on the bed, trying to coax him to come out of the cold attic to the fire downstairs.

'You're down in the dumps,' she said. 'Is it about that money still?'

He sighed. 'It's people, Daisy. They tell you one thing, and you think that's right, that's the right way to behave. I dunno. I bin seriously thinkin' about givin' this life up.'

'But what would you *do*?' Dismay was in her voice.

'Thought I might join the army. My brother's a soldier, Middlesex Regiment. He says it's a great life.'

She moved nearer to him. At that moment Rose entered without knocking, her eyes snapping with censure.

'What are you two up to? You shouldn't be in here, Daisy!'

'She wasn't doin' no harm, Rose.'

'No, I just come in to look for him, Rose.'

Rose regarded them tight-lipped. Lolling on the bed, indeed!

'Yeh, well, now you've found him, you can come out. I got work for you.'

'See what I mean?' said Edward behind her retreating back. 'People, Daisy. I'm goin' out. Get drunk.'

She touched his hand gently. 'You get drunk, you deserve it. Only don't – please – go and join the army!'

Richard was not pleased to be telephoned by Geoffrey Dillon to the effect that Harry Tewkesbury had heard about the attempted bribe, and was publicly blaming Richard for complicity. He was, indeed, furious.

'I don't condone what Gilmour did,' he said, 'but my God, I understand his reasons!'

'All right, keep calm. The point is, it's common knowledge that your footman accepted a bribe. He was seen to accept it.'

'It was thrust into his hands! He brought it straight back to Hudson, who gave it to me. We'll clear that up right away. I want to see Tewkesbury again, Geoffrey, and you'll arrange it, at the earliest possible moment. Tomorrow.'

'Tomorrow's Saturday.'

'Exactly. Which is why I want this rumour scotched, before the weekend's social arrangements.'

Edward, true to his word, had got drunk. As he was staggering towards the door of the Crown and Anchor, homeward bound, he was intercepted.

' 'Evening, Edward,' said Clough.

Edward blinked. 'Don' want to talk to you.'

'But I want to talk to you.' The detective pushed him into a chair and drew up another. 'Ever been in a Court of law? They make you swear to tell the truth – now listen, lad – on the Bible, see.'

'I know that.'

'And if you don't tell the truth, the whole truth and nothing but the truth, even though it's against your master's interests, well . . . you've heard of conspiracy to pervert the court of justice – perjury? That means prison, a long time in prison.' He had Edward by the lapels and was all but shaking him. 'That's why, when you get into the witness-box—'

'Take your hands off that boy,' came an incisive Scots voice from behind him. Mr Hudson loomed into view, a calm and commanding figure most welcome to Edward's wavering sight. Clough stood back, uncertain, as Edward got up.

'Mr Hudson, this was the bloke that started it all, asked me questions and give me the half-sovereign. And now he's threatening me—'

'All right, Edward.' Mr Hudson turned steely blue eyes to Clough. 'I am Mr Bellamy's butler, and I suggest you stop molesting and threatening young servants in public houses, unless you want the police after you.'

Clough looked, hesitated, and began to move off, saying, 'I'll see you in court, my lad.'

'Come, Edward,' said Mr Hudson, in fatherly fashion.

While Edward was being persecuted in the Crown and Anchor, Richard Bellamy received two visits. The first was from Sir Geoffrey Dillon, calling to tell him that Tewkesbury had agreed to meet him at Dillon's office the following morning. The second visitor, arriving just as Dillon was leaving, was Lady Prudence.

'I'm sorry to rush in like this, Richard,' she said, 'but I must talk to you.' Dillon took his hat and coat from Rose. 'I'm just going.' He was not fond of the society of verbose ladies.

'Just a minute, Geoffrey. Is it about Harry and Natalie, Pru?'

'Well, yes . . .'

'Then I think you should stay, Geoffrey.'

Reluctantly Dillon followed him back.

'Well,' Lady Prudence began before they had even had time to sit down, 'it's more about something else, and rather disturbing—'

Dillon was interested now. 'Lord Charles?'

'Yes. Natalie had arranged to see him today – a discreet little restaurant in Curzon Street for luncheon. Well, he didn't arrive, so in some consternation she went to his flat in Mayfair. Her ring wasn't answered, though she was certain he was in, and you can imagine her humiliation, just standing on the pavement. Anyway, she came home to me, and at five o'clock she had a letter by messenger, that vulgar valet of his. Not a very good letter for someone of whom the country has such high hopes. I don't know what happens now, but one thing's certain – our dear Lord Charles emerges with no credit at all.'

Dillon's face spread in a slow, smug smile. 'Still think you're backing the right horse, Richard?' he enquired.

Richard was not, indeed, happy to hear this story. But it didn't deter him from meeting Harry Tewkesbury the next morning.

'Thank you for agreeing to meet me, Tewkesbury,' he began. The other man was brusque.

'I can't give you too long. I've other appointments.'

'Won't you sit, gentlemen?' Dillon was producing chairs, of the uncomfortable kind common to solicitors' offices.

'First of all,' Richard began, 'you owe me an apology, don't you?'

Tewkesbury glanced at the impassive Dillon. 'Is that so?'

'I can appreciate you've been under considerable strain recently, but it can hardly excuse the unpleasant rumours you've evidently been spreading about me and my supposed collusion with Charles Gilmour.'

Tewkesbury bridled. 'Unpleasant rumours? Rubbish.'

'I simply want you to know – in the presence of our mutual solicitor – that if I don't receive a retraction, I shall take out an action for slander against you.'

'If your source for these rumours is Geoffrey, then you must take out an action against him, too. It's as much a slander to pass on gossip as to initiate it. That's the law.' Dillon, alarmed, held up a cautioning hand, but Tewkesbury went on.

'One thing I don't do is blab my mouth off in public-houses for all the world to hear!'

'And I don't employ snoopers to hang about public houses and threaten people's servants!' Richard snapped back. Tewkesbury looked at Dillon for arbitration.

'It is sometimes necessary to determine the truth,' the lawyer said carefully.

'Not when it threatens the integrity of my footman, Geoffrey!'

Tewkesbury went turkey-cock red. 'My God, we didn't pay your man to suppress evidence! That was your doing, to protect your protégé.'

Richard half rose in his chair. 'That's false assumption and a downright slander!'

Tewkesbury surveyed him with angry contempt. 'It's very hard to understand you, Bellamy. You take the side of a young rake, a philanderer who seduces young married women, and you champion him in the name of vigorous, progressive Toryism. Good God, if the country ever fell into his hands, I'd emigrate. And I don't think you'll find many to disagree with me after what happened yesterday!'

'I'm not in a position to comment on that. I don't wish to.'

Dillon intervened. 'Gentlemen, gentlemen, I really must put in a word. I don't think Richard has quite grasped the point that the divorce will not take place.'

Richard stared.

'I've taken her back, Bellamy,' Tewkesbury said. 'If you must know, I never wanted to lose her in the first place. We've had our difficult times before, got over them, but I couldn't stomach this one. Fellow comes up, buys a house twenty miles away from where I live – makes love to my wife blatantly – makes me the laughing-stock of the district. And to cap it all, he has the effrontery to be setting himself up, on the quiet, as my political rival. Not only my wife, but my constituency. *You* talk about rumours. Good God, Bellamy, you should've heard what I've had to put up with. I had to take some action. Either my wife behaves herself, or she ceases to be my wife. I put it to her in those terms. Well, the rest you probably know.'

Richard nodded silently.

'When the heat's on, the fellow shows his true colours and drops her. Last night she comes quietly back. No fuss. People have a wrong idea, you see. They assume – well, let them assume what they damn well like. We'll work it out our own way. Now I must go. Taking her home.'

With a brusque nod to both of them he left.

Richard's interview with Charles Gilmour was brief. Charles appeared quite unrepentant, and professed himself glad that Natalie had gone back to her husband. 'I had to break it,' he said, 'and a quick clean blow is always the best, isn't it?'

'Your timing was unfortunate.'

'Now there *is* a note of censure.'

Richard was angry. 'It can hardly be anything else, can it? You haven't played your cards altogether wisely.'

Charles smiled. 'But you see, I'm not like you, Richard. You've always played your cards wisely, and look where it's got you. You're a disappointed man at heart, looking at life through other people. It may be that I shall be judged as an arrogant whipper-snapper who lived dangerously and perished ignobly. But I was always my own man. Never for me the epitaph "He played his cards wisely".'

Mr Hudson was giving a heavily overhung Edward a sermon on morality.

'You see, Lord Charles Gilmour is one of our most brilliant politicians. Now if a man can achieve great things in his public life, who are we to judge his private life. It's no concern of ours, is it?'

Edward was confused. 'N-no, Mr Hudson.'

'And when the two, the public and private, get tangled up, then it's only reasonable that he should take steps, albeit unorthodox ones . . . you see what I'm getting at?'

If the truth were told, Mr Hudson didn't see it clearly himself. But Edward meekly agreed, and promised that he wouldn't join the army and would keep out of public-houses in future. It had been the worst week of his life, but now it was over. He borrowed a shilling from Rose and took Daisy to a picture-palace, where they held hands tightly through eight thrilling reels of *Quo Vadis*.

CHAPTER ELEVEN

Rose gave another touch to the holly wreath, gay with scarlet ribbons, which she had hung on the front door of 165 Eaton Place, and stepped back to admire the effect. The voices of carol-singers came to her on the cold air from the Square. Soon they would be on the doorstep, and Mr Hudson would bestow on them the usual sum. When they returned on Christmas Eve, two days hence, they would be invited down the area steps for a jug of steaming cocoa.

She went into the house and encountered Mr Hudson in the hall, looking unusually flustered. 'Is everything ready upstairs?' he asked.

Rose nodded.

'And the room is well warmed? You know how her ladyship dislikes the cold.'

Rose knew only too well. She had been a child at Southwold in the days of the old Earl, and remembered his lady, now the Dowager Countess, very vividly. Thank goodness, she thought, it's easier doing for her now. People either get better or worse with old age, and Lady Southwold had softened up quite a bit. A regular Tartar, she'd been. Rose closed her eyes patiently as Mr Hudson said 'You've put a hot-water bottle in the bed, I hope. At her age she'll be tired after a long journey, and may wish to retire at once. We must have everything prepared.' His accent was growing more and more Scottish, always a sign of agitation. Having been reassured that Rose had carried out all her duties, and that the new parlourmaid, Daisy, was being kept under supervision, he bustled off to attend personally to the morning-room fire.

Entering the kitchen, Rose mimicked him to herself. '"Is everything ready, Rose? Yes, Mr Hudson. Meek heest then, girrl, we're a wee bit leet."'

Edward, shoe-polishing, grumbled 'Honestly, all this fuss. Anyone'd think we had Queen Mary coming.'

Mrs Bridges turned from the pan she was stirring, red of face. 'Now, Edward, don't you be impertinent. Old Lady Southwold's very particular. She likes her comforts. And she's used to good service, so you'd better be on your toes.'

'It's a long time since she's been here, Edward,' said Rose. 'We don't want her to think we've got slovenly since—' she didn't finish her sentence, but the others knew the end of it. Her eyes encountered Daisy, standing forlornly with the coal-scuttle in her small dirty hand. Daisy was pretty in a flower-like way, the way Rose would like to have looked; already Edward was casting eyes at her. From Rose she got far more scoldings than praise.

'You can put that outside in the area,' Rose said sharply, 'then get yourself cleaned up. They'll be here soon.'

'Is she bringing old Hodges with her?' Edward asked. Rose sniffed. 'No, Miss Hodges will not be coming. *I*'m to see to her.'

Mr Hudson approached, checking off on his fingers. 'One more thing, Rose, did you remember the extra pillow in her ladyship's room, and the spare blankets?' Rose had to smile; he was such an old fuss-pot. 'I've remembered every blessed thing, Mr Hudson,' she said.

'Good.' He addressed them all. 'We shall be on trial for the next few days. The Dowager Countess has high standards which each and every one of us must live up to.' Daisy came in from the area; some of the coal-dust had transferred itself to her face, more on to her apron. Her hands were filthy and her cap askew, causing soft tendrils of brown hair to escape in what Edward considered a very becoming way. But Mr Hudson had other views. Not for him the poet's declaration that 'A sweet disorder in the dress Kindles in clothes a wantonness' more charming than precise order. He fixed her with a stern blue eye.

'And *you*'ll do well to remember that, Daisy, if you're to remain in service here.' Daisy quailed. When he had gone, she whispered to Edward: 'What's Lady Southwold like? Is she very fierce?' Edward felt like petting her consolingly, but decided to tease instead.

'Oh, she's dreadful. A real monster. She has these terrible rages, you see. Once,' he lowered his voice to a melodramatic whisper, 'when her bath wasn't as hot as she wanted, she went for one of the maids with a red-hot poker. Maimed her for life.'

Poor Daisy's lip began to tremble. As she went to the sink to wash her hands Edward followed her, and whispered:

'And she's got a beard. A red one. And one eye much larger than the other. I've heard tell that she's a witch.'

At that moment the front door bell rang. Daisy gave a muffled shriek and all but leapt in the air. Hastily Mr Hudson shepherded them all towards the stairs except Mrs Bridges, who remained in charge of the hot posset which was to be administered to Lady Southwold after the rigours of her journey.

They were lined up in the hall as Lady Southwold entered on her chauffeur's arm. Daisy could hardly believe her eyes at the vision of a small, elegant, extremely pretty old lady, charmingly dressed, utterly feminine. It dawned on her that Edward wasn't always to be taken seriously; but what a relief!

Richard, emerging, embraced his mother-in-law.

'Mabel, my dear. You must be frozen to the marrow.'

She gave him her bright smile. 'Nonsense, Richard, don't fuss. I was well wrapped, and Masters kept me liberally supplied with brandy. I really feel quite merry!'

'It's wonderful to see you looking so well.'

'Am I?' She knew the answer, of course, being as familiar with her looking-glass as any girl of eighteen. Her delicately-rouged cheeks were always the same becoming pink, her once devastating eyes still bright. She greeted Mr Hudson. 'I believe,' she said, 'there are some hampers of Christmas fare in the back of the motor, sent up by Mr Coombes. Perhaps you would be good enough to look after them.'

As Hudson, Rose and Edwards busied themselves with the luggage Richard led Lady Southwold into the morning-room.

'I'm afraid it will be rather a quiet Christmas – James and Hazel left for Paris yesterday, but they'll be back on the 27th, so you'll see them . . .'

The food hamper had safely reached the kitchen, and Mrs Bridges was summoned to witness the opening of it. Mr Coombes, the Southwold estate agent, was a generous provider, and this year he had surpassed himself. From the big basket they pulled a brace of pheasants ('very handy' commented Mrs Bridges) a hare, woodcock, and a curiously-shaped parcel which Mrs Bridges identified.

'Venison! That's a nice surprise. Ah, and here's the turkey.' She dragged it out and peered into the hamper. 'Something else at the bottom. You get it out, Ruby.' Ruby obeyed, gasping, and revealed the lingerer to be an enormous goose, still in its white feathers.

'Like the one in the panto!' she exclaimed.

'Pity it won't lay no golden eggs,' said Edward, 'or we'd all be millionaires for Christmas.'

'Now careful, my girl,' Mrs Bridges was superintending Ruby's nervous conveying of the bird. 'Straight to the larder, and later on you can pluck it.'

'Here, where's the tree?' asked Rose. 'We always get a Christmas tree from Southwold every year. Where is it?' She was investigating another hamper full of holly, ivy and mistletoe. Mr Hudson overheard the enquiry.

'Use your brains, Rose. They could hardly fit a nine-foot high Christmas tree in the back of a motor-car, now could they? Mr Coombes has dispatched it from Salisbury by train, and it is at this moment at the station awaiting collection. So there is no need to worry, is there Rose?'

As he moved majestically away, Edward held a sprig of mistletoe over Rose's head, with a playful request to be given the season's greetings, but all he received was a smart rebuff. He pocketed the sprig in the hope of better luck with Daisy.

The Dowager Countess had enjoyed her dinner. There had been a time when she had fought her daughter's determination to marry the comparatively poor and obscure Richard Bellamy, and for years afterwards there had been stress, political and personal, between them. But time had tempered things; Richard had been a good husband to poor Marjorie, and had carved his career – not without some wifely pushing. He was a thoroughly presentable and amiable creature, and it was pleasant to be at the little town house (for so it seemed to her) instead of at the lonely Dower House which looked across at the stately home that had once been hers. She settled among the cushions and put her small feet up.

'I'm glad you could have your old mother-in-law, Richard. It's not very – well, cheerful – to be alone at such a time. Sometimes, when I think of Christmas in the old days, when Hugo and Marjorie were in the nursery...'

'I know.' Richard sipped his brandy. 'But we have Georgina to look forward to.'

'Yes. At least poor Hugo left me a step-grandchild.'

'You know,' Richard said, 'I find the thought of having a schoolgirl here for Christmas somewhat alarming.'

'No need. Georgina is a very easy child, young for her age in some ways, but you'll take to her, I'm sure. I'm only afraid she'll find it too dull, after all the young company she's had at finishing-school. When does she arrive?'

'Tomorrow afternoon, from Geneva.'

If Richard was faintly alarmed at the thought of his step-niece's stay, she was even more so. Coming to England wasn't a bit like coming home, really, now that Mummy and Hugo weren't there. She had learned to live with the sorrow of the *TITANIC* disaster; it wasn't done to bore people by grieving. But to come for Christmas to a house where that disaster had also struck – for Aunt Marjorie had drowned with her mother and step-father – well, it made one feel a bit dreary, un peu triste, or even sehr traurig, as Minna would say . . . she tore her mind away from her schoolmates and smiled nicely at Hudson, who looked to her several miles high but had a kind face.

'Mr Bellamy apologises for his absence, miss,' he was saying. 'He was called out but hopes to be home shortly. Her ladyship is in her room, and will see you at teatime.'

Mr Hudson looked down benevolently on the girl who stood very straight and correct among her luggage, a round school hat on her dark curls, her travelling coat of utilitarian rather than fashionable cut. She looked very vulnerable, while trying hard not to show it. Nothing so young and tender had entered the house for many a year, he reflected (without a thought for Daisy downstairs, almost exactly Miss Georgina's age and considerably more vulnerable.) A sentimentalist at heart, he compared her with a girl who had come into his life long years ago, and had left it too soon. Just such a wild-rose complexion had been Lindsay's, just such an air of fresh youth . . .

'I have had your trunks sent up to your room,' he said. 'The maid will be up shortly to unpack.'

She followed him upstairs, to the prim, now characterless room which had once been Elizabeth Bellamy's. At the door he paused.

'Will there be anything further, miss?'

'No. No, thank you.'

'Well, if you should require anything, the bell is here. I will send the maid up to you.'

Alone, she looked round at the unfamiliar room where she had never been before. There was a small fire in the grate, but the air was cold and unwelcoming. She saw her own trunk, the only thing she could recognise, and laid her hand on it affectionately. Outside, the tall London houses were fading in a grey winter dusk, yellow lights gleaming here and there, and somewhere there was singing.

'It came upon the midnight clear,
That glorious song of old,
From angels bending near the earth
To touch their harps of gold:
"Peace on the earth, good will to men
From Heaven's all-gracious King!"
The world in solemn stillness lay
To hear the angels sing.'

Georgina knelt up on a chair with her nose pressed to the window-pane. A few flakes of snow began to tap against the window and fall wetly on the sill. Tears began to well up in Georgina's eyes. A timid tap at the door made her pinch herself sternly. 'Stop it, you silly thing,' she said sternly to the Georgina who would like to have cried like a baby.

'Come in,' she called. It was a relief to see nothing worse enter than a shy-looking little maid.

'The butler – Mr Hudson – sent me up to unpack for you, miss,' said Daisy.

'Oh, thank you.' Georgina smiled at her. 'That's my trunk, there.'

Daisy began to busy herself with taking things out of the trunk and laying them on the bed as gingerly as though they were made of spun glass. Georgina watched her interestedly, sensing a nervousness and dread near to her own.

'What's your name?'

'Daisy Peel, miss.'

'Mine's Georgina Worsley.'

'Oh yes, miss.'

'How old are you, Daisy?'

'Eighteen, miss.'

Georgina was delighted. '*Are* you? So am I. When's your birthday?'

'March the seventh, miss.'

'Mine's in November, the twenty-eighth. So you're older than me.'

'Yes, miss.'

Georgina surveyed her. 'You don't look it.' Suddenly she jumped up and pulled off her coat. 'Shall I help you? Where does everything go?'

'Oh no, miss, I'm to do it, Mr Hudson sent me up to unpack for you. He said I wasn't to disturb you, and if – well, if Rose or anyone came in—'

'You'd get into trouble? I see.' Georgina subsided. 'They wouldn't mind if I just sat and talked to you, would they?'

'Oh, no, miss.' They smiled at each other. Georgina flopped down on the bed. 'Well, then,' she said, 'who's Rose?'

'The head house-parlourmaid, miss. I'm the under house-parlourmaid. I'm new, I only came last week.'

'I only came today, so I'm newer than you. Do you like it here?'

'Oh yes,' Daisy said virtuously, adding, as she caught Georgina's sceptical eye, 'Well, it takes a bit of getting used to.'

Georgina sat up. 'You know, I may be coming here to live, Daisy. In the summer, when I've finished school, so I can do the Season. Be presented at Court, you know.'

'Where's your Mum and Dad, then?'

'Oh, they're dead. My father was killed in a hunting accident when I was six, and then my mother married Hugo – Lord Southwold, that is – and they both went down in the *TITANIC*.'

'Oh. Like Lady Marjorie.'

'Yes. Hugo was her brother. They were all going to Canada together. And they all got drowned.'

Daisy was embarrassed. 'That's very sad.'

'Yes, it is rather. So I haven't got any relations – except Mr Bellamy, who's a sort of uncle-in-law, I suppose. He said I could come here for Christmas and perhaps come back in the summer.'

'That's good.'

'Where do you live, Daisy?'

'Here, miss.'

'No, I mean where's your home? Where do your parents live?'

'Oh.' This was something Daisy didn't want to talk about. 'In Hoxton.'

'Where's that?'

'East End of London, miss. A long way from here.'

'Is it nice?'

Instead of answering, Daisy lifted from the trunk a tired-looking teddy-bear, which Georgina eagerly seized on.

'Oh, let me have him! His name's Mr Gladstone – I've had him since I was five, and he goes everywhere with me.' She rocked him for a moment, then laid him on the bed with his head on the pillow. They both admired him.

'Will you be looking after me all the time, Daisy?'

'No, miss. Rose'll be looking after you. She's very nice, miss, I'm sure you'll like her.'

Georgina was disappointed. 'It'd be much nicer to have you. Where's your room, Daisy?'

'Upstairs, at the top. I share with Rose.'

'Do you? I share at the convent. With a girl called Anne-Marie. She talks in her sleep.' Daisy giggled. 'Does Rose talk in her sleep?'

'Oh, no. Rose is very quiet. But – she does snore a little bit.'

It was Georgina's turn to giggle. 'You should hold her nose.'

'But she might wake up!'

'That'd be funny, wouldn't it – if she woke up, and found you holding her nose?' They both began to laugh, Georgina kicking her legs in the air in a most unladylike manner. It was thus that Rose found them, opening the door suddenly. The laughter stopped as though cut with a knife.

'Tea is about to be served, miss,' said Rose icily. 'In the morning-room. If you'd like to follow me, I'll show you where it is.'

Meekly Georgina followed, while Daisy burrowed in the trunk. As Georgina went through the door, Daisy's head came up and they exchanged sympathetic glances.

It was a bit like the French Revolution, Georgina thought; Sydney Carton bravely going to the scaffold. In deathly silence she and Rose went downstairs. Rose ushered her into the morning-room and announced 'Miss Georgina.'

There seemed to be a lot of silver in the room – tray, teapot, cream jug, sugar-bowl, kettle-stand – and plates of tiny sandwiches and sticky cakes. For a second or two Georgina felt hungry, then caught sight of the grown-ups and lost her appetite.

Lady Southwold, smiling on the sofa, beckoned graciously. 'Come in, child, and greet your Uncle Richard.'

It could have been a great deal worse. Everybody was very kind, particularly Uncle Richard even though he wasn't exactly her uncle, and old Lady Southwold, even though she looked slightly witchy at times. But it was awfully, awfully dull. Christmas Eve, and nothing to do but play Patience. Lunch was over, Lady Southwold dozing in her chair, Uncle Richard reading *The Times*. Georgina laid out the cards with a sigh that was no more than a breath. It wasn't done to let people know you were bored.

In the hall a confused noise could be heard; Georgina looked up hopefully as Mr Hudson entered.

'Excuse me, sir, I just thought I should inform you that the Christmas tree has arrived and the staff are putting it up in the hall – in case you should wonder at the commotion.'

'Yes. Thank you, Hudson.'

Mr Hudson lingered. 'Also, might I remind you, sir, that this afternoon we were intending to put up the Christmas decorations?' she suggested. Georgina's face lit up.

'Oh yes – I'd forgotten. Well, I'm going out in a moment, Hudson, so it won't disturb me. How about you, Mabel?'

Lady Southwold yawned delicately. 'I shall go up soon. It's time for my rest.'

'And you, Georgina? What are your plans for the afternoon?'

'Oh, none. I mean, I'm not doing anything.'

Lady Southwold caught the note of dejection in Georgina's voice.

'Perhaps you would like to help the servants with the decorations?' she suggested. Georgina's face lit up.

'There you are, then,' Richard said. 'Another helper for you, Hudson. Run along and join them out there, Georgina – see what they're up to.'

Politely Mr Hudson stood aside for Georgina to precede

him into the hall. The reason for the commotion they had heard was immediately obvious. Rose, Edward and Daisy were united in a heroic struggle with a nine-foot fir-tree, tied round with string and paper. It had got itself stuck firmly in the service-door, and seemed determined to stay there throughout the festive season. Georgina watched with lively interest their efforts. It took Mr Hudson to suggest that if Edward lifted his end of it the thing might be manoeuvred round the corner. This worked satisfactorily; at least the tree was prone on the hall floor. Edward set about placing the tub in position.

'Miss Worsley,' Mr Hudson announced, 'is kindly going to assist you all with the decoration of the tree.'

They all looked up in surprise. Only Daisy was pleased. Rose and Edward resented the intrusion of Upstairs on what was their own bit of fun. Georgina stepped forward shyly.

'Please, I'm Georgina.'

'*Miss* Georgina,' Mr Hudson corrected. 'There's a chair over there, Miss Georgina, if you would like to sit and watch while they put up the tree.'

'Oh, thank you. Yes, I will.'

When he had gone a silence fell. Georgina felt unwelcome, Rose and Edward were inhibited by her presence, Daisy wanted to talk to her but dared not. At last Rose said impatiently 'Come on, then, let's get started. Daisy, you take the other end.'

'Ooh, it's heavy!' Daisy squeaked.

'Of course it's—' at that moment the string round Rose's end of the tree snapped, and a branch sprang out, hitting her across the face, to the unconcealed enjoyment of Daisy and Edward. Other branches followed it, scattering needles and causing both girls to drop the tree. They all burst out laughing, and Georgina joined in. At last the ice was broken; but the tree was unconquered. As often as they lifted it, it slipped from their grasp, lying with irritating complacency on the ground. Rose abandoned her attempts and stood back glaring at it.

'Well, *I* don't know. How are we going to get it up, then?'

A small voice broke in. 'Can I make a suggestion?' Georgina left her ringside seat. 'If you put the tub over here, by the stairs, and I go up the stairs and lean over, I can catch the tree when it's out of Daisy's reach – and then I can help you to hold it, Rose.'

Rose was furious with herself for not having thought of this obvious solution. 'All right. Yes, miss, that's a good idea. Let's try it.'

The scheme worked perfectly, with some panting and puffing and many complaints from Edward as he hammered it into place. Now it was decorated, no longer a sombre fir but a great isosceles triangle of colour and sparkle. Its branches, powdered with mimic snow, were laden with bright glass baubles of every colour, balls and pear-drops, fragile coffee-pots and trumpets; birds of silver with blue or pink wings and white spun-glass tails swayed at branch-ends, gold and silver tinsel wreathed about their perches, and coloured candles in spring-holders waited to be lit. A tiny Christmas angel in wax held out his arms in flight; he was treated with phosphorus and would be luminous when the lights were out.

Watched by the admiring Mrs Bridges and the others, Georgina, her cheeks pink with excitement, climbed the step-ladder to place the Fairy in position. This was no mass-produced plastic object, but a beautiful doll with a face and bust of tinted wax, a shapely body sawdust-stuffed, and porcelain forearms and legs. Her 'real' hair was golden, her ballet-dress of stiffened pink muslin dotted with spangles, and her crown and wand each tipped with a tinsel star.

'Oh, it's lovely!' cried Mrs Bridges, her eyes touched by the start of tears. Her childless state struck home to her at this time which was made for children, the festival of the Holy Child. And Mr Hudson remembered the days when there had been a little Master James and a little Miss Lizzie and their friends to exclaim with wonder at the Tree and pick their presents from it. Rose thought of Miss Lizzie's child Lucy, far away in America; perhaps she would never even set eyes on her. And of Lady Marjorie, at the bottom of the Atlantic.

But Georgina and Daisy, who were still almost children, rejoiced in the Tree. As the others were going downstairs Georgina called Daisy back.

'Daisy! bring some holly and we'll do my bedroom next.'

Christmas decorations made Georgina's bedroom look a lot

more homely. The waits were singing again. Georgina threw up the window to hear them better.

'Isn't it funny,' she said, 'to think that out there, all over London, people are doing the same thing tonight – wrapping up presents, decorating their homes – your family – this family, every family in the world – well, the Christian world, I suppose. Daisy, you're awfully quiet. What is it? Are you sad?'

Daisy shook her head.

'Homesick?'

'No, Miss Georgina. I haven't been home – not for three years. There was seven of us, you see. And not enough to eat, not with my Dad unemployed. He worked in the docks, when he could get work. Used to worry ever so bad, when he was out, 'cos of Mum and us kids, you see.'

Georgina was listening, shocked. 'So that's why you don't go home now.'

'I'd just be another mouth to feed. But Christmas time, I do think of home . . . At least Mum and Dad used to cheer up a bit, Christmas Day. A neighbour used to let them have half a bottle of gin, so they'd sing and laugh a bit, and stop bashing us and fighting, and that. It was better – Christmas time.'

Outside the waits were singing 'O Come, all ye Faithful'. Georgina pondered.

'Don't you think, Daisy, you ought to give them a nice surprise and go home this Christmas? I could ask Mr Bellamy to give you time off.'

'I've got Christmas afternoon off, we all have. But . . . better not go, miss, thanks all the same.' And Daisy began to cry. Georgina ran to her and put her arm round the thin shoulders. 'Oh, Daisy, you mustn't. Come on, now . . .'

The door opened and Rose was on the threshold, viewing the scene with high disapproval. Daisy jumped up from the bed and turned away to hide her tears.

'Excuse me, miss, but her ladyship is waiting in the morning room.'

Georgina blushed hotly at Rose's tone. 'Yes, Rose, all right.'

'Daisy!'

Daisy brushed a hand across her eyes and followed Rose.

Over tea, Richard told Georgina about the arrangements for Christmas.

'Tomorrow evening we shall be dining out and leaving them to have their own Christmas dinner downstairs. Lady Southwold's sister, Lady Castleton, has kindly invited us.'

'Not that poor Kate's much company nowadays,' said his mother-in-law, bisecting a finger of toast. 'She's stone deaf and practically blind.'

'Yes, well . . . We shall have our own Christmas dinner at lunchtime tomorrow after which, Mabel dear, I shall have to leave you for a couple of hours, while I visit the Infirmary in my constituency. I'm so sorry.'

'My dear boy, you know perfectly well that I spend every afternoon asleep in my room, and I'm sure Christmas Day will be no exception.'

'Then, Georgina,' said Richard, 'at five-thirty, after tea, the servants will get their presents in the hall. I expect you'd like to be there.'

'Oh yes.'

'So, if there's anything you'd like to do in the afternoon—'

'Oh, I'll just stay in and read a book,' said Georgina mendaciously.

That night Rose combined the brushing-out of Georgina's hair with a veiled homily on the relationship between mistresses and servants. Georgina realised that she was being told off for showing friendliness towards Daisy; and she was right.

'Take Daisy, for instance, miss. She's a good girl but she's not been long in service. I don't know whether you've noticed, miss, but sometimes she's inclined to be a bit too familiar. She means no harm, mind. It's just that she hasn't learnt how to conduct herself properly yet. The point is, miss, that we all have our place, and we have to keep to it. It's no good pretending that isn't so, is it, miss?'

'I suppose so,' Georgina said, supposing nothing of the kind.

'Daisy needs a bit of help, that's all. Perhaps – if you could help her to know her place, miss. Be a bit more distant with her. That's all she needs.'

Rose peered down to see how Georgina was taking it.

'It's for her own good. You do understand, don't you, miss?'

'Yes, of course, Rose.'

'Well, if there's nothing further you want I'd better be getting downstairs, miss.'

Her departure crossed Daisy's entrance. Daisy looked frightened as usual when she met Rose's eye.

'Is it all right to turn the bed down?'

'Ask Miss Georgina.' And Rose swept out.

'Of course it's all right, Daisy. I'm glad you're here. I want to talk to you.'

Daisy advanced. 'Yes, miss?'

'I've been thinking about your family. And I've quite made up my mind that you're going home to Hoxton tomorrow afternoon to see them, and I'm coming with you.'

Daisy's eyes widened in alarm. 'Oh no! We can't – it wouldn't be right – begging your pardon, miss.'

'Why not?'

Daisy plucked at her apron. 'Well, I'm not sure if they're still at the old address – they may have moved, you see . . .'

'If they have, someone will tell us. Now. After lunch tomorrow, when everyone's either gone out or gone to sleep, we're going to creep out, you and I, and take some food from the larder, and some holly and crackers, and perhaps a bottle of wine, and we're going to burst into your parents' home and surprise them. Then, when we've been there long enough, we'll catch the tram back and nobody will be any the wiser. Isn't that a good idea?'

From Daisy's expression it would seem that she didn't think so.

But Georgina had her way, as she had been determined to do all along.

At half-past two on the dark afternoon of Christmas Day she was sitting on her bed, warmly dressed and wearing her new red hat, waiting for Daisy's tap on the door. At last it came. Daisy was clad in a rusty-looking shapeless coat, with an awful hat which turned up at the front; it would have done nothing for a beaming face, and Daisy's young brow was furrowed with anxiety.

'*There* you are. Did anyone see you?'

'No, miss. It's all quiet downstairs.'

'Cheer up, Daisy. Aren't you looking forward to seeing your family – the look on their faces?'

Daisy allowed herself a little smile. 'Yes, miss.'

'Well, come on, then.'

Their progress downstairs was admirably silent. Everyone was out, Daisy said, except Mr Hudson, and he was asleep in the butler's pantry. They tiptoed down the service stairs, past his door into the kitchen, where in a corner stood an empty hamper placed there by Daisy. Georgina had just opened her mouth to speak when, horror of horrors, the unmistakeable footsteps of Mr Hudson were heard in the passage, approaching.

'Quick! under the table!' Daisy hissed. They shot under its ample cover and lay prone, still as mice. Humming softly, Mr Hudson entered. He saw with satisfaction that a teapot stood on the stove, and found with even more satisfaction that it was still hot. Smiling, he bore it off to his pantry.

'Phew!' Georgina drew a deep breath of relief.

'Has he gone?' Daisy whispered.

'Yes. That was close. Come on, where's the larder?'

Daisy, still shocked, could only look at the larder's store of food. It was Georgina who seized an almost whole Christmas pudding and dropped it in, followed by mince-pies, cheese, apples, and, to Daisy's alarm, the remains of the goose.

'Oh no miss, we shouldn't!'

'Why not? It's finished with. Well, almost.'

She shut the hamper; they each took a handle, and crept out.

Nearly an hour later their footsteps echoed on the stone staircase, iron-railinged, of a tenement block in Hoxton. The building had a strong, stuffy smell: a blend of stale cabbage, cats and dirt, unfamiliar to Georgina. They reached a peeling door with scribbled writing on it, and Daisy said 'This is it, miss. Number Three.' The door was open, despite the cold weather. As Georgina was about to knock a child appeared beside them on the landing. It was a boy of about eight, filthy of face and ragged of clothing. He shot a malevolent look at them before dashing through the door. Sounds of loud argument and a baby crying came to them from within.

'Who was that?' Georgina asked.

'One of my brothers, miss. Must be Tommy. He was five last time I was home.'

Georgina refused to be daunted. 'Do you think you should go in first? I'll follow you.'

They entered a dark lobby which led to what might aptly have been called the Peels' living-room, for it was their kitchen, bedroom, sitting-room and bathroom all in one. The smell outside was as nothing compared with the reek indoors. Torn, faded wall-paper hung in tatters from the damp walls, and the only lighting came from a high cracked window and a broken gas-mantle in the middle of the ceiling. A line of grey washing hung in front of an empty grate. On a bed in the corner, its missing fourth leg replaced by bricks, lay an unshaven man, asleep. At the table sat Daisy's mother, a woman of thirty-five whose emaciation and wrinkles made her look fifty, a baby sucking at her fallen breast, while two filthy children, one of them Tommy, crawled about the floor.

Georgina was shocked to the core. Hurriedly she collected herself; at all costs she must not show it. Daisy shot a rueful sideways glance at her.

'It's me, Mum, Daisy. Come to wish you Happy Christmas and bring you something nice. Is it all right to come in?'

Mrs Peel stared vacantly at her with bloodshot eyes. Georgina stepped forward. 'I'm Georgina Worsley – Daisy's friend. We've brought you some things for Christmas. Would you like to see?'

'Christmas,' the woman mumbled.

'Shall I wake Dad?' Daisy asked. But the man on the bed was awake, sitting up and looking at them. Daisy's face was shocked.

'Who's that? Where's Dad?' she said.

Mrs Peel roused herself a little. 'Died. In the Infirmary. Last year. His lungs give out. He's buried out Barking way.'

Georgina saw that Daisy wanted to cry, and took her hand comfortingly. The man got off the bed to investigate the food hamper. Before Georgina could protest he had plunged his hand inside and pulled out the goose carcass, which he proceeded to rend and devour piece by piece. The children scrambled to him and howled for some of it.

'Git aht of it!' He kicked them away and threw a piece to each, and another to Mrs Peel, who chewed it slowly, spitting out the bone.

'Anythink else?' he asked the girls.

'Yes,' Georgina said, 'pies and fruit.'

He helped himself lavishly, throwing small pieces to the children, who ate it on the floor like animals.

'Who's that man, Mum?' asked Daisy.

'Bill, that is,' returned her mother listlessly.

'I live 'ere, that's who I am,' the man said, his mouth full.

Daisy timidly touched her mother's arm. 'Are you all right, Mum?'

Mrs Peel turned her head with a faint sketch of a smile. 'What do you think I am – bleedin' joyful?'

'Is there anything we can do?' asked Georgina desperately. 'I mean, tell someone – to come and help you . . . There must be something . . .'

'Clear aht,' said Bill, chewing. 'She don't want you 'ere. Clear off.'

'Get back to your work, Daisy, and leave us be,' the mother whispered. 'There ain't nothing you can't do for us – not now . . .'

Georgina gently urged Daisy towards the door, then went back and awkwardly put some money on the table. Bill's dirty hand came down over it. She stammered 'We'd like to wish you a happy Christmas once again – and hope that next t—' But, overwhelmed, she couldn't finish. She ran outside and leaned against the landing wall, sick, faint and tearful. Now it was Daisy's turn to comfort and take charge.

'Come along, Miss Georgina. You mustn't distress yourself. I can't help them – not on me own. Come on, now. We must try and walk quick back to the tram stop . . .'

The grandfather clock in the hall at Eaton Place was striking a mellow six. Richard paced to the morning-room window and stared out anxiously.

'She might have told *someone* where she was going. It's too bad.'

Lady Southwold refused to be flurried. 'I'm sure there's no need to worry, Richard.'

'It's snowing now. Where *is* the child?'

Lady Southwold propelled herself to her feet with the aid of her stick. 'Well, we can't keep the servants waiting any longer for their presents.'

The servants were indeed waiting by the brilliantly-lit

Christmas tree, but they were too absorbed in discussion to notice the passing of time.

'Little minx!' muttered Mrs Bridges. 'Just wait till I get my hands on her!'

'She won't come back now,' said Rose. 'Wouldn't have the nerve.'

'That beautiful bird, what I cooked so special! It makes my blood boil.'

'At least she didn't take our turkey,' Ruby reminded them.

Mr Hudson hushed them as Richard and Lady Southwold emerged into the hall. He stepped forward.

'M'lady – begging your pardon, sir. I'm afraid that Daisy is missing, sir. I would have informed you earlier but we hoped she might return. Some items of food are also missing from the larder, sir.'

This was news to Richard. 'Miss Georgina also has not returned home, Hudson – she said nothing of going out this afternoon. Is it possible they could have gone out somewhere together?'

'They are of an age, sir. Possibly—'

Lady Southwold tapped the floor with her stick. 'Come along, come along. They want their presents.'

One by one the parcelled gifts were dished out, with a Christmas wish, and each was received with a bow or curtsy. When the presentation was over, Richard went to telephone the police. He rejoined Lady Southwold with a haggard face.

'They don't know anything. They're going to search the Park, and – and the Serpentine. Mabel, we can't go out to-night with Georgina not back, or the maid. I shall have to telephone to Kate. She'll understand.'

He ordered cold supper on a tray, and together they sat down to wait.

Downstairs Christmas Dinner was proceeding with verve. The missing Daisy forgotten for the moment, the staff ate their way through the courses, demolished the huge turkey, consumed a fair amount of beer, and then were led by Rose in the singing of 'The Twelve Days of Christmas'. They had reached 'Nine swans a-swimming' when a rapping at the window-pane stopped them.

'Someone at the back door,' said Rose.

'Edward, go and see who it is.' Mr Hudson had a fair idea, even before Edward opened the door to admit two pitiful figures. Daisy's coat had a great tear in it, and she was covered with mud and lying snow, while Georgina, equally soaked and bedraggled, and without her gay red hat, might have been taken out of the river. Speechless, they stood awaiting judgment.

It was Mr Hudson who took command, the others being too startled to do anything but stare. 'If you'd care to come upstairs, Miss Georgina. The master asked me to inform him the moment you returned.'

'Yes.' Georgina's whisper was hardly audible as she followed him out. When they were gone Mrs Bridges and Rose closed in on the wretched Daisy, who retreated until she fell into a chair. They advanced on her like birds attacking a wounded member of the flock, in strophe and anti-strophe of accusation.

'You know you've ruined the whole of Christmas!'

'All my mince-pies gone!'

'What about that goose?'

'Leading Miss Georgina astray like that!'

'The police are out lookin' for you, do you know that, madam?'

The miserable Daisy did nothing to defend herself. Huddled in the chair, she sat with tears pouring down her face, twisting her hands wretchedly. It was Edward who took pity and spoke to her reasonably.

'Come on, Daisy, what happened?'

'It'd better be good, or Mr Hudson'll have the hide off you!' Rose said.

'And so he should,' put in Mrs Bridges, an avenging Fury with arms folded, 'and throw you out in the street, you wicked, wicked girl, stealing my goose, and my pies, and ransacking my larder—'

Mr Hudson was behind them, calming the tumult. 'Now then, Daisy. What is all this?'

Sniffing and gulping, she began to tell them the story. She left out the part of it that dealt with the visit to her family; it was too awful to speak of. She only said 'We took this food to my – my Mum, and – we didn't stay long, we started off back before it got real dark. Then – then some men come at us and snatched Miss Georgina's purse, so we had no money and I said we'd have to walk . . . but Miss Georgina thought if we told the tram conductor what had happened, he might let us go on the tram without paying the fare. But when – when we got to the stop – the last bus had gone, so we had to w-walk.' She broke down again and Edward slipped a napkin into her hand. Noisily she blew her nose and wiped her eyes.

'All the way from Hoxton!' he said with wonder.

'And then – half way along Newland Road three boys chased us – and threw stones, and Miss Georgina lost her hat – and I fell over and grazed my knee,' and she lifted her skirt and showed the bloodied stocking. Then it – started to snow – hard . . .' Her sobs recommenced. Mrs Bridges, no longer a Fury, put her arms round Daisy, who buried her damp head on the comfortable shoulder.

'There, there. Don't cry. It's all over now. Edward, get us that hot-bottle that was going in her ladyship's bed. I can heat up another one.'

Georgina was in bed, a hot toddy untasted by her side. Her eyes were red and swollen, her head dropped. She had just had the telling-off of her life from Richard and her step-grandmamma, who could be a very formidable lady indeed when occasion warranted it. She had exonerated Daisy from all blame and begged that the girl should not be punished, a request which Richard passed on to Mr Hudson.

'I'm sorry,' she said for the twentieth time. 'I suppose I didn't really think—'

'No, you didn't,' said Lady Southwold sharply. 'If you had you would have realised how unfair you were being, persuading a maidservant to steal from her employer's larder.'

'She didn't steal it. I took it.'

'Who took it doesn't matter. You must understand, child, that in life you cannot simply do what you think is right, regardless of anybody. You must learn to consider others.'

'But surely – it's more important that hungry people should eat.'

Lady Southwold sat back and surveyed her. 'I wonder. How much were you really thinking of Daisy's family? If you'd truly wanted them to have food over Christmas, wouldn't it have been better to ask your Uncle Richard? He might have stopped you going yourself, but surely you didn't think he would refuse to give them anything?'

'I'm sure she wasn't thinking of herself, Mabel,' Richard put in.

'I wanted to help them, that's all,' said Georgina quietly.

Lady Southwold crossed the room and sat on the bed. 'You've ruined the servants' Christmas, kept them waiting for their presents. You've caused me and your uncle and the police a great deal of anxiety by your thoughtless behaviour.' Suddenly she smiled. 'But what you did was prompted by a kind heart and concern for those less fortunate than yourself; so you may kiss your step-grandmamma, and take this with my best Christmas wishes.'

She handed Georgina a small jewel-case, open, to display a necklace of diamonds glittering against dark blue velvet. Georgina gasped. Lady Southwold kissed her. 'Take care of it. It's been in our family for four generations. Good night, Georgina. Good night, Richard.'

Richard stood looking down at his niece. 'I don't think we need to say any more, my dear. I just think it would be a good idea if you could leave Daisy alone for a bit. Let her take her place with the other servants, settle down and make friends. We want her to feel this is her home, now.'

Georgina nodded.

'And you must try to feel that this is your home too, Georgina. That you're one of the family now – that you belong here.'

Georgina looked up with a radiant smile. 'Oh yes, please!' she said.

CHAPTER TWELVE

Mrs Bridges stood back and surveyed her own handiwork with admiration. The plum cake was newly out of the oven, golden brown and flecked with the ivory of almonds. It looked totally mouth-watering.

'Very nice indeed, Mrs Bridges,' remarked Mr Hudson. 'Are we to have the pleasure of sampling it at teatime?'

Mrs Bridges shook her head. 'No, it's for my old friend Mrs Beddowes, poor old soul. She's ninety-three today and I wanted to send her something she'd really appreciate.'

'Generous to a fault as usual, Mrs Bridges. Let me pack it for you.' Mr Hudson produced as if from the air a folding cardboard cake-box, lined it with a doyley, and tenderly conveyed the cake into it. 'Yes,' Mrs Bridges went on, 'she took me under her wing when I was startin' out in life. She was cook to Lady Templeman, you know.'

'Ah, yes. Were not lobster patties her speciality?'

'They were. *And* her gooseberry trifles. But them Templemans – I don't care to mention their name if I can help it. Letting her end up forgotten, in a basement room in Camden Town! There ought to be a law about such things.'

Rose appeared in her coat and hat.

'Got it ready, Mrs Bridges?' she asked.

'Here we are, all nicely packed. Got the address all right, Rose? Now careful how you go with it!'

'I will, Mrs B.,' Rose called back, almost bumping into Edward outside as she carried the precious box before her. Edward, also bound for the door, was burdened with a large bunch of purple grapes, which Rose surveyed with raised eyebrows.

'You're not takin' those to Daisy?'

''Course. Hospital visitin' time at half-past two. Want to see what she looks like with her adenoids out.'

'Same as with 'em in, I should think. But what you taking them for? She won't be able to eat anything.'

'Oh.' Edward was nonplussed. 'Well, what *can* I take her?'

'Nice pretty bunch of flowers, I should think, if you want to show how much you care.'

'Oh, don't be rotten, Rose!' he called after her. He did care for Daisy, a good deal.

On the Camden Town tram Rose sat rigidly upright, the box on her knee. She was wearing her best clothes, which she considered as becoming to her as was necessary, but which, in fact, only emphasised the severe look which had become second nature to her. The dark green suit was plain, the flat pancake cap sat on top of her head uncompromisingly.

As the tram lurched round a corner, a young man who was moving towards the empty seat beside her was thrown off his balance and landed heavily on top of her. He was substantially built, and Rose gave a loud cry of protest as her hat shot on to one side and her face came into contact with his broad chest. But what concerned her more was the effect of the impact on the cake. The cardboard lid was now dented in, an ominous sign. To his embarrassed 'Sorry!' she snapped 'Oh, look what you've done! You've ruined it.' This was all too clearly confirmed when she lifted the lid and disclosed the cake, its round beauty now concave and its neat sides spreading outwards. Almost crying, Rose repeated 'Look at it!'

The stranger glumly obeyed. With an attempt at propitiation he asked 'Did you bake it yourself?' Rose turned huffily away. 'Clumsy, that's what you are.'

He sighed. 'Too right. Just what my mother used to say.'

She snorted. 'You can joke. Someone was expectin' this, a poor old lady.'

'Well, it's not the end of the world, is it. I'll buy you a replacement.'

'You can't. Not one like this, it was special.' Her face crumpled. 'Oh, what am I going to do?'

The stranger had a manner which lay between the forceful and the persuasive. Within ten minutes Rose was reluctantly surveying the wares of a teashop in Camden Town, the large young man hovering helpfully behind her.

'What sort was it?' he asked.

'Plum, if you must know. With almonds.' He passed on the description to the assistant, who went off in search, returning with the news that there was no plum. 'Only a nice lemon sponge or a gingerbread, or some California Jumbles.'

'They sound good,' said the stranger cheerfully. Rose

scowled. 'Not them. They've got wine in 'em, and she's ninety-three.' He chuckled. 'Just the ticket. Give her a lift, eh?'

They were becoming unpopular with the assistant, who pointed out that other people were waiting. 'All right,' said the stranger, 'we'll have the lemon sponge.' It was wrapped for him, and he presented it to Rose, saying 'Best I could do.' But she was not mollified. Undeterred, he said briskly 'Right. Now, how about having some tea with me?'

Rose looked startled. 'Tea? No, I can't. I got to deliver this.'

'Oh, have some tea, first. Come on.' He took her elbow and led her firmly into the tea-room. She was seated at a table before she found breath to say 'But I don't know who you are!'

'Gregory Wilmot's my name.' Rose surveyed Gregory Wilmot. He was somewhere in the mid-thirties, well-built, with a sturdy, outdoor look about him, a thatch of fair curly hair and bright humorous eyes. His suit was a good one, and there was an air of prosperity about him. His voice had a tinge of what Rose thought of as Colonial; it was actually Australian.

'What's *your* name?' he asked.

'Rose. Rose Buck.'

'Nice bumping into you, Miss Buck.'

Rose was instantly on the defence. 'I want to make it clear, I don't normally . . .'

'Neither do I,' he broke in, 'so we're both safe from each other.' He surveyed the squashed cake-box. 'What are we going to do with this? Have it now?' He nibbled a crumb. Rose took him seriously. 'Not in here!'

'Well, I could take it back to my hotel. I often get peckish, middle of the night.'

'Your hotel?'

He smiled. 'I'm on a visit. From Australia. That's why I fell over on the tram – not used to confined spaces. I'm English, actually, but I've been out of the country six years now.' All the time she felt him looking at her. Suddenly he asked. 'You're not married, are you?'

Rose gave an unreal giggle. 'Me? Do I look like it?' She was quite sincere.

'Can't think how you slipped the net,' he said; and the

admiration in his eyes was quite undisguised. He began to tell her about himself, as they ate the tea which was promptly served to them. His father had owned a small farm in Yorkshire, struggling with hard times and poor industrial conditions, making good in the end by changing over from agriculture and cattle to dairy produce. It was quite clear that Gregory's political sympathies lay with the Labour Party. He himself had emigrated, with his father's approval, and having done well had stayed out in Australia until a few weeks before, when he had come back to deal with affairs left unsettled by his father's sudden death.

Then he asked Rose for her own life-story. She told him briefly of her origins and her present work, pausing only when she came to the words 'head house-parlourmaid.'

'No point in pretending different,' she added defensively. Gregory laughed. 'Why should you want to? It's a very respectable job, and worthwhile too, if you're good at it.'

Rose was half-pleased and half-embarrassed. It was a relief that the tearoom clock showed half-past three, high time she was delivering the cake. She resisted Gregory's attempts to accompany her, but before they parted found herself pledged to meet him tomorrow. He was a very persuasive young man.

When she got back to Eaton Place in time for supper her feet were unwontedly light and her face had lost its normally controlled look. Mrs Bridges was too busy to notice anything. Busy with the meal, she asked 'Did you find my friend all right, Rose?'

'Oh yes, Mrs B. She was very pleased with the cake.'

'Well,' said Mrs Bridges complacently, 'plum with almonds was always her favourite.'

'Yes,' said Rose guiltily. And, to Mr Hudson, who was adding up accounts, 'Mr Hudson, do you know anything about Australia?'

He was always pleased to be asked for information. 'Australia, Rose? What a strange question. What prompts it?'

Rose improvised. 'Nothing, I just heard an Australian talking, on the tram. And you're always going on about how we should be curious about things and interested, and I didn't know much about it, that's all.'

Mr Hudson removed his glasses and prepared to expound.

'Australia is a large uncomfortable place with a hot and dusty climate, full of convicts and swindlers and bad living conditions, and certainly no place for a woman. If you're thinking of emigrating,' he added by way of a joke. Rose blushed. She was not good at lying.

Gregory's own version of Australia, when they met next day, was somewhat different. He told her about his sheep farm, with about a thousand head of sheep, a hundred miles or so west of Melbourne, but near a smaller town.

'We make our own company, anyway. There's my brother Tim, and three jackeroos who help us out—'

Rose was delighted. 'I've got a brother called Tim!' she exclaimed. 'He went to Canada, doing forestry.'

Gregory was delighted too. 'Well, isn't that amazing? What a coincidence. It has to be fate, doesn't it?' Their eyes met. 'You know, I think you'd go for it out there – the sheer size and beauty of the place. And the colours – delicate, soft, faded . . .' Rose's eyes were getting bigger and bigger. She shivered with a kind of ecstasy.

'You cold?' he asked, and put his arm round her shoulders. She didn't resist. 'No cold and damp out there,' he said, his mouth very close to her ear in the warm, intimate taxicab, a vehicle in which she was not used to riding. It was all becoming more and more like a beautiful dream. On Wednesday, her half-day, they were to meet again and go to a thé dansant.

But back at Eaton Place it was not easy to say so; indeed it became impossible after Mrs Bridges had flurried her by exhibiting a letter from old Mrs Beddowes in Camden Town. 'She thanks me kindly for the "lemon sponge", but asks me why couldn't I have baked one myself. What does she mean by that?'

'I don't know, Mrs Bridges,' Rose replied nervously. 'I – I think she must have got muddled in the head. You do, don't you, when you're ninety-three?'

Mrs Bridges glanced over the top of her glasses. 'The rest of her letter's sharp enough. It's very sharp indeed.' Rose pretended to be absorbed in something else. 'You coming to Richmond Park with us Wednesday?'

'Richmond Park?'

'Yes. To see the deer. We usually go this time of year,

you know, with the weather getting warmer.' Rose had an inspiration.

'Sorry, I can't. I got to see some friends. Er – friends of my brother, over from Canada – married couple. Got to look after 'em.'

'Bring 'em to Richmond Park!' suggested Mrs Bridges triumphantly. 'Make a lovely outing.'

Rose struggled mentally. 'Well – I would, only – only they want to see the Tower of London.'

'Oh.' Mrs Bridges looked round, disappointed. 'Sorry I can't take you, Mrs B.,' said Edward. 'Got to visit Daisy in hospital.'

Mr Hudson came to the rescue. 'I'll accompany you, Mrs Bridges. As Spring is in the air.'

'Thank you, Mr Hudson. That's kind of you – yes, I'd like that.' As Rose made her escape, the cook's sharp eyes followed her. 'Friends from Canada? Tower of London?'

The thé dansant had been an unqualified success. Neither Rose nor Gregory was a championship dancer, but their steps suited reasonably well, and the atmosphere was delightfully frivolous. As they took tea, Gregory gazed round the room, taking in the little orchestra, the ladies in their feathered hats and hobble skirts, the men with them, some considerably younger than they were themselves.

'Well,' he said, 'this time in ten days, all this will be a memory – a dream.'

Rose looked shocked. 'Ten days?'

'Right. I'll be sailing out of Tilbury, to the open sea.'

'So I won't see you again.'

His tone was light. 'Why not come with me?'

Rose laughed. 'Oh yes, of course.'

'No, I'm serious. Where's your spirit of adventure?'

She temporised, not understanding. 'I get quite a lot of adventure in my life – you'd be surprised.'

'With Mr Hudson and Mrs Bridges and Edward?'

Her chin rose. 'Oh, they're not all stick-in-the-muds, like you seem to think!'

'I never said they were, Rose. I wouldn't judge people before I met them. Let's go and meet them now. I want to see this famous house of yours.'

Rose's face was shocked. 'But – you can't. We haven't finished tea!'

'What's the matter? You ashamed of me?'

There was nothing Rose could say. As he waved for the bill, she put on her gloves.

And, after all, when they got to Eaton Place, the house appeared to be empty. Rose was deeply relieved until she saw Ruby peacefully snoring in a kitchen chair. 'What are you doing here?' she asked sharply. With a snorting start, Ruby woke. Dazedly she took in the presence of Gregory. 'Mrs Bridges said I was to stop in,' she said sleepily, 'mind the place while they was out.'

'Well, I'm here now,' Rose snapped, 'so you can go out for a walk. Go on.'

Ruby didn't in the least want to go far a walk, but Rose was obviously determined to be alone with her gentleman friend. 'Yes, Rose.' She eyed Gregory.

'This gentleman's just come to see Mr Hudson about something,' Rose said.

'Mr Hudson's out.' Rose shooed her. 'Off with you, go on . . .'

Gregory had found himself a chair and was gazing round. 'Aren't *you* going to sit down?' But Rose remained standing. 'Somebody might come in.'

'Thought they were all conveniently out.' Gregory smiled.

'Conveniently?'

He was very gently mocking her. 'You don't want me to meet them, do you – your "family"?'

Rose bridled. '*I* don't care if you meet them. It was your idea coming back here. I was really enjoying it at the thé dansant.'

'Aren't you enjoying it here, alone with me?' He looked round. 'You know, this could almost be my house. I made my own furniture. Rose – I meant it when I said come with me. How about it, eh?'

'It's ridiculous,' said Rose faintly.

'I don't see why. I'm not such a bad fellow. I'm thirty-five, and doing quite well for myself. I'd look after you.'

'It's not that. It's – well, I mean, why me, when you could do so much better? I'm only a house parlour-maid—'

'Just about the best qualification I can think of for a wife.'

She gasped. 'A wife?'

'Well, we don't have to get married right away. You can come out, look around before you make your mind up. I'll pay your fare back, if you don't like it – buy you a return boat ticket tomorrow. Well?' He got up and approached her, but she backed away. 'You're not frightened of me, are you?'

'No, 'course not.' But her voice was trembling.

'No reason to be.' He grinned. 'I wouldn't do anything to upset you, against your will. Not till after we're married, anyway!'

'You would then?'

'You know what I mean.'

Rose twisted her fingers together. 'Don't know what Mr Hudson would say.'

'Oh, the heck with Mr Hudson. You can make your own mind up, can't you?'

Rose was thoroughly flustered by now. 'You don't know what you're doing to me. I never been like this before, not with anyone. Don't make fun of me.'

Gregory put his hand on her shoulder. 'I wouldn't do that, Rose, I swear it. I've never been more serious in my life. Do you think I'd take the chance of making you unhappy? Do you think I'd lumber myself with an English girl, out there in the wilds . . .' He caught her enquiring look. 'In the not-so-wilds, unless I was certain we could make a go of it? *I* was certain, the moment I saw you in that tram.'

Rose prevaricated, fighting her own wish to believe him. 'I still can't help feeling you want a – a housekeeper, not a wife. Someone to sew, cook, scrub the floors for you and your friends . . .'

'That's not true!'

' "Pick up some housemaid" they probably said.'

'How can you think that of me, Rose?' Gregory turned her face towards him. 'Look at me. How can you think it?'

She pulled herself away. 'Because you haven't mentioned the word Love yet. It may sound stupid, but I always thought, if this ever happened to me, and I didn't think it would, I'd hear the word Love.'

Gregory laughed indulgently. 'But of course I love you. I wouldn't be asking you if I didn't. I love you, I do love you. There now, I've never said it before to anybody. Now I've done my bit. Let me hear *you* use that word – because no one's ever said it to *me* before.'

Rose hesitated. 'Well – I'm very fond of you, Gregory—'

'Don't you love me?'

She was like a trapped animal. 'I don't really know you. Only known you four days, and you're asking me to uproot everything, leave all my friends, the life I know – go to a strange country, thousands of miles away, with – with convicts and swindlers, and – and living conditions . . .'

Gregory took her firmly in his arms and implanted on her mouth a long kiss. Her struggles died away and she went limp in his arms. It was her first kiss, ever, not counting Mr Hugo's clumsy embrace all those years ago when they'd picnicked at Southwold. Poor Albert had never been man enough. Up to this moment she had never been kissed; and now she found it was the most wonderful, exhilarating thing that had ever happened to her.

When Gregory released her she was dazed, and hardly heard him saying that he'd have to have her answer next day, in time to book her passage.

Ruby had resented being sent out for a walk just because Rose wanted to be alone with a fellow. When Mr Hudson and Mrs Bridges came back she lost no time in telling them about it. Mr Hudson, in turn, lost no time in challenging Rose.

'Rose, apparently a man was looking for me yesterday.'

Rose tried fibbing. 'Oh yes, that's right. Said he'd call back, it was nothing important.'

'That isn't what I heard from Ruby!' Mrs Bridges broke in. 'Tell us about this man, Rose.'

Rose looked down. 'Told you all I know.'

'I don't think you have!'

'Oh, all right. He was a friend of mine.' In the background, Edward nudged Ruby in the ribs. Mrs Bridges set her arms akimbo in a warlike manner.

'And you said you was going to the Tower with a married couple, friends of your brother. That's not very truthful, Rose!'

Rose tossed her head. 'Just an acquaintance, after all. Nothing wrong, is there?'

'An acquaintance whom you brought back here,' said Mr Hudson in a grim tone, 'when the rest of the house was deserted. You know my opinion of that, Rose.' Mrs Bridges joined the accusations. 'If it'd been an old friend, that might've been different. But—'

Suddenly Rose's temper flared and she turned on them. 'Since you're all being so flamin' nosey, he wasn't just a casual acquaintance, he's – he's my fiancé.'

Their faces were a study in shock and incredulity.

'But why didn't you tell us, Rose?' Mrs Bridges asked.

'Well . . . he only asked me yesterday, and I haven't quite made up my mind. I didn't want to tell you till it was official.' Still nobody offered any congratulations. 'Well, don't say you're pleased for me,' she snapped.

'Naturally,' said Mr Hudson, 'we're pleased. But you can't expect us to be overjoyed till we know a wee bit more about him.'

Question by question they got it all out of her, Mr Hudson approving Gregory's business, Mrs Bridges all consternation that Rose might go to live in Australia, Mr Hudson scandalised that the acquaintance had been so short and that it had begun by Gregory falling on her in a tram. Before she knew it, she was under orders to bring him to tea on the following day.

The tea-party started off well enough, with everybody dressed in their best and a splendid chocolate cake, deemed ideal for the occasion by Mrs Bridges, on the table. Gregory's greetings were warm, but his offering of a bottle of whisky was met with astounded expressions. Rose, leaping into the awkward silence, said 'Thank you, Gregory. That'll be most welcome,' and put it on the sideboard. Tea begun, Gregory politely answered their questions about his sheep farm.

'I believe,' ventured Mr Hudson, 'that it's hard to find satisfactory labour,' and Edward chimed in 'Yeh, I've heard they're all convicts and ticket-of-leave men.'

Gregory was not pleased. 'It's a great exaggeration, all this about convicts; I've got as loyal a bunch of fellows working for me as you could ever hope for. And Rose'll find that there's no class consciousness. She'll be treated like an equal at last.'

Mr Hudson bridled. 'An equal to what, may I ask?'

'I mean, she won't be a house parlour-maid, at everyone's beck and call all the time.'

'But that's what she's used to, Gregory, 'put in Mrs Bridges. 'That's all she knows how to do.'

'I don't believe that, Mrs Bridges! She'll be free. A free woman at last.'

Mrs Bridges's brow wrinkled. 'But she's free now – free as is good for her.'

Gregory tried to hold the reins of his hobby-horse. 'I mean no disrespect to you, Mrs Bridges, or Mr Hudson.' The hobby-horse became restive. 'It's the system you live under – the whole outmoded class-structure of this country.'

Mr Hudson drew himself up sternly. 'You're a Socialist, then?'

'I am,' said Gregory proudly, Rose adding hastily 'Only in Australia. Because the Labour Party's in power. He wouldn't vote Labour in England.'

'Oh yes, I would!' Gregory flung back at her. Mr Hudson leant back, his tea cooling, as he prepared to enlighten the heathen.

'Being out of this country for so long, Mr Wilmot, I don't think you quite realise what's happening here. If the working-classes are allowed to organise themselves into powerful Trade Unions, they begin to disrupt the nation with strikes. Why, this past year—' He looked outraged as Gregory interrupted, the hobby-horse by now rampant.

'But they only want better living-conditions, man! A decent wage for their wives and families. *You*'re a working man. You may be comfortable enough, in Eaton Place, but think of your fellow-workers, outside, in the cold.' As Mr Hudson opened his mouth to reply Mrs Bridges saved the day by saying quickly 'Well, I think we should stop talking about politics and have some chocolate cake.' By this time Mr Hudson had decided that it would be beneath him to wage war.

'Naturally,' he said, 'everyone's entitled to his own view. When are you returning to Australia, Mr Wilmot?'

'Friday.'

Mrs Bridges threw up her hands. 'Not this comin' Friday?' He nodded.

'You goin' with him, Rose?' Edward asked.

Rose was torn between rapt admiration of Gregory's strength and courage in defying Mr Hudson, and the awful problem of making up her mind. Gregory smiled down at her.

'She'd make me the happiest man in the world if she did,' he said.

'Go on, Rose,' Edward urged. 'I'd go if I was you.'

Mr Hudson shook his head. 'Take great care before you answer, Rose. It's a decision that will affect your whole life.'

'I know that, Mr Hudson,' she said sharply. 'I'm not a child.' Then, suddenly, feeling the unbearable pressure of their various wills upon her, she said 'I'll go.'

There was an outburst of congratulations, smiles and embraces. 'As it so happens,' Gregory said, 'I've got something in my pocket to seal the bargain with.' And he brought out a little heart-shaped box and placed the ring it contained on Rose's finger. Overcome, she began to sob on his shoulder.

When she took Gregory upstairs for the formal presentation to the mistress of the house, Hazel made her happy by her unforced pleasure. Warmly she admired the ring. 'But, mind you,' she said, 'I can't imagine this house without you. I suppose I formally have to accept your notice, do I?'

This was another aspect of the mighty changes that were coming which had not struck Rose before. 'Yes, I'm sorry, Mrs Bellamy – I should've mentioned.'

'How long does it take to get to Australia?' Hazel asked Gregory.

'Fifty days out of Tilbury.'

'Cape of Good Hope?'

'That's right. Las Palmas. Cape Town. Adelaide. Melbourne.'

'I envy you. I love travelling by sea.'

As Rose ushered Gregory out she turned back to look at Hazel, who stood looking after them, her eyes wistful. She looked unusually pale, Rose thought, and fatter than usual, she who had always been so slim.

And Hazel thought of the day James had put the ring on *her* finger, and of how sadly different things were now.

And of the child she was carrying.

As Rose was brushing her hair that night in front of the mirror Mrs Bridges tapped and entered.

'Just wanted to make sure you're all right,' she said. 'I like your man, and I just want you to know, if your mind's truly made up, then you can count on my full support.'

Rose turned in gratitude. 'Thank you, Mrs Bridges, I knew I could.'

'Just hope that climate's all right for bringing up babies in.'

Rose was startled. 'Babies?'

'Well, he'll want sons, for the farm.'

'Yes . . . Hadn't thought about that.' She hadn't, indeed. Gregory's kisses – were they to lead to something Rose, country-bred as she was, could hardly picture, applied to herself and a man. And all the rest of it . . . she remembered her mother lying on the bed, pale and cold, and two women washing a new-born baby . . . and then young Lady Marjorie, so pretty and sweet-scented, comforting her and taking her and Tim up to the big house for a meal. She remembered Gregory's words to Mrs Bellamy: 'Fifty days out of Tilbury. Cape of Good Hope. Las Palmas . . .' The wide ocean, and somewhere under its depths, between England and another continent, Lady Marjorie lay. Despite her warm flannel nightgown, Rose shuddered.

It seemed impossible that Friday morning could have come so soon. Dressed for travel, Rose looked round her bedroom, bare and neat, everything personal removed, the bed-clothes folded. The reflection in the mirror, with a veil over its best hat, didn't look like her. Even the luggage was unfamiliar, the cabin-trunk that Mrs Bellamy had appeared with the day before, Rose had been astonished to see her, panting, with sweat on her brow, the heavy trunk at her feet.

'Mrs Bellamy! You never been and brought that thing down from the attic by yourself!'

Hazel wiped her brow. 'There wasn't anyone about – and I – wanted you to have it, Rose. It was Lady Marjorie's. One she didn't take with her. I thought you'd like it.'

'Oh, that's ever so kind of you, Mrs Bellamy. But you shouldn't have. Here, sit on the bed. You've gone and hurt your back, haven't you.'

Hazel winced and leaned forward, her hand on her side. 'It's nothing. Just a pulled muscle, something like that. Now you'd better start your packing.'

And now it was time to go. She had said goodbye to Hazel and James, who had rather stiffly given her a parting present of money. Richard was away but sent her his good wishes. In the servants' hall Ruby was sniffling, Mrs Bridges weeping openly, and Mr Hudson trying to conceal his own sadness under a brisk and jaunty manner. As Rose appeared with her luggage he handed her his personal gift; a shiny new Bible with a neat inscription. For the first time in history she kissed him.

'Oh, it's lovely. I'll treasure it and remember you, Mr Hudson. You'll always be with me now.' He replied, typically: 'Well, if it's a comfort to you in the days to come, then it's money well spent.'

Mrs Bridges had given her copies of all her recipes, a noble gesture indeed; while Edward had arranged for the halting strains of 'Waltzing Matilda', played somewhat waveringly on a fiddle, which were now wafting in from the area, the performer being a street musician friend of Edward's. Choking, Rose said 'Thanks, Edward. It's a lovely thought. Goodbye, Ruby, goodbye, everybody,' and ran to the door, Mr Hudson shepherding the others to wave her off; all but Mrs Bridges, who remained, overcome, in her fireside chair.

Gloom reigned over the servants' hall all that day. They talked of Rose, of her qualities, of their memories of her, just as they had talked of Lady Marjorie after the tragedy. It was as if Rose were dead. Edward said, with rare insight: 'The funny thing is, really, that we won't remember anything after a bit. I mean we'll remember *her*, Rose. The fact that she existed. But nothing *about* her. I suppose that's the way it is, with people. They just fade away.'

They brooded on this depressing theory. Outside in the street a cab was heard, stopping. 'Can that be the new girl arriving in a *cab*?' queried Mr Hudson. 'Go and see, Edward.' Edward went out. A few moments later strange cries were heard, and Edward's startled face appeared round the door. 'It's *Rose*, Mr Hudson!' he gasped.

Before the group had time to take it in he was leading her through the door. Mr Hudson leapt to assist him, for Rose looked hardly capable of standing. They supported her to a chair, where she lay back white-faced and haggard, barely conscious. Mr Hudson bustled round her.

'All right, Rose, you're quite safe. Edward, take her bag. Don't crowd her, now.' Mrs Bridges was spilling out frantic questions.

'What's gone wrong? Hasn't the boat sailed? Is there fog? Where's Gregory?'

It was Mr Hudson's task to break the incredible news to James and Hazel. Rose had now recovered, he said, though still very shaken, and had given them a somewhat muddled explanation. 'It's difficult to know for certain, madam, but it seems the gentlman, her fiancé, already has a wife. In Melbourne.'

James stared. 'Well, well, well. How on earth did she stumble on that?'

'From some friends of his who came to see them off. It was hard to get a clear account of what happened, but it would seem she's had rather a lucky escape.'

Hazel was looking thoughtful. 'How is she?'

'Rather less overwrought than she was, madam. She's in her room. I – er – took the liberty of turning away the new applicant for the post of house-parlourmaid.'

'Yes, of course.'

When he had gone James said 'Poor old Rose. Just her luck to get caught up with a scoundrel.'

Hazel turned to him sharply. 'Do you believe that?' she asked.

She went upstairs and tapped at Rose's door.

'Rose, it's Mrs Bellamy. May I come in for a minute?' After a pause the door was unlocked. Rose was unpacking, her usually smooth hair hanging untidily about her face, traces of tears on her cheeks.

'Hudson has just told me what happened. I'm very sorry.'

'Yes,' Rose's voice was shaking, 'I'm sorry I've caused so much trouble. I'll – I'll give you your trunk back.'

'Oh, Rose, please don't worry about that . . . may I sit down?' Painfully, her hand on the small of her back, she lowered herself on to the bed. 'So he had a wife, in Melbourne. Those friends of his told you.'

'Yes.'

'But he's separated, isn't he? Perhaps divorced? I mean, she's not living with him on the farm?' She was watching Rose keenly, noting the wary expression in her eyes, the air of nervousness which didn't seem to be the product of her state of shock. There was something almost – could it be relief?

'I don't know about that,' Rose said flatly.

'I know one can be wrong about people. But he seemed so clearly a man who'd worked hard and built something up for himself, and was looking for a wife to share it – and found what he was looking for in you.'

'Yes. But he wasn't honest with me, was he.'

Hazel's tone was gentle. 'Are you being honest with me?'

Rose gasped. 'Mrs Bellamy!'

'Rose, we're good enough friends to be frank with each other. I want to help.'

Rose began to throw garments out of the trunk on to the bed.

'You can't help. It's all over and done with. The boat's gone.'

Hazel forced Rose to meet her eyes. 'Rose. He *was* free, wasn't he?'

There was no answer. The feverish unpacking went on.

'Why didn't you go with him?'

'Like I said, he had a wife. He didn't want me. Just led me on. Making fun . . .' she began to cry, and subsided on the bed beside Hazel, who put a comforting arm round her shoulders. 'It was awful – the docks – people pushing, couldn't get through – that dirty old boat . . . And his friends, laughing – I felt I didn't know him. It wasn't real. I felt sick, I had to get away – started running – back.'

Hazel went on patting her shoulder until her sobs quietened.

'Mr Hudson was right.' Rose wiped her eyes. 'It's ridiculous thinking you can get to know someone so quick. Silly to throw away all your friends, all you know about – for a perfect stranger.'

Hazel shook her head. 'I know, Rose. But sometimes it's important.'

Rose turned to her almost savagely. 'It's *silly*. Don't tell them downstairs, will you? Please don't tell them, or Captain James.'

'Of course I won't. It's between you and me. You must get some rest now – you must be very tired.'

Downstairs it was agreed in council that when Rose reappeared among them, all was to be as before. Gregory's name was not to be mentioned, and the whole incident forgotten. It had been unfortunate, but Rose had learned her lesson and returned to the fold. There was no harm done.

Next morning Hazel did not come downstairs. James telephoned for Dr Page, who came promptly when he heard the symptoms. Having examined her, he joined James in the morning-room, his face grave.

'Mrs Bellamy is suffering from what may be merely an isolated attack of bleeding. On the other hand, it could be the first sign of a miscarriage, which at her stage of pregnancy could be serious. We must do all we can to prevent this, of course, and the most important thing is that she should have complete rest until the bleeding stops. She must not put her feet to the ground.'

James nodded dumbly.

'Would you like me to send in a nurse, Mr Bellamy?'

But when Hazel was consulted, she shook her head weakly. 'I want Rose to look after me. Nobody but Rose.'

In spite of Rose's skilful nursing, within a week Hazel had a painful and dangerous miscarriage. The doctor said it had probably been caused by a strain.

CHAPTER THIRTEEN

An early summer hot spell had brought airlessness to the basement of 165 Eaton Place. It was a relief to Rose to emerge from the pass door into the slightly more airy hall, but she puffed and panted with the effort of climbing the stairs. Her collar clung stickily to her neck, and there was an unbecoming film of sweat on her brow and cheeks.

'Must be getting old,' she observed to Mr Hudson, who had just retrieved the evening paper from the letter-box, and was reading it with a frown of disapproval.

'We're in for a storm, I shouldn't wonder,' he said. 'Ach, these cursed Suffragettes! They've smashed up the British Museum now. If they claim the right to vote like men, they ought to be flogged like men.'

Rose, who had painful memories of her one excursion into Suffragism with Miss Lizzie, didn't take up the challenge. Mr Hudson glanced at the bottle she was carrying. 'What have you got there?'

'Liniment. For Mrs Bellamy. She's a bit more cheerful today, bless her, but her back still aches pretty bad.' She went upstairs, slowly, to Hazel's bedroom.

Hazel looked pale and tired. The disappointment and pain of her miscarriage, and the constant nagging of the strain which had caused it, had put lines on her face. As Rose expertly massaged her back, the lines were gradually smoothed out, and she turned her head contentedly on her arm. Rose's hands had a hypnotic effect, stroking and pressing the knotted muscles, locating the worst spot with gentle force. She smiled up at her masseuse.

'You ought to take massage up as a profession, Rose. It's quite the thing now. Go on for another minute or two – it's very soothing.'

Rose continued the rubbing, chatting quietly to her mistress. No, Captain James hadn't come in yet. Yes, he'd probably been kept late at the office.

'Have you written that letter yet?' Hazel asked.

Rose's lips tightened. 'Not yet, Madam.'

'I think you owe it to Mr Wilmot. Otherwise he'll spend

the rest of his life wondering why you changed your mind. Rose – did you love him very much?'

Rose nodded. 'He was most girls' idea of a dream come true, Madam. But when he asked me to go off abroad with him and everything, I – well . . .'

The door opened, and Hazel, her face against the pillow, asked eagerly 'Is that you, James?'

But it was Richard, embarrassed to have interrupted the massage. He vanished hastily, as Rose helped Hazel back into her nightdress.

'All's well, now, Richard!' Hazel called. 'You can come in.'

'I'll go down and see Ruby about your dinner, Madam,' said Rose, as Richard entered.

'Thank you, Rose. Tell her something very light, though – I'm not hungry.'

'I'm afraid it's Irish stew, Madam. She's been stewing it since eleven o'clock this morning,' she added censoriously, as she departed.

Richard stood by Hazel's bed looking down at her. She was smiling, but Richard knew how little joy there was behind the smile. Her illness had been a great anxiety to him. The loss of Marjorie had darkened his life; was there to be another great shadow on it, if Hazel died? He tried not to admit to himself how much she meant to him – she, his son's wife! He must force himself to think of her only as a dear daughter-in-law.

'How are you feeling?' he asked.

'A little better, thank you. But Dr Page says I'm to rest for another day or two, helpless and useless.'

'Never useless, my dear!'

Tears cracked her voice. 'I haven't been much use as a wife, have I? I'm still haunted by James's bewildered stare, when Dr Page broke the news to him in here. Like a little boy, who's had his new toy taken away from him. It was so . . . pathetic.'

Richard took her hand and patted it consolingly.

'You mustn't feel like that. Nobody's to blame – it was God's will. You'll have another chance. Page told me there was nothing to stop you having twins next time. So cheer up and let's change the subject, eh?'

'Yes. Let's. How was your day?'

'Somewhat frustrating. If we poor mortals could only influence events—'

'You mean "we poor Tories"?'

'No, my dear. All men. We have the vote. Some of us have the chance of questioning and opposing the Government's policies. But *events* continue to gallop forward unchecked, like stampeding bulls, and there's nothing any of us can do to stop them. I sometimes think the future of our civilization so grim and dangerous that I'd rather not face it.'

'You mustn't be depressed. One of us is enough.'

'I suppose so.' His face was gloomy. 'All the same, I see little to be cheerful about. This country is spoiling for war.'

'War?' Hazel was shocked. 'Oh, surely not.'

'I feel it. Even the civil disruptions are pointers to it – the Irish gun-running in April, the Suffragettes and their home-made bombs. Even the children . . . in the Park this morning I saw a small boy dragging a toy cannon on the end of a string. Once it would have been a wooden horse. Ah, well! I rather think I'll escape from it all in another biography. Lansdowne, perhaps.'

Hazel brightened. 'Then I'll type it for you, and help you with the papers.'

'Would you?'

'Yes, in your study. As I used to do. They were – such very happy days!'

Their eyes met.

Georgina was painfully toiling away at a letter, with frequent pauses for inspiration, when she heard James's latch-key in the door. A moment later he entered, with a cluck of affected surprise.

'Well, well! Miss Georgina Worsley writing letters! Didn't know you *could* write.' She put out her tongue at him.

'Bread-and-butter letters,' she said disgustedly. 'Look – I've put "Dear Lady Renham, thank you so much for my stays . . ."'

'Oh, you left them behind in a drawer, did you?'

Georgina giggled. '*Stay*. Now let me see. "It was—"'

'"Such hell and I loathed every minute of it,"' James suggested.

'Stop it, James, you're muddling me.' She went on writing. '"—such fun and I enjoyed . . ."'

'Spelt E-N-G-O-I-D'.

Half-cross, half-mischievous, Georgina jumped up, snatched a cushion and began to thump James with it, while he fended off the blows with his arm. 'Shut up! I can't – concentrate – if you keep saying – silly things!'

James snatched the cushion. 'Hey, you've crushed the evening paper – how dare you! Come here—' and he began to chase her round the furniture, while she shrieked with delight and dodged him nimbly. 'Can't catch me!' she chanted, 'can't catch me!'

'Oh, yes, I can, and will, and you'll be punished!'

He grabbed a fold of her rose-pink dress, caught her and flung her across his knee, where he smacked her soundly with the rolled-up paper to the accompaniment of her delighted squeals. Both were thoroughly enjoying it, when the door opened and Mr Hudson broke in upon the unseemly situation. They broke apart and both began to stammer explanations, to which Mr Hudson listened impassively. He took the crumpled paper from James.

'I'll ask Rose to run an iron over it, sir.'

'If you would, Hudson, before my father comes in. Er – did you want something?'

'Just about this evening, sir. I understand Mrs Bellamy will be requiring dinner upstairs on a tray.'

'I suppose so, yes. If she's still in bed.' James looked as though he would rather not have known where Hazel was, or discussed her at all.

'She is still confined to her room, sir,' Mr Hudson informed him. 'Mr Bellamy has gone up to see her, I believe.'

'Oh. Very well, Hudson.'

Georgina had resumed her writing, the flush of the chase cooling on her cheeks. James wandered over to the mantelpiece and surveyed the white flock of invitation-cards ranged on it.

'Six dances. Four dinner-parties. Three garden-parties, and two receptions, all for the month of June. Are you going to all of them?'

'Oh, I hope so – the dinners and dances, anyway. I love going to them.'

'You're a very lucky and rather spoilt little girl. Aren't you?'

Georgina pouted. 'Why?'

'Going to so many parties.' They were two of a kind, he and she.

'Those cards aren't *all* for me.'

'Most of them are. There's the Life Guards at Ranelagh for me, which I can't go to anyway.'

Georgina swung round sympathetically. 'Oh, James, how sad. Why?'

'Well, it's tomorrow night – to dine with the Newburys and go on to the ball. But Hazel won't be fit to go, you see.'

'I suppose she won't . . . Oh, dear. You'll miss seeing all your old Army friends.'

'Yes. Might be my last chance to see them all before I go to India.'

Georgina's lively face was usually thoughtful and wistful. 'When will that be, James?'

'If I accept the post, in the New Year – January, 1915. It'll be a Junior Directorship.'

'How grand!'

James was unwilling to express whole-hearted pleasure in anything. 'It'll be stinking hot and stuffy out there, like it is in London today.'

Georgina rose, put her arms round him, and gave him a gentle kiss. 'Poor old Jumbo,' she said, 'I'll miss you.'

'You're not to call me Jumbo. I dislike it – intensely.'

'Very well. I'll try and get myself out of the habit.'

'You will – unless you want another spanking.'

Georgina's eyes twinkled with merriment and anticipation; she had enjoyed the spanking. 'I promise, Jum—' she began, and hurriedly clapped her hands to her mouth. 'No, no, I didn't say it! James, Cousin James!'

But James didn't respond as she wished. The unspoken attraction between them was telling on him. He knew that if he touched Georgina again the romp would turn from play to earnest. 'I think,' he said, 'you'd better get on with your thank-you letters – don't you?'

As she went back obediently to the desk he threw himself down in a chair, and stared into vacancy.

Hazel's modest meal on a tray had looked vastly preferable to the mess which Rose, Daisy and Hudson were contemplating, as it lay palely on their plates. Ruby had acted as cook in the absence of Mrs Bridges, who was nursing a violent sick headache upstairs; and between Mrs Bridges's writing and Ruby's own unfamiliarity with reading-matter, the excellent recipe for Irish stew had strayed far from its appointed path. For one thing, Ruby had interpreted the word 'butter' as 'bitter', and had soused the ingredients with ale before Mr Hudson had pointed out the error. The meat had got burnt in the frying-pan, which gave it a very nasty flavour, in addition to which it was tough, while the thickening might very well have been glue, from the look of it.

Rose impaled a fairly edible-seeming piece of onion with her fork, and slowly ate it. Mr Hudson chased a slice of carrot round his plate, with no very fixed intention of catching it; and Daisy, who even at home had never eaten such food, gazed at it dumbly.

Only Ruby, ever-hungry and sublimely unaware of the others' distaste, tucked heartily into her portion and took another helping.

'Will Mrs Bridges be up soon?' Daisy enquired plaintively.

'Let us hope so.' Mr Hudson's speech amounted to a prayer. He pushed the slice of carrot aside.

Neither Richard, James nor Georgina had enjoyed the stew in the dining-room, but Georgina ate anything on principle and the two men balked at creating a fuss in the kitchen. In any case, they could drown the memory of it in brandy. Georgina looked over the table at James, staring broodily into his glass.

'Poor James, missing the ball,' she said.

Richard's head came up. 'What ball?'

'The Life Guards Ball at Ranelagh, tomorrow,' Georgina answered.

'Oh. Why can't you go, James?'

'I can't, not without Hazel,' James snapped. 'We were to have dined with the Newburys beforehand – I've refused already.'

'You could still go to the ball,' Richard said.

'Haven't got a partner. Too short notice.'

'Take Georgina.' He turned to her. 'Unless you're otherwise engaged?'

Georgina's face was bright. 'Tomorrow? No, nothing. I was only thinking of going to the Earl's Court Exhibition with a rather boring young man. Oh, please could I come, James?'

James was pleased, both at the idea of partnering Georgina and at his father's unwonted approval of something that he, James, wanted.

'I can see no objection,' he said, 'as long as Hazel doesn't mind.'

Hazel didn't mind; or so she said. James looked in on her before leaving for work next morning, just to reassure himself. Uneasily moving about the room, never quite catching Hazel's eye, he said:

'You're *quite* sure you don't mind me trotting off to this wretched ball tonight?'

She smiled. 'Of course I don't. You'll enjoy it – see all your friends.'

'Yes.' He struggled with himself, hating himself for not saying the things a husband should say in the circumstances: 'I shan't enjoy it without you.' 'Wait till you're about again, we'll do something to make up for it.' 'Being ill makes you look very beautiful.' But instead he said 'Well, I must go, or I'll be late for work.'

As he reached the door she called him back. 'James. Dr Page told Richard I could still have children – did you know? There's nothing wrong, you see.'

Now was the moment when he must go to her, kiss her, tell her how happy he was to know it, how sorry for what had happened. But, without moving his hand from the doorknob, he said 'Oh, good. That's splendid news, isn't it. Well . . . I'll be on my way.'

The door closed behind him.

Georgina was humming 'After the Ball', which was silly, she thought when she caught herself at it, because this was actually the night of the ball. She sat in front of her dressing-table mirror, the reflection of her brilliant face smiling back at her, her ball-dress, scattered with sequins, glittering on its hanger behind her. In the mirror Rose's face was reflected, demure, as she applied talcum powder to Georgina's bare shoulders – a pleasant task which reminded Rose of how she used to do the same for Miss Lizzie. Only Miss Lizzie had been such a fidget, not enjoying dressing up or anything. As the thought crossed her mind Georgina began to wriggle with impatience.

'Oh, that's enough, thank you, Rose!'

'I haven't done yet, Miss.' Rose laid on again with the powder-puff.

'Why do we have to be all covered in powder, just to go to a ball?'

'In case you perspire. Wouldn't look very nice, if you was waltzing about with sweat pouring down your back, would it? Specially this weather.'

Georgina nodded. It was really very enjoyable, if she could restrain her impatience to be dressed and ready, this soft tickling of swansdown on her skin; like a cat being stroked. She said over her shoulder: 'Mrs Bellamy said last night you might have healing powers in your hands, Rose.'

Rose smiled. 'Me? I don't think so.'

'She says you've done wonders with her back.'

'That's time and rest, not me. I'm not a magician, Miss.'

Georgina gazed sadly at her reflection. 'It must be very sad to lose your first baby – or any baby.'

'Very sad,' said Rose. (Or not to have a baby at all, she thought, when one could have had two or three, or any number, of Gregory's children, some with his fair curly hair and some like her; instead of turning into a sour old maid, as like as not . . .) She shook herself angrily. 'Slip the frock over your head, Miss, then I'll do your hair.'

In the hall, half an hour later, Rose watched them ready to set off, a handsome pair; James elegant in white tie and tails, his Indian General Service Medal well in evidence, Georgina radiant, flushed with happiness, the diamond earrings and Granny Southwold's necklet out-glittering the decorations on her black dress. James, Rose could see, was struck all of a heap by his step-cousin's beauty. He was looking at her in quite a different way, as though seeing her for the first time, and she was twinkling up at him, flirtatiousness embodied; or, as Rose put it, asking for trouble. And poor Mrs Bellamy lying upstairs alone; no baby, no husband, nothing.

They were leaving, Georgina on James's arm, going to the waiting taxi. Rose and Mr Hudson waved them off, and returned downstairs. It seemed very quiet now that Georgina's laughter and chatter had gone.

'You'd never take him for a young husband what's recently lost his first-born child,' Rose said. Mr Hudson looked reproachful, though inwardly he agreed.

'Young gentlemen, Rose, especially officers, are trained to conceal their true feelings – a tradition necessary on the field of battle – lest the men sense their officer's fear or anxiety, and lose heart.'

Rose snorted. 'If *I* was a man and my wife had a miscarriage, I'd either sit with her all evening or stop in my room, having a good cry. Not go gallivanting off to a ball.'

'You're not a man, Rose.' Mr Hudson's tone was enough to quell anyone but Rose, who snapped back 'No, I'm not, am I?' and she turned to go upstairs. Mr Hudson called after her.

'If you're going up, you might just pop in and see if Mrs Bridges needs anything.'

'Last time I looked in, she said her head was splitting. I'd better give her a couple more aspirins tonight.'

Rose found Mrs Bridges in a poor way, still racked with a migraine headache, and slightly feverish. She was hardly able to answer Rose's enquiries, and when offered the aspirins said that the last ones had made her sick. Rose, shaking her head, went downstairs to report, and after a conference with Mr Hudson knocked at Hazel's bedroom door.

Inside, she could hear Richard Bellamy's pleasant voice reading to the invalid. He stopped as she entered.

'Beg pardon, Madam,' Rose said, 'but Mr Hudson was wondering if Mr Bellamy would mind coming downstairs for a moment. Only Mrs Bridges is worse, and she's got a temperature – Mr Hudson thinks she ought to have the doctor, sir.'

Richard got up. 'But of course. I'll telephone for Dr Foley at once, tell Hudson.'

The door had no sooner shut behind Rose than Hazel was getting out of bed. 'I must go and see to her, of course.'

'Hazel, get back into bed – at once!'

'No, Richard.' She slipped her feet into her mules and reached for her dressing-gown. 'It's my duty. I should be with her.'

Richard was seriously alarmed. 'Hazel, you're *not* to get up! Dr Page forbade it. You'll only injure yourself.'

She was half-way to the door. 'I'm responsible for the

household now. If our cook's ill, I must go up and see to her.' Richard was standing between her and the door. She tried to push him aside. 'Richard, please.' But he had caught hold of her arms, and was propelling her back towards the bed.

'I forbid it,' he said firmly. When Richard used that tone there was no fighting him. With a certain relief she gave in. 'Do you?' she asked, searching his eyes with hers. So should a good husband behave, she thought, not without bitterness. Gently Richard urged her back into bed. 'I'll go and see to Mrs Bridges,' he said. 'After all, I've been responsible for things in this house for a number of years.'

She looked up at him. 'Yes. You are still – the master – aren't you?'

He was at the door. 'And – allow me to look after you. *Someone*'s got to.'

Through the drawn curtains of Hazel's room the first light of dawn was filtering. She had not slept, except for a few fitful snatches. She was hot and uneasy, her back aching, thoughts tumbling into her mind regardless of sense. The sound of a taxi approaching brought her upright on her elbow, listening. Voices, a key in the door, and the door quietly shutting. She lay down again, wide awake, staring at the ceiling.

Richard saw the taxi arrive. As troubled as Hazel, in his own way, he had given up all attempts at sleeping, and was standing by the window, smoking a cigar. He watched the two figures leave the taxi and cross the pavement to the house, the smaller one looking up at the other, laughing.

Georgina and James were having a quiet nightcap, Georgina drinking barley-water, James a whisky-and-soda.

'Thirsty work, dancing,' he said, 'especially if you dance every one on the card. Like you did.'

She laughed. 'Did I? Yes, I suppose I did.'

'Well, you certainly were the belle of the ball. I should have claimed a few dances myself before we set out.'

She pouted. 'Then why didn't you?'

'I was just going to, when I saw you stifle a yawn and realised it was time I took you home.'

'That was only because that boy with red hair, Giles Everton, was telling me how he landed a twelve-pound salmon on the Spey. He went into every gory detail.'

James set down his glass. 'Perhaps there was another reason why I didn't ask you for a dance. But I'm not sure that I ought to tell you.'

She ran over to him and shook him by the lapels.

'Oh, come on, James! You've got to tell – you're not allowed to keep secrets from cousins – well, step-cousins.'

'All right.' He put his hands on her shoulders and looked down at her. 'Because I'm not sure that if I had to take you in my arms to dance with you – I could quite trust myself not to kiss you – not as a young step-cousin should be kissed – like this . . .' he stooped and gave her a light kiss on the cheek. 'But as one would kiss a beautiful young woman of whom one is growing – dangerously fond.' He kissed her on the lips. Her eyes closed and she remained pressed against him until he released her.

'And now, since we were denied our dance together at the ball, I would like to ask you formally, Miss Worsley, for the pleasure of the next waltz.'

She joined in the game. 'Yes, please, Captain Bellamy.'

Dreamily, they began to waltz slowly round, Georgina humming a snatch of a Viennese waltz. They were playing with fire, Georgina's instincts told her; suddenly she detached herself, saying lightly 'That was fun.'

They were sipping their drinks decorously when Richard looked in on them.

'Enjoy yourselves, you two?'

'Very much, thank you,' said Georgina. 'It was a lovely ball.'

'Sorry if we woke you up, father.'

'I was awake. Couldn't sleep. This close atmosphere.'

After a few desultory words, and a warning not to waken Hazel, he drifted back upstairs, half-satisfied, half-uneasy.

They didn't waken Hazel, for she had not slept. Wide-eyed in the dark, she heard their soft footsteps and whispers as they passed her door, and a smothered laugh from Georgina.

It was after nine when Daisy woke Georgina with her breakfast-tray. Roused, she sat up in bed.

'This is such a treat. Thank you very much. Oh, Daisy – I was having such a horrible dream when I woke up.'

'Then it's just as well you did wake up, Miss.'

Georgina's face was clouded, remembering. 'I was on a swing in a big park somewhere. And there was a young man beside me, tall and good-looking. And as we swung to and fro, higher and higher in the air, he was – well, kissing me. All the time.'

Daisy giggled appreciatively.

'But down below, people were cheering and waving flags at us. Then I saw that the young man's face was dreadfully white – all the blood drained away. Then – he toppled off the swing and fell down, down, miles below to the ground. I wanted to go down there and help him, in case he wasn't dead. Then I saw that by falling he'd knocked down all the other people waving flags and cheering. But they were all young men too, with terrible white faces . . . and some of them were bleeding, and crying out. But I couldn't get off the swing. Then I woke up.'

'I'd call that a nightmare, Miss, not a dream,' Daisy said, awed.

Georgina began to nibble toast. All the pleasure of the evening before seemed to have melted. Only a dream – but it had spoiled things. She hoped she would soon forget it.

When James came in that afternoon he learnt from Mr Hudson that Hazel had got up that afternoon for the first time, and had been writing letters in the morning-room. But she was not there, or upstairs. James's usual feeling of guilt and of duty only half-done assailed him. Sharply, he called her name in the hall. Rose appeared.

'Ah, Rose. Have you seen Mrs Bellamy?'

'Yes, sir. She's gone down to the kitchen.'

'The *kitchen*? Well, she shouldn't!' James returned sharply. Rose opened her mouth to speak but he was already striding towards the pass-door.

In the kitchen Ruby, red-faced, tousle-headed and with traces of tears on her face, was doing something with a frying-pan. At the stove stood Hazel, stirring the contents of a saucepan. Beads of sweat were on her brow from the heat of the stove; she looked weary and untidy, and, James noted with fury, she was wearing one of Mrs Bridges's aprons.

'What are you *doing*?' His voice was gritty with anger.

'What do you think I'm doing? I'm helping Ruby out. All this cooking's too much for her.'

'And who said you could get up?'

'Dr Page did.' Her eyes met his defiantly.

Even in a rage, the maxim 'not in front of the servants' governed James. 'Leave us, please, Ruby,' he said. Ruby, flustered and apprehensive, took herself out of the way, casting a frightened glance back to the two by the stove, James standing over Hazel and shouting at her.

'You're supposed to be the mistress of this house. How the hell do you expect the servants to respect you and carry out your orders, if you come down here and try to cook the meals?'

She shouted back. 'And how do you expect that wretched little kitchen-maid to cook all the meals for upstairs *and* down – all by herself?'

'That's nothing to do with you. It is not your place to come down here and cook!'

Hazel was white with temper. 'Not my place? I note your choice of expression.'

'What expression?'

'You said it was "not my place" to cook the meals – just as you'd say of a domestic servant. Yet in the same breath you tell me I'm not to soil my hands doing servants' work. Well, it *was* my place to type your father's book for wages, and you didn't object to that, did you?'

'What's that got to do with it? Damn it all, you're my wife, not a cook!'

'Wives *are* cooks where I come from. They have to be.'

'Well, they're not in this house and never have been. So you can put that ladle down and go upstairs where you belong – and leave the meals to Ruby.'

'I'll do nothing of the sort! *I* am responsible for the domestic running of this house.'

He looked as if he were about to strike her. 'You are responsible for running this house with dignity, as Mother did – from upstairs – not messing about in the kitchen like a scullery-maid!'

'How dare you say that!'

'You'll do as I say and go upstairs. As my wife, you owe me obedience.'

'And don't you owe *me* something?'

He looked blank. 'What? What's the matter with you?'

She dragged off the apron and threw it on the floor. 'If you can't understand, then perhaps it's just as well our baby died. Just as well!' Sobbing, she flew past him and up the stairs. He heard the pass-door slam behind her.

The anger which had erupted in the kitchen was still raging in the morning-room. Hazel had gone to her room and locked the door, refusing James's demands to come in. James, storming down again, had been confronted by a furious Richard, and the morning-room rang with argument.

'How I live my life in my own house is my own affair!' James shouted.

'I have every right, James. You're still my son and as long as I live under this roof I reserve the right to comment on your behaviour.'

'Father, my relations with my wife are none of your business.'

'Hazel's suffered the agony and distress of losing her baby. She is weak, depressed, and in need of all the love and care she can get from her husband. Yet you behave as though she'd suffered nothing worse than a slight cold.'

'That's monstrous! Do you think I don't know how she's feeling?'

'Then why in God's name can't you show some concern for her? I can only say that in my opinion you are not worthy of her love. She's too damned good for you. And that is my last word on the subject.'

James's tone and look were dangerous. 'And my last word,' he said between his teeth, 'is that I'm beginning to think the time has come for us to go our separate ways.'

'Just what do you mean by that?'

'I mean that instead of endlessly quarrelling and feuding with me about the running of this house, you might find life more to your liking in a set of rooms in St James's. It might just be better for all of us.'

A silence fell between them. The fury had died down; a cold reality enveloped them.

'Very well, James,' Richard said quietly. 'If that's what you want. I'll move. I've no wish to stay on here, if I'm not welcome. But I shall need a few days to find suitable accommodation. I trust you'll grant me that.'

James was silent. Suddenly he had realised what he had done, like a boy who breaks something in anger and regrets it.

'There's no hurry. It was – only a suggestion. I didn't mean . . .'

Richard turned on his heel and left the room. James looked after him, helpless and miserable.

Dinner that night was an outwardly peaceful, conventional function. The game of bridge that followed was equally decorous. But between the four who played, James, Hazel, Richard and Georgina, a tension vibrated in the close evening air. Nobody spoke much; Hazel's eyes were red. Georgina, desperately uncomfortable and embarrassed, broke the silence at the end of the first game.

'Phew – I'm stifled.' She blew the hair back from her forehead.

James took up her lead, with relief. 'I know. It's warmer than ever tonight. I'll go and open the window a bit wider.'

Through the opened window floated in the sound of a small band of street musicians. They were playing 'Who were you with last night?' Over and over went the banal tune, until James threw them a handful of coins. He returned to the table.

'Three chaps, one blind and two on crutches. Wounded in South Africa. Reduced to – that. Recognize the tune, Hazel?' Awkwardly he bent and kissed her neck. As a propitiatory move it was a failure. He had meant to remind her of their long-ago courtship; but to Hazel it was a cruel reference to his night out with Georgina. She ignored the remark and the kiss. Crestfallen, James returned to the table, picked up the cards Richard had dealt, and stared at them, unseeing.

Richard wiped his brow.

'It must be in the 'eighties tonight,' he said.

'It can't last much longer,' said Hazel. She looked round at the others. 'Can it?'

Nobody answered.

CHAPTER FOURTEEN

Ruby, an ecstatic smile on her face, was painfully reading from the newspaper to Edward, who was engaged in polishing glasses.

'"Their Majesties, the King and Queen, accompanied by members of the Royal Family, entered the ballroom at ten o'clock when dancing commenced immediately. The King wore the uniform of the Colonel-in-Chief of the Scots Guards. The Queen wore a gown of grey and silver b – broché with a corsage of silver embroidery and a crown of diamonds with the lesser stars of Africa, the Koh-i-Noor with diamond bows arranged as a stomacher . . ."'

'Quite a sparkling em-bom-pom,' commented Edward, arranging the wine-glasses on the servants' hall table. Ruby eyed them with wonder.

'What you doing with them good glasses?'

'Haven't you heard?' Edward struck an attitude. 'Mr Lyons, our purveyor of fish and poultry, is honouring our humble servants' hall for luncheon.'

Ruby pulled a face. 'What's so special about him?' Edward put on a mock-shocked expression, his finger to his lips.

'Sssh. Mr Lyons has got a "sole", and his heart's in the right "plaice", and his "mussels" are as hard as iron. And take care you don't tread on his "eels" 'cos they're jellied – and what's more, if you ask me, there's a certain lady not a thousand miles from here that he'd like to catch in his net.' He paused for breath. It had taken him quite a time to work all that out, and he was justly proud of it.

Ruby giggled gleefully. 'Ee, he pinched my bottom when I went round to t'shop last week!'

'Not *you*, Ruby!' Edward looked down his nose at her. 'Why'd Mr Lyons want to throw himself away on you?' His voice dropped to a conspiratorial whisper. 'Mrs B. He fancies her.'

'Fancies Mrs Bridges?' Ruby's eyes opened even wider than usual. 'Oh, go on!'

'Honest.' Edward's tone was low but something in it communicated itself to Mrs Bridges, who was preparing an eel pie just within hearing distance. She turned and issued a short warning about talking too much. Edward and Ruby subsided, but Ruby's eyes soon wandered back to the Society columns of the paper.

'Here, listen, Edward!' she whispered. '"Some of the gowns . . . Miss Georgina Worsley wore a dress of black tulle, with a coat, embroidered in white and grey shaded diamante, and crystals in a grape design. Ee, I wish I'd seen her!'

Round about the same time, Rose and Daisy were folding and smoothing that very dress, casually left on the floor overnight by its owner. Daisy viewed it admiringly.

'Miss Georgina ought to've gone all in white – virgin white!' she said romantically.

'How could she?' asked Rose tartly, 'when the Court's in mourning? Royalty has to stick together and show respect like anyone else, or they'll *all* get murdered. Anyway, it's only half-mourning, not like after the King died.'

'Why's it only half-mourning?'

'Well, he was only a Serbian Arch-Duke, wasn't he?' returned Rose. The bullets that had killed two Balkans, man and wife, one day at Sarajevo, had not disturbed the sleep of the British, however significant they were to politicians. Who were Rose and Daisy, to realise that the consequent clash between the Dual Monarchy of Austria–Hungary and Serbia presented to Britain a threat worse than any since Bonaparte had encamped at Boulogne, ready to invade? The author Maurice Baring had been in Berlin when the news of the assassination broke. He bought a newspaper, of which the whole front page was taken up with headlines in thick black letters, announcing the murder of Archduke Franz Ferdinand and his wife. But when Baring arrived in London 'the whole population appeared to be thoughtless and gay, and rumours of war were forgotten.'

And so, as fleecy clouds sailed over the blue skies above Eaton Place, Daisy sentimentally regarded Georgina's dance-card from the Royal Ball. 'Quadrille, Methusalem,' she read. 'Strauss Waltz, The Cinema Star . . . Look, Rose. B.L., four in a row. That's the Honourable Billy Lynton! I bet she'll treasure that card all her life – the memory'll be like a beautiful dream.'

Rose set her lips. 'There's too much dreaming going on in this house as it is. You know what I'm talking about, don't you? You want to wake up and be sensible.'

'Well, I can't help it if I love him, can I?' Daisy retorted.

'You want to watch it, Daisy. If Mr Hudson finds out about you and Edward, there'll be trouble, and that's for sure. He'll have you both thrown out into the street.'

Daisy bridled. 'Well, it's not so awful, is it? We might get married.'

Rose banged the pillows of Georgina's bed into place. 'Servants can't get married – not junior servants. You'll both end up in the poor-house, or like your pa and ma, as if that wasn't example enough.' She handed Daisy a pile of sheets. 'The top ones for Mrs Bellamy's bed and the bottom for Captain James. Separate bedrooms – and they haven't been married two years. There's another example for you.' She shook her head.

In the morning-room James was haranguing his father on major political issues. 'You people in Parliament drive me mad,' he was saying. 'First you turn a blind eye when the Belfast crowd land enough rifles and ammunition to arm themselves to the teeth, and now when the Dublin crowd does the same and the British army shoots a few of them, all you people say is "We'll have to wait and see." It's incredible.'

'I'm not actually in the Government, James,' his father reminded him testily.

'Still, you could do something about it,' James said. 'God! Ireland on the verge of civil war, the Empire going to the dogs, half the country on strike and women throwing bombs in Westminster Abbey – what a country! We're up the spout. Well—' he looked at his watch 'I must sweat off to the sweaty city. In Bombay at least I wouldn't have to wear these ridiculous clothes.' He sketched a salute to Richard and Hazel, and departed.

They sat in silence for a moment.

'Poor old James,' Richard said.

'Poor old James.' Hazel sighed. '"Up the spout". That just about sums us up.'

'Not your fault, my dear!'

'Just as much as it is his. I haven't provided him with any children, for one thing. Isn't that considered to be the principal duty of a wife?' She looked wryly at Richard. 'He should never have fallen – I mean I should never have married him. I'm not the right sort of person for James, Richard.'

'Is anyone?'

'Oh, yes. One of those bright tough blueblooded hunting ladies who would have provided him with a brace of tough hunting children and then amused herself with lovers – and if James had complained, she'd have told him to stop whining and find himself a mistress.'

'Sounds an ideal marriage. Marriage à la Mode. It didn't happen to me.'

She looked up and smiled. 'I'm glad it didn't.' She meant it, deeply.

'I'm afraid,' said Richard, 'that James's malaise, whatever it is, goes deeper than that. In Biblical times they'd have said he was afflicted by a Devil.' He shook his head, as if shaking out of it the thought of his son. 'Well, I must sweat off to sweaty Westminster and listen to Mr Redmond telling Mr Carson that he's a murderer and Mr Carson telling Mr Redmond that he's an ignorant Papist cattle-driver.'

As he moved towards the door Hazel went after him. 'Richard, I don't know if James is serious about this directorship Jardines have offered him in India. But – if he is, I'm not going with him.'

'No,' Richard said quietly. 'I don't see you as memsahib.'

'Even if he doesn't go, I shan't stay with him. I wouldn't be still here now if it wasn't for you – and Georgina. It gets worse all the time – we're nearly driving each other mad – just by existing.'

Richard nodded. 'What shall you do? Not – back to your parents?'

'Out of the frying-pan . . . no. I'll do whatever James wants, divorce, desertion, separation. Perhaps I could find refuge with my typewriting machine . . .'

Richard seemed to be summoning up courage to say something he very much wanted to say; something Hazel wanted to hear.

'I just wish . . .' he began. A long look passed between them; eager hope on her part, desire blended with pity on his. In a few seconds their eyes silently talked of their unspoken attraction to each other, of the protective love which had grown in Richard as he had watched Hazel's sufferings under James's callousness; of Hazel's deep need for a strong and loving man who could be all to her that James was not. And Richard mentally saw the headlines that would blast his career were his name to be linked with the name of his daughter-in-law, whether divorced or separated. Both knew it was an impossible situation.

'Nothing,' he said abruptly. Then, almost as a groan, 'Oh dear.'

'Yes,' she said softly. 'Oh dear.'

In the servants' hall Mr Albert Lyons, fishmonger, was tucking into Mrs Bridges' faultless eel-pie. If tradesmen grow to resemble their goods, Mr Lyons might well have been mistaken for a butcher, being portly, red, and beefy. He was dressed in his sporting best, a rose in his buttonhole, and his grey moustache was waxed and perkily curled up at the ends. Mrs Bridges was beaming at his compliments and pretending modesty.

'It's the eels that make the pie – and there's no one in London can touch you for eels, Mr Lyons.'

Mr Lyons simpered. 'Well, I have to admit when it comes to eels and handsome women I am a bit of a connoisseur.' He winked broadly at Mr Hudson, who smiled politely in return. Albert Lyons was not his personal choice of company, but it was obvious that Mrs Bridges liked him. She listened with respectful awe as he discoursed of the eel trade and of a letter which had appeared in *The Times* that morning.

> "Bribery and corruption," it said, "among servants and tradespeople are rampant in London, especially in the great houses of Belgravia and Mayfair. A gift to a servant as an inducement to show favour to a tradesman dealing with the master and made without that master's consent is corruptly given."

Mr Hudson raised his eyebrows, and Mrs Bridges's cheeks turned an even deeper pink with indignation. 'That's libel, that is! That's blackmail and slander! Making out the tokens what such friends as Mr Lyons here presents us with from time to time is bribes!'

'I'm surprised at *The Times* printing such blethers,' said Mr Hudson. 'How about a wee drop of port for you, Mr Lyons?'

'That would be very nice, I must say. I trust that it won't be construed as bribery and corruption!' They both laughed as Mr Hudson conducted him into the butler's pantry. As he watched the ruby liquid being poured, the fishmonger said: 'A woman of some spirit, your Mrs Bridges.'

'Oh yes indeed, Mr Lyons – a fine person.'

'Mr Bridges was a very lucky man. I take it he's passed over?'

'To my certain knowledge there has been no Mr Bridges – the title Missus being the usual honorarium enjoyed by cooks of a certain class. A cigar, Mr Lyons?'

Mr Lyons accepted graciously, and returned to his subject. 'I take it some lucky man has already found favour in her eyes?'

Edward, who had just brought in their coffee, paused outside the door to hear the reply.

'That is a delicate question, Mr Lyons, which only the lady in question can answer.' Mr Hudson's tone gave nothing away. Edward hastened to Ruby in the kitchen. 'I was right!' he told her excitedly. 'Mr Lyons has baited his hook and is going fishing – and not for no tiddler, neither!'

If there had been any doubt in the servants' hall about Mrs Bridges' state of mind, it was dispelled that afternoon when she appeared in her best costume, the grey striped one, her freshly-frizzed hair topped with a magnificent pink hat decorated with navy feathers, and carrying a green sunshade. 'I'm just slipping out for a few minutes,' she said self-conscious under their stares. 'I'll be back after tea.' Their eyes followed her out of the door.

'Well, if that titfer don't do the trick,' said Edward, 'nothing will.'

Hazel was disappointed to hear from Richard that after all he wouldn't be able to accompany her and James to Goodwood. Always shy in company, she had been dreading the ordeal; only the thought of Richard being there had made it bearable. But Richard had been invited to the home of Bonar Law, leader of the Conservative Opposition.

'Things are getting rather tricky,' he told Hazel. 'It's this Balkan business.'

'But that's nothing to do with us, is it?'

'Not yet. But Austria's ultimatum to Serbia expired yesterday, and she declared war today; and Russia is Serbia's ally and hates Austria. If Russia comes in, Germany's bound to help Austria, and France has an alliance with Russia, and we have an entente with France.'

Hazel shook her head in bewilderment. 'It all sounds a terrible tangle.'

'It is. Let's hope the only way to untangle it isn't with gunpowder.'

Like sunshine in gloom, Georgina burst in on them, radiant and excited, her arms full of parcels. She accepted eagerly the cup of tea Hazel offered her.

'Oh, lovely, I'm dying of thirst. Oh, Uncle Richard, the Lyntons have asked me to stay over the Bank Holiday. Please can I go?'

Hazel said 'But I thought that after the Salisburys' ball you were going to come back here for a proper rest?'

'Oh, but I'm absolutely boiling with energy, and anyway Lady L. is the beadiest chaperone there is, and they've got a maid for me and everything. Oh, please say yes, Uncle Richard!'

He smiled. 'I don't seem to have much alternative, do I?' Georgina flung her arms round him. 'You *are* a darling – I don't think there can be a nicer uncle in the whole world. Oh, it's going to be such fun, there are tons of dances and we're going to play charades at the Trees, and the Fox-Bredons are having a masked ball – I've bought a splendido mask, I must show you . . .' She opened a box and produced a grotesque papier-maché head, red-nosed and witch-chinned. 'Guess who?' she asked hollowly from within it.

'Judy,' Richard said.

'Yes.' She removed the mask. 'Because Billy Lynton's going as Punch.' She was blushing a little.

'So,' reflected Hazel, 'there won't be anyone here over the weekend.'

'Nice for the servants. They can all go on holiday too!'

The choice of a resort for the Bank Holiday outing was a vexed one. Rose was fixed on Clacton, but Daisy's suggestion of Herne Bay was taken up enthusiastically by Mrs Bridges.

'Well,' she said, in a state of what could only be described as girlish confusion, 'that's a funny thing. Albert – er – Mr Lyons is going to Herne Bay – they've got a Club outing.'

Mr Hudson was not slow in taking the point. 'Well, if it's good enough for Mr Lyons's Club outing, I believe it'll be good enough for us. Let's have a wee show of hands.'

The wee show of hands was in favour of Herne Bay.

That night Mr Hudson's modest nightcap of brandy was interrupted by Mrs Bridges, requesting a word with him.

'Come away in,' he said. 'How about a wee brandy, in anticipation of our holiday, so to speak?'

'Well, I won't say no.' They drank companionably. Mrs Bridges's face was unusually grave; something was obviously weighing on her mind. Suddenly she came out with it.

'Mr Hudson. I been seeing Mr Lyons.' Mr Hudson showed no surprise.

'There's indications he's serious – straws in the wind, you might say.'

'I see. Such as . . .?'

'Well – I been to tea twice now – and the second time his only living relative, his sister, come up from Wanstead special. And then there's his manner – his general behaviour, you might say.' Head bent, she was nervously tracing a pattern on the tablecloth. 'I been very perturbed.' She looked up at him appealingly.

'I'd have thought it was more a time for rejoicing.'

'On account of *you*, Angus. I mean – when I had my bad trouble and you was so very kind – and so very very gallant – well, we did make a sort of agreement, didn't we, that we'd reserve ourselves for each other until such time as we retired from service . . .'

Mr Hudson smiled. Whatever disappointment he felt, he was not going to show it. 'Reservations can always be cancelled, Kate. Don't worry your head about it. I can't deny that I shall miss you very much. But nothing must be allowed to stand in the way of your future security and happiness.'

Mrs Bridges's eyes glistened. She put her hand over Mr

Hudson's. 'Thank you for those words,' she said. 'You're a good, generous man.'

Monday, August 3rd, 1914, was a perfect Bank Holiday. The small shingly beach of Herne Bay was almost invisible, hidden beneath the crowd of holiday-makers. Eastwards, towards Margate, the ancient towers of Reculver stood sentinel; westwards, the coast of Sheppey glimmered in heat-haze. The sea reflected a sky so blue as to be hardly English.

On the Promenade the stalls were doing a roaring trade in buckets and spades, celluloid windmills and – a novelty – miniature Union Jacks. Bathing machines with 'Ladies Only' notices stood at the edge of the water. Rose and Ruby (in a daring dark-blue costume) were splashing about with happy shrieks, while Mr Hudson paddled gently, trousers rolled up, a straw hat tilted back on his head, letting the sun bring out his redhead's freckles. From one of the bathing machines Mrs Bridges emerged, bathing-costumed and turbaned. The two girls hailed her with delight. 'Come on, Mrs Bridges, it's lovely!'

She took a step forward, hesitated, and with a loud cry slipped and fell into the water with a splash that attracted notice from everyone in sight. Her friends laughed heartlessly, but Rose went to her assistance, and soon she was right way up and swimming confidently. It was all very, very different from Eaton Place . . .

Daisy had not gone swimming. She and Edward were sitting together by a breakwater, watching Rose repelling a local 'masher'.

'Doesn't she look ripping!' Daisy said.

'It's you that looks ripping, Daisy love.' Edward looked fondly down at the pretty face beneath the summer hat. He touched a strand of her hair. 'I love you, Daisy. Honest.'

'I know you do, Ed. I love you too. But what's the use – Rose says that if Mr Hudson finds out—'

'Rose isn't marrying you, is she? I'll be a butler soon and there's plenty of places in the country where they'll take a married couple, good wages, too.'

She sighed. 'And then there's this war.'

'Don't worry about that,' said Edward cheerfully. 'It's just the newspapers exaggerating – the war won't affect us.'

Distant cries of 'Edward!' 'Daisy!' reached them. Edward kissed Daisy and hauled her to her feet. Together they moved off towards the picnic party further up the beach.

A newspaper boy was stumbling along the shingle; he was calling 'Invasion of France! Germany marches! War latest! Invasion of France!'

Mr Hudson's attempts to read the newspaper he had bought were frustrated. Mrs Bridges advised him to give up warmongering and interest himself in her chicken pie. Soon they were all eating contentedly, Daisy playfully feeding Edward. The pie was excellent, the sun hot; France seemed a very far-away place.

The picnic over, they strolled towards the entertainment pavilion where a pierrot troupe was amusing a small audience. Mr Hudson paid for deckchairs for his party, and they settled down comfortably. Unseen by him, Rose made her way swiftly to the back of the pavilion and spoke to the troupe's leader, 'Uncle Claude.' The two pierrots on stage came to the end of their rendering of 'Gilbert the Filbert' to a round of applause, after which Uncle Claude advanced.

'And now,' he said ringingly, 'by special request, I am calling on Uncle Angus to give us one of his famous monologues.'

Mr Hudson looked thunderstruck, then began to smile as the party from 165 rolled about with laughter. Settling his straw hat more firmly, he went up to the stage and took his place on it, more pleased than embarrassed at Rose's trick. After all, he didn't get a chance to recite every day . . . He spoke briefly to the plump lady pianist, who nodded and rattled off a rousing, dramatic introduction. Into the expectant silence that followed Mr Hudson began to declaim.

'"There's a one-eyed yellow idol to the north of Katmandu;
There's a little marble cross below the town;
And a broken-hearted woman tends the grave of 'Mad' Carew,
While the yellow god for ever gazes down.
He was known as 'Mad' Carew by the subs at Katmandu,
He was hotter than they felt inclined to tell,

But, for all his foolish pranks, he was worshipped in
the ranks,
And the Colonel's daughter smiled on him, as well . . .' "

Mr Hudson was getting into his stride and beginning to enjoy himself thoroughly. But his euphoria was short-lived. A hand touched his shoulder, and he found 'Uncle Claude' beside him.

'Sorry to interrupt Uncle Angus, boys and girls,' said the pierrot, 'but I have some news just come on the wire.' He consulted a piece of paper. 'The King of the Belgians has appealed to His Majesty King George the Fifth for help!'

A cheer greeted his announcement. He went on: 'Remembering all our brave Jack Tars manning their guns in the Atlantic, let us stand up and sing a verse of "Rule Britannia"!' He began to conduct them, leading the singing himself.

' "When Britain first at Heaven's command
Arose from out the azure main . . ." '

They began raggedly on the unfamiliar verse, but soon picked it up and sang lustily.

' "This was the charter, the charter of the land,
And guardian angels sang the strain.
Rule, Britannia! Britannia rule the waves,
Britons never, never, never shall be slaves." '

Later that afternoon the party from 165 were still singing, but the song was a different one.

' "Come, come, come and make eyes at me,
Down at the old Bull and Bush . . ." '

they chorused, along with the others in the bar of the little public-house.

They were hot, tired, and thirsty. Edward, bringing a tray of refills to their table, whispered something in Mr Hudson's ear; and Mr Hudson turned to see a familiar face, that of Albert Lyons, entering the room. Mr Lyons and the friends with him bore every sign of having refreshed themselves already, somewhere else. Mr Lyons, very flushed in the face, was supporting himself on the shoulder of one of the ladies, who in turn was leaning on the bar.

Mr Hudson frowned. It would never do for Mrs Bridges to see her suitor like this. Hastily he gulped down his beer and consulted his watch.

'It's late,' he said. 'We'd best get down to the station.'

Mrs Bridges began 'But the train doesn't leave till . . .' As she spoke, Mr Lyons saw the party. He advanced on them unsteadily.

'Well, I never did!' he exclaimed. 'Rose!' and he planted a smacking kiss on her face. 'Don't you smell lovely!' She recoiled furiously as his friends burst into laughter, and Mrs Bridges stared at him in disbelief. He pointed rudely at her.

'Crikey, they're all here – my old bag of lard and all!'

'*That*'s not your intended, Albert?' asked the man behind him.

Albert Lyons attempted to look serious. 'It is, you know. It's not the way she looks – it's the way she cooks . . .' He roared with laughter. 'She may call herself missus – but she's as pure as – as driven snow, aren't you, my love?' He made towards her, as she shrank back, crying 'Don't you touch me, Albert Lyons!'

Egged on by his friends' amusement, he gestured largely towards her.

'Lovely bird, eh? Nice plump breast. What d'you price her at, Bill?'

'I'll give you tenpence a pound unplucked,' Bill replied.

'Unplucked? I'll soon pluck her – you wait till I get her between my legs . . .'

Mr Hudson, who had been choking with silent rage, now exploded.

'How dare you, you drunken oaf!'

Mr Lyons's reply was coarse in the extreme. Edward leaped up and seized him by the shirt-front, shouting 'I'll knock your block off! I mean it!' And as the ladies screamed, and Lyons retreated with some feeble fist-waving, Edward pursued him into the next bar until recalled by Mr Hudson. Clustered round the sobbing, shaking Mrs Bridges, they made for the door. It was an ignominious end to a perfect day.

When Rose heard next morning that Albert Lyons was at

the back door, asking to see Mrs Bridges, she set her lips in an ominous line. Through the window she could see him, looking much the worse for wear, and anxious of expression. She opened the door just a crack and said 'Well?'

'Where's Mrs Bridges, Rose? I want to speak to her.'

'She doesn't wish to speak to *you*,' Rose snapped.

He essayed a quavering smile. 'Rose – you and me have always been the best of friends, eh?'

'That's news to me!'

'If – if you come along to my shop – there'll be something special for you – something you'll like . . .' he was almost on his knees to her.

'I'm sure there will,' she rapped back. 'Thank you for nothing, Mr Lyons.'

Desperate, the fishmonger tried to get his foot inside the door. Rose gave it a savage kick and Mr Lyons yelped with pain. From inside, Rose informed him loudly:

'Mrs Bridges has asked me to tell you that she's not available to you, and she don't want to see you no more, ever again. And furthermore, Mr Lyons, your services to this household as purveyor of fish and poultry are no longer required.' She gave a satisfied smirk at his fallen, mortified face, slammed the door, and turned the key ostentatiously. Mrs Bridges was avenged.

It had been a bad morning for Mr Hudson. A very different James Bellamy had returned from Goodwood than the one who had gone away. James was bright, eager, and pleasant. 'We're back early,' he had told Mr Hudson, 'because I'm going soldiering. Will you look out all my army kit, please – all my camping stuff – and I'll wear service dress.'

Dazed, Mr Hudson went to obey.

James's high spirits grew. Over coffee in the morning-room, he was saying to his father and Hazel 'Thank God for something positive at last! Even the damned pacifists in the Government can't get out of it now.'

'Morley and Co. resigned yesterday,' Richard said. 'It was Edward Grey's speech did it – you never heard such a reception. After that there was no doubt that if Germany went into Belgium we'd go in.'

James's eyes were alight with enthusiasm. 'It's like a breath of fresh air – in the street, at the station, everyone smiling and happy. I mean, it's brought everyone together, we've got a job to do at last. Instead of fighting each other we can get on with thrashing this damned Kaiser!'

Hazel sighed. 'I wish it could have been decided peacefully.'

'It couldn't. They *want* war, don't you see. And we've got to win or the world won't be fit for a human being to live in. Let's do it properly while we're about it – smash or be smashed – the war to end all wars!'

They saw him off that morning, smartly uniformed and kitted. He and his father bade each other a brief, embarrassed farewell. He gave Hazel a long, regretful kiss; the tenderest he had given her for a long time.

'Don't worry about me – and look after yourself. Keep an eye on father, make sure he doesn't work too hard . . .'

With a cheerful wave, he was gone. Hazel was dry-eyed.

'You can't go now,' Richard said.

She shrugged. 'No. I can't, can I.'

During the course of that day, August 4th, the people of Britain learned that Sir Edward Grey had given the Germans until midnight to abandon their aggression against Belgium. Hazel and Richard had spent the evening quietly, she working at her embroidery. Sometimes they talked, sometimes they were silent, listening to the distant roar of excited crowds gathering round Buckingham Palace.

'Is it going to be very bad?' Hazel asked.

'Very bad for very long. At least, that's what I think – and so does Kitchener.'

He came over and sat beside her.

'Last night Grey looked out across the Park and said "The lamps are going out all over Europe; we shall not see them lit again in our lifetime." I'm too old for war, Hazel. This means the end of that pleasant order of things that I have known, and lived, and loved . . . the end for ever.'

She kissed his cheek gently.

The door burst open and Georgina rushed in, flushed and happy. Behind her was young Billy Lynton. During the idyllic weekend their flirtation had become something else; they had discovered that they loved each other, and Georgina was in the seventh heaven of delight.

'The whole of London's gone mad,' she told them. 'We've been to a gorgeous war party at the Ritz, *everyone* was there, and Billy met a nice colonel who promised to help him get a commission in the Grenadiers – and I've come to a great decision, Uncle Richard – I'm going to be a nurse so that I can be with the army!'

Mr Hudson entered, bearing a tray with champagne and glasses.

'Thank you, Hudson. Have a drink downstairs, if you feel like celebrating.'

'Thank you, sir. The time is five minutes to eleven, sir.'

At Richard's request Billy opened the champagne and poured for them. Richard raised his glass. 'I refuse to drink a toast to war,' he said. 'From battle and murder and from sudden death – Good Lord, deliver us!'

In silence they drank the toast.

As Mr Hudson descended into the servants' hall Edward, Daisy and Ruby almost tumbled down the area steps, babbling excitedly to Mrs Bridges and Rose, who each held a glass of beer.

'You've never seen anything like the crowds outside the Palace, all shouting their heads off and singing!'

'We saw the King and Queen and the Prince of Wales come out on the balcony!' Ruby gasped.

'And Winston and Mr Asquith and Lloyd George . . .'

The clock of St Peter's Church, Eaton Square, tolled the first stroke of eleven. Somewhere rockets were exploding, and the crowds were singing 'Land of Hope and Glory'. Mr Hudson took up a glass and the others fell silent.

'This,' he said solemnly, 'is a great moment in the history of our country and our Empire. We are at war with Germany. Our cause is a righteous one. May the Lord mighty in battle give us victory! God save the King.'

Rose and Mrs Bridges echoed him. Edward's eyes were on Daisy; and Daisy was weeping.